Temporarily Insane

by

Vicki Batman

A Hattie Cooks Mystery

Temporarily Insane

Cover Art by *Debbie Taylor*

The Wild Rose Press, Inc.
PO Box 708
Adams Basin, NY 14410-0708
Visit us at www.thewildrosepress.com

Publishing History
First Crimson Rose Edition, 2016
Print ISBN 978-1-5092-0915-6
Digital ISBN 978-1-5092-0916-3

A Hattie Cooks Mystery
Published in the United States of America

"Stop it, Hattie!"

Trixie had some nerve. Her reprimand, the one which skewered a stabbing pain to my right eye, sounded terribly out of character, like she had little patience for me.

Maybe she felt rushed.

Ordinarily, she was the nicest person I knew who didn't have a mean bone in her body. The kind who rescued animals, picked up trash at Sommerville Park, and delivered Meals on Wheels to the elderly during her lunch hour.

Not today. I narrowed my eyes and crossed my arms over my chest in a school-girl flaunt.

Trixie tilted forward in her ergonomically designed chair, her bosom almost resting on her desk. "This nonsense has to end. Your moan sounded like an obscure breed of a bizarre…untamed…wounded animal." She returned to an upright and seated position. In tiny increments, she rotated from side-to-side, waiting for me to say something not insane.

In truth, Trixie had pounded the nail on the head.

I had nothing to add. My whole life had turned into an obscure, bizarre, bad reflection of itself, thus wounding me to my core. I sighed and pouted an *if only*.

Don't go there.

Dedications

As always, to Handsome.
Every minute, every hour—the best.
~*~
To Susan Ard.
I'm still having fun, thanks to you.
~*~
To the Guilty Girls Book Club
~*~
To The Wild Rose Press, Inc.
and editor Leanne Morgena

Chapter One

"Stop it, Hattie!"

Trixie had some nerve. Her reprimand, the one which skewered a stabbing pain to my right eye, sounded terribly out of character, like she had little patience for me.

Maybe she felt rushed.

Ordinarily, she was the nicest person I knew who didn't have a mean bone in her body. The kind who rescued animals, picked up trash at Sommerville Park, and delivered Meals on Wheels to the elderly during her lunch hour.

Not today. I narrowed my eyes and crossed my arms over my chest in a school-girl flaunt.

Trixie tilted forward in her ergonomically designed chair, her bosom almost resting on her desk. "This nonsense has to end. Your moan sounded like an obscure breed of a bizarre...untamed...wounded animal." She returned to an upright and seated position. In tiny increments, she rotated from side-to-side, waiting for me to say something not insane.

In truth, Trixie had pounded the nail on the head.

I had nothing to add. My whole life had turned into an obscure, bizarre, bad reflection of itself, thus wounding me to my core. I sighed and pouted an *if only*.

Don't go there.

My Funsister friend owned the employment agency Jobs Inc., and on occasion, she'd—mostly—happily assisted me in finding temporary work since my dream job had been flushed down the proverbial toilet a few months back, thus soiling my picture-perfect life. For this newest offered assignment, I'd be employed as an administrative assistant for the managing partner at Northside, Lancaster, and Brookside, Certified Public Accountants, headquartered in my hometown of Sommerville.

At first, she'd sounded *oh-so* pleasant when we began our chitchat about the opportunity.

"Think accounting," she'd teased, followed by a small chuckle.

Her laugh had spoken volumes of Encyclopedia Britannica proportions. My imaginings took me to Trixie's delicate hand brushing across the blue sky, creating a large banner decorated resplendently with a glittery rainbow, playful butterflies, and springtime flowers dancing in the breeze.

Gag me with a spoon.

Now, face-to-face to hash out the details of what she'd stashed up her black suit sleeve, the designer one I'd scored for her at a consignment store, I sprung to my feet and planted my hands on the edge of her desk. I huffed which puffed my side-swept bangs out of my eyes, then squeezed my orbs into python-like slits. "Are you crazy? Me...in accounting? You must be on drugs."

"Not hardly. However, I am considering a mood enhancer after our meeting." Her gaze held a hard-metal edge as her pen drummed a faint staccato on her desk's mahogany top. "I said accounting and"—she held up her hand like a traffic cop bringing on-coming cars to a halt—"*and* before you go ballistic, I do know how you feel about the profession. Newsflash: everyone in the entire stratosphere knows." She dropped her hand to her lap and watched and waited for me to respond with…whatever.

I couldn't do anything but stare. Stare at my friend and nothing else. Stare so hard, I'd bore a hole through her forehead and find spaghetti instead of brains.

So, on some occasions, I'd pontificated a little too much about how I didn't want to be employed at an accounting firm. *Sue me.*

From the bowels of my being, the wounded wild animal sound "aaarrrggghhhh" threatened to erupt Mt. Capulin-style, albeit I lacked experience with *any* wild animals. My past sole camping experience had been limited to day camp where the only bizarre, untamed, wounded animals I'd encountered in nature were the occasional armadillo, skunk, cow, and raccoon from really, really far away.

I tossed my hands in the air for emphasis and rotated from her desk to pace. I had little choice but to join the legions of geeks, especially if I wanted a paycheck.

I desperately needed one.

I walked to the sofa table positioned in front of the picture window. Sitting on top were various brochures and today's newspaper. The bold headline caught my eye, hooking me into reading further. The opening paragraph said something about a lead on a case involving an accountant who'd been found dead in Louisiana, apparently poisoned.

Was the saying *the only good accountant is a dead*

accountant true?

I massaged my forehead and wished for a normal life before turning to face the music Trixie would impart. I crinkled my nose and swiveled her way.

Trixie tossed her pen on her desk. She held up her left hand and ticked, "One: I know accounting isn't your career of choice, which I completely understand. Two: We all have different kinds of talents, and advanced number computation eludes you. Three: Your mom will take to the streets and do a riotous dance in celebration complete with a megaphone when she hears about this opportunity. She loves and adores the profession and wishes you were employed as one—"

"Trixie, that's not—"

"Ah-ah-ah." Her index finger tick-tocked. "Let me finish." Pausing, she took a deep breath, dropping her arm. "Hattie, set aside your feelings for one teensy-weensy moment. This is a tem-po-rar-y job until you're back on your feet, until we find the one you really, really want. Don't let the last—uh, the last two fiascos—hold you back. You're an intelligent girl, and we both know other jobs exist in the great big wide world in which you can be successful. Somewhere, out there, is the perfect retail job."

I snorted, tucked a strand of hair behind an ear, and let my gaze wander to look beyond the window. A scattering of leaves danced in the road along the curbing with a few lifting and twirling in a delicate air ballet. The women walking amongst the tall buildings had added autumn-colored scarves and light sweaters to their clothing like I had. Summer had ended, and before we knew it, winter would be peeking around the corner. Evening tiptoed in earlier and earlier, taking away the bright days of sunlight and bringing the long dark nights of cold.

A squeak from Trixie's chair interrupted my random musings.

"You can do this if you really want to," she said. "I have complete faith."

Don't you just love a woman with confidence?

Sure, I could *do this*. And would someone please pass a butter knife so I could stab myself in the eye? I turned from the window and ran both my hands in my hair. My fingers curled to yank out strands.

If I wanted to.

But *if* I wanted to get where *I* wanted to be…

Dammit. Realizing I'd ruin my new hairdo—a cheer-me-up birthday present—I uncrimped my fingers. After scraping together cash by pet-sitting a former co-worker's Great Dane, totally loveable even if larger than most people, I'd managed to convince my hairdresser to squeeze me in at the last minute to add much needed golden highlights to the plain ol' brown the family genes had blessed me with.

My elevating efforts had worked right up until Trixie had spoken the one little word I didn't want to hear: *Accounting.* With firm steps, I trod across the floor in front of her desk, the back of my hand lying against my brow with flair as I heaved and sighed worthy of a drama queen. Trixie had found me a job working for an accounting firm. Only I didn't want to be employed there.

Maybe I secretly liked the idea of thwarting Mom's education desires.

Maybe my dislike for the vocation was because accounting involved complex math which would never be my strong suit.

Maybe…

No. To be totally honest, adding and subtracting wasn't really why.

The real truth? The stigma attached to the profession—accountants were nerds.

Who wanted to work with a bunch of nerds? I certainly didn't.

Their conversations revolved around *numbers* and *books*. And technical terms like *depreciation* and *fiscal year*. For gosh sakes, they wore pocket protectors stuffed with an assortment of pens and pencils, displayed proudly on their chests like—my gaze traveled along the ceiling where I spotted a red splotch of gum, possibly cinnamon flavored—*the crimson badge of courage.*

Trixie understood why I didn't like accounting, but she had dismissed my reasoning. She had determined this job was the best choice and for a darn good reason—money.

Money. Money. Money. I needed lots of it. *Now.* My money well had run dry, in almost drought-mode in fact, and this temporary job thingy would provide a steady income to pay the bills like car payments and rent. Trixie wouldn't put me in an accounting job just for grins. I thought about that for a sec. *Yea, she would.*

Why can't I do what I want? My unspoken bellyache reached an invisible audience. Therein lay the real dilemma. I couldn't do what I wanted. With great restraint, I bypassed stamping my foot like a four year-old.

I wanted my old career back. I wanted to be a buyer for a large department store, not a stenographer—

excuse me, administrative assistant—at a nerdy accounting firm. I wouldn't be happy there.

I missed the camaraderie of my former co-workers.

I missed the enjoyment of placing orders for new clothing at market.

I missed seeing the merchandise attractively displayed on the racks and shelves and the subsequent sales.

But most significantly of all, I missed the excitement of Christmas time in the stores.

I loved Christmas and the holiday season at Tucker's Department Store spelt *MAGICAL*. At the beginning of every November, freshly cut Fraser Fir trees, curling ribbons, glass-blown ornaments crafted by the very best vendors, and twinkling lights too numerous to count delightfully decorated each store's floor along the escalator well and on glass countertops. Joyful shoppers and sales personnel happily hummed along with the classic carols sung by our favorite singers, broadcasted over the store's sound system. An utterly pleasurable atmosphere permeated the store.

Year-after-year, the holiday merchandise flew in and just as rapidly flew out. I'd found great reward when I assisted customers as they searched in a hurried, frantic way for the perfect gifts for their special someones.

Another sharp breath escaped my barely parted lips. I'd had a hard time accepting the fact some things weren't meant to be. My nose scrunched with wistfulness while recollecting those happy days.

Ironically, my sister, Tracey, was the accountant in my family. Not me, Harriette, mostly known as Hattie Cooks. My sister wasn't geeky, nerdy, and all other colorful phrases which came to mind when describing bean counters. My sissie had a distinctive flair and some fashion sense—thanks to style lessons from me, the pro-shopper extraordinaire. I had to admit on occasion, she'd ruined my efforts with her unique shoe selections. Her black platform pair—*ick!*

Mom continually reminded me of how disappointed she'd been with my degree of choice, Bachelor of Science in Home Economics from State Tech University. She expressed her annoyance in a nasal tone, the hoity-toity one I'd heard when she'd pinched the bridge of her nose and asked with great frequency, "Why did you pick a Fashion Merchandising degree? You'll never make any money working in retail."

I'd grown sick and tired of defending my position. *Why couldn't Mom be satisfied I'd graduated and was employed in a career I adored?*

Hadn't she heard about big-time jobs in New York City, aka Retail Haven? Heaven forbid other successful careers—as Trixie so graciously had pointed out— could be found "in the great, big, wide world."

Apparently, Mom's ultimate goal was to raise a whole flock of accountants. Only God knew why because the accounting gene didn't run historically in our family tree.

Dad—employed as a mechanical engineer at an architectural firm.

Mom—employed as M. O. M. also known as Monopolizing Overbearing Mother.

"Accounting has a good future," she'd explained, "and desirable marital prospects can be found at accounting firms."

Aha! Marital prospects. With crystal-clear clarity, every single girl in America understood her line of thinking.

Mom would be deemed a huge success if she achieved the goal of finding prospective mates for her offspring, because one never knew *when your parents might pass on. Who'd care for you then?*

What was Mom thinking? Not thinking seemed more like it—I wouldn't dare utter that particular phrase out loud. I could take care of myself, even if I had very little money streaming in. I'd been employed since age thirteen when I'd babysat the neighborhood tots.

I glanced around Trixie's office space on the lookout for listening devices. As a charter member of the Mother's Always Know Network, my Meddling Obsessive Mama possessed an uncanny way of acquiring information I didn't want her to know.

Alas, everything circled back to accounting. I'd nearly failed Accounting 101 at State Tech, because numbers weren't my strong suit. Even with a calculator, the columns never did add correctly.

I set a finger to tug my bottom lip. Realistically, retail management jobs were hard to come by in Sommerville. However, I'd done something proactive in my career of choice. I kept this possibility a secret. Mom didn't know. Jenny, my roommate, didn't know. Trixie didn't know. Absolutely, positively no one knew.

"Hello? Hello?" Trixie rapped her desk. "Hattie, are you there?"

I faced her. I needed a job, and Trixie had found one for me just like I'd asked her to. To calm my nerves, I centered my mind on a happy peaceful place, similar to meditating in yoga, and breathed. Innn...and out. Innn...and out. Once composed, I said, "I'm listening."

Trixie angled toward her computer monitor and clicked her mouse. "We need to wrap this up because I have another client coming in"—she frowned at the screen then shifted her gaze back to me—"fifteen minutes. If you weren't such a good friend, I would have dumped you. Quit being obstinate. This job's perfect."

Obviously, Trixie seemed overjoyed with her efforts to match me.

She continued her sales pitch with assurance. "You're highly organized. Great with people. Professional. A true asset. Just think of all the typing, filing, and phone answering—skills you excel at."

Typing, filing, and phone—*oh my!*

"And you dress sooo well."

Trixie knew how to stroke my ego. I loved clothes. I especially loved expensive clothing I'd purchased at bargain prices, which qualified me as a pro-shopper—my take on the crimson badge of courage.

"It's just temporary," she explained, "like six weeks. Mr. Hiram Northside, the Managing Partner at Northside, Lancaster, and Brookside, is about fifty years old, a well-respected family man, and a pillar of the community. He needs an administrative assistant while the current one is on medical leave.

"I've personally spoken with Mr. Northside about you. He agrees your qualifications sound ideal. It's a slam dunk. Show up for the interview, and you're in." Trixie paused and tilted her head. "Hattie? Say something. Anything. Hattie!"

I stood like a lump on a log, mentally rehashing her argument, the one she reiterated for what was most likely, the hundredth time. The job didn't appear too bad, certainly better than the other ones where I'd recently temped. The good news was no number crunching required, and the much-needed cash would be flowing in. Otherwise, I'd be crawling on my hands and knees to ask Mom and Dad for a handout, because the never-ending bills of rent and food kept streaming in. More importantly, I needed to skim a bit off the top to procure chocolate.

Horrendously horrible. My body quaked involuntarily.

At my first venture into the world of temporary employment, Trixie had placed me as a data-entry specialist for Buy Rite Automobile Insurance Company. In my second, I worked as a printing expert at Button and Bows Stationary Company. On a personal rating scale, I would consider the past jobs a two and six respectively and this new placement a seven point eight three.

In the positive column, I noted opportunities to meet new and interesting people. And yes, especially men. Lots of handsome young men were employed in the accounting profession. And it was true, not all business professionals were nerdy and geeky. *Well...* Tracey's stuck-out-all-over hairdo looked geeky.

I released another sigh. No number crunching eliminated the math aspect. And Trixie was right. I did excel at typing, filing, phone, and dress. I could do this if I really wanted to, which appeared to be the key— *wasn't it?*

If I really wanted to.

"Hattie, if I don't hear a *yes* in the next fourteen seconds, I'm calling someone else." Trixie's words carried a note of irritation. She touched her handset. "One. Two. Three…"

More numbers. "Yes."

"Great!" Her hand retracted. "You'll be pleased to know this job pays really well, probably better than an assistant buyer."

Trixe quoted a superlative figure which sent my eyes wide. If she'd said the salary first, this conversation might have been over quicker. Done. Finito. *Just like that,* as I faux snapped my fingers.

"Think of all the shopping damage you could do."

I did. I could do excessive amounts of shopping damage with the kind of money she'd mentioned. And on the plus side, tons would be left over for the rent, food, and chocolate!

I loved shopping and even better, pro-shopping. But in order to be an expert pro-shopper, cash had been deemed major, indispensable equipment, along with good quality shoes, a big shopping tote, and heaps and heaps of stamina.

My *Once Upon a Time* dream job had been fulfilled when Tucker's Department Store recruited me in college to groom me for their buying program. I worked as a department manager then did a stint as supervisor before moving to the assistant buyer's position in men's sportswear. I'd worked long hard hours to prepare for advancement to buyer, the next big rung up the corporate food chain at Tucker's. Instead, my boss had called me to his office and laid me off due to staff reorganization in an economic downturn.

A shocking surprise!

Passionately, I wanted another dream job in retail; unfortunately, none could be found in Sommerville. National chain stores, headquartered in large metropolises like New York City, the heart of the fashion industry, were where incredible careers in retail proliferated.

An outside possibility was to apply for a job with one of those companies. A friend of a friend knew someone I could contact. But I didn't want to leave Sommerville, not unless I ab-so-lute-ly, pos-i-tive-ly had to. My life in my hometown was perfect. I was content. I truly desired to be here, where my family and friends resided.

I'd interviewed with other area stores, even Tommy's Best Value Hardware.

"You want to do what?" The manager clutched his ribs and bent over, dying with laughter.

Noticing his overly red face, which suggested high blood pressure and/or possibly a stroke, I'd retrieved my phone from my handbag and contemplated punching 9-1-1 to be on the safe side.

None of the family businesses I'd met with were employing buyers or assistant buyers "at this time" for the same economic reasons. I'd left those interviews, feeling discouragement draping over my shoulders.

I'd toyed with an alternate idea, a secret one I called *Plan D*—open my own store. I would scour antique shops, flea markets, and estate sales for old linens. The well cared-for tablecloths, bedding, and scarves would remain the same. Damaged goods would be recycled into pillows and shams, pictures, and clothing. I would supplement with accessories like vintage jewelry, silver trays, and possibly, bath products and high-quality candles I bought at market. I could even stock my favorite accessory—handbags.

My *Plan D* was good. But in actuality, I knew myself too well. The demanding schedule of retail ownership required *extreme* self-motivation and *extreme* dedication, putting everything else low on the priority list.

Considering the current economy, opening a store wouldn't be the prudent move since I didn't have a good down payment saved to launch the venture. If I had gone to the bank for a loan, I knew for a fact they would want to know my contribution. I'd set aside a little bit for personal emergencies like car repairs and insurance. But not enough to cover both at once. Certainly, not enough to apply for to finance a store.

And horrors upon horrors, accounting would be involved. I would have to keep store books through— *what's the name of the accounting software?* Or hire someone. Someone like…

Allan Charles Wellborn. My best friend's older brother. A former CPA. Mr. Perfect. A police detective. Probably out saving the world like he felt compelled to. *I wonder if he knew something about the death of the poor man in Louisiana, the one in the Sommerville News—*

I shook my head. *So not going there.* I'd be the last to know because he wouldn't tell.

Perhaps, I should develop my *Plan D* some more. I sensed my forehead pleating, which Mom said would cause wrinkles. While rubbing the spot, I toyed with the idea of working garage sales. Set up an on-line shop.

A while back over lunch, Maggie, another Funsister friend set for life with her career of choice as a doctor, had suggested I implement *Plan B*, working temporary jobs. Her hand had slid through her shoulder-length hair, streaked various shades of red and gold. "It's a great way to make some cash, scope out possible opportunities, and acquire needed new skills. Call Trixie."

Since unemployed people always needed cash, I'd taken Maggie's sensible advice. The assistant buying job had a decent salary, but I hadn't accumulated enough savings for months on end of unemployment. Instilled with a strong sense of economy, sensibility dictated I leave my sparse savings alone in case of a real emergency.

The accounting job didn't sound ideal. Generally, it sounded ordinary. But I found myself in the ultimate quandary: I wanted to find the dream job; yet, I felt bound to my current lifestyle and needed money to support it. A lot of real world, grown-up stuff to consider.

Sensibility prevailed. With great reluctance, I asked Trixie, "When do I start?"

"Excellent!"

Trixie's enthusiasm burst like sun rays breaking through dissipating rain clouds. I asked with an uninspired, monotone voice, "Do I need to interview?"

"Yes, but it's a no big deal, follow up, look-you-over one. You'll consult with...hmm, let me check." Trixie mouse-ed through a calendar program. Pausing, she scrutinized her screen. "Here it is. You'll interview with a Mr. Stuart Steems, Senior Audit Manager."

What kind of name was Stuart Steems? *Sounded goofy. Reminds me of a cleaning service Mom uses.*

Trixie examined me.

Possibly sensing my thoughts and possibly in an effort to mollify them.

"He sounded nice when I called," she said. "Maybe geeky. Probably geeky."

Great. I rolled my eyes heavenward. I'd had enough of dweebs and nerds to last a lifetime. "You know the difference between a geek and a nerd?"

She leveled on me a suspicious gaze. "No."

"A geek doesn't know he is one."

"Very enlightening."

I laughed a long time. "I think T-shirt worthy."

"You would." She bounced her pen on her desk. "Mr. Steems interviews all prospective hires for NLB. I'll set up an appointment for tomorrow at nine A.M." She drew in a short breath. "There's a slight hitch—"

"What?" My insides grabbed.

She shrugged. "Nothing."

"S-swell." I suppose I could show more excitement about this thrilling opportunity. After all, Trixie had performed way beyond the normal call of duty for a friend. Not wanting to sound totally ungrateful, I added with the courtesy Mom had instilled with her little talk on politeness, "Trixie, I really appreciate your taking care of me like this. I hope I'm not inconveniencing you in any way."

"Inconveniencing me?" She shoved away the wireless mouse which skidded to a stop. "Are you kidding? I live to be entertained by you and your jobs. You have an interesting...track record."

"Track record?" Now, my Funsister friend had decided I had a weird-assed track record with two temp jobs bagged?

Did she not have any hope I would land

somewhere?

Did she think my life resembled a swinging singles sitcom where the heroine flits from one job to the next?

Stay tuned for next week's episode of Hattie Cooks, Temporarily Employed. Watch out below as Hattie takes a job as a window washer!

Fixing my gaze on the popcorn ceiling, I imagined myself garbed in white Dickie overalls, red Converse hightops, and a matching striped baseball cap with the company logo embroidered above the bill. Suspended precariously on a scaffolding platform, I would flutter my lashes at attractive executives working in their offices, who paused to eyeball me while I cleaned their windows.

Not-so great.

Sounded like an *I Love Lucy* episode.

Trixie ushered me to her office door, squeezing my shoulders with a quick *bye*, and then returned to her desk. Her laughter lingered in the air behind me.

Laughter. I wondered if my Funsisters laughed behind my back. So unfortunate things happened at some of the jobs where I'd worked. The mishaps…accidents…whatever weren't entirely my fault.

My last job with Buttons & Bows had seemed ideally suited, especially considering my extensive retail background. Customers couldn't help but *ooh* and *aah* over the clever items found in the store's inventory of greeting cards, computer stationary, and invitations.

However not that long ago, I'd had an unfortunate accident. A small boo-boo really. Due to my inexperience. I'd endeavored to console the hysterical bride over the simple mistake I'd made, a misprint of her mother's name on the wedding invitation. Regrettably, she had a huge temper tantrum. The word had sounded similar to a woman's unmentionable body part. However, the fateful fiasco ultimately resulted in me leaving Buttons & Bows Stationary Company…involuntarily and without a paycheck.

Before Buttons & Bows, I'd worked at Buy Rite Automobile Insurance Company. I typed, filed, copied, and answered the phone and email, following normal office procedures. Only I'd discovered the boss ran a far-reaching embezzling scheme which involved employing thieves who procured parts off cars or stole whole cars. On the side, he'd pocketed a portion of the money from the settlement checks.

By accident, I'd exposed his scheme and the murder of the woman I'd replaced. As a result, his insane assistant thrust and slashed at various places on my body with an unusually sharp letter opener, a complimentary giveaway from Buy Rite.

The cop assigned to the case, Detective Allan Charles Wellborn, had investigated the stolen cars and the murder of the Buy Rite employee, coming at it from another angle. We ended up becoming more than friendly, making my heart and other body parts go thumpa-thumpa. Hot things almost took place under the covers until his phone interrupted.

I'd battled the crazy woman, and Detective Wellborn rode to the rescue, shooting her dead, dead, dead.

I'd been badly hurt physically. Stitches were involved.

And emotionally? Well… Let me state, eventually, I'd healed.

So what happened to the cop I made more than friendly with? The one who made my heart go thumpa-thumpa? Much to my dismay, in the end, he hadn't chosen me.

Why?

Chapter Two

The morning of my interview with Northside, Lancaster, and Brookside, CPAs dawned bright and clear. I stood by my beloved Jeep Wrangler and unlocked the door as a wind gust, bending with a nip from the north, wove my skirt's hem around my knees. Countless migratory birds flew overhead to the South, a *caa-caa* squawk accompanied them.

Weather always changed in Sommerville. We could be freezing cold one day and in the nineties the next.

"That's why we live here," Dad always said. "Keeps things interesting."

Hopefully. I crossed my fingers and sent a prayer skyward, this cool air was a one-time thing before Saturday. Excellent weather needed to prevail throughout the weekend for a very good reason. Fall's arrival coincided with my highly anticipated—I did a tiptoe happy dance—birthday. I climbed in my carbaby and took off for the appointment at NLB.

Like Trixie had expressed, she'd arranged a nine A.M. appointment with Stuart Steems, Senior Audit Manager of Northside, Lancaster, and Brookside. The firm's headquarters were situated fifteen minutes from my apartment in a nice part of town. Several large office towers and a trendy hotel had been built in this area to take advantage of the convenience to five-star restaurants, late-night entertainment, banks, and most important of all, exceptional boutique shopping.

My route took me past Allan Wellborn's townhouse complex. An emptiness rooted in my belly. I drew in a deep breath, and something propelled me not to exhale until I'd passed. My chest tightened to the point I had to force myself to breathe again the second I drove by his street. I rubbed my tummy to assuage the pit of despair for I'd found deep hurtful feelings were hard to shake.

I pointed an imaginary finger in the general direction of his place and said softly even though no one would hear me, "He lives...right...there."

Every single time I'd motored past his home *why-why-why* thoughts about our relationship occupied my head, leaving me perplexed about *why* whatever hadn't developed between us like I'd supposed would have.

I'd really believed Allan and I as a couple would be different. With him, I'd mulled over feelings like *this could be the one* and *this could be for real*. We were ideally suited. Everyone had said so. Our mothers had matched us since almost birth...well, since the Wellborn family had moved to Sommerville.

I could not mention these musings out loud to anyone, because if my mother had caught even a sniff, she would have planned our wedding in three seconds flat.

Heck, she most likely already had.

Allan had said things like "I've wanted you for forever," and "I've waited for you all my life."

Sure, this guy talk sounded like regular lines in order to get into a girl's panties—which he sorta did. He wasn't that way...most days. But we're talking about Allan Wellborn here. He really meant what he'd said. From my growing-up years, I knew his family intimately. My mom thought him an upstanding guy on the fast-track to sainthood. Turned out, she was totally wrong there. He'd demonstrated he was not Mr. Perfect at all.

Still, I had an undeniable attraction for him I couldn't shake. Everyone made mistakes. And sometimes, they can be redeemed.

My mental mind loop drove me crazy. I needed to stop. I wasn't obsessed. I needed more time, sorta like the quote *time heals all wounds*. Time would get me past.

Actually, a new route would be a superb idea.

I managed to squish the uncomfortable ruminations to my brain's subterranean recesses in order to concentrate on the drive and my interview. Upon arriving at my destination, I maneuvered my car into a marked visitor's space in the parking garage of the twenty-story glass tower which housed NLB's offices. I approached the building's main entryway decorated with enormous cast stone planters filled with exotic blue agaves, the biggest I'd ever seen. I eyeballed the three sets of double bronze doors which looked extremely heavy. Easily, one opened at my touch which surprised me.

While I waited in the lobby for the elevator to arrive, I scrutinized my reflection in the mirrored panels. Turning slightly to my right, I paused, seeing a nice tall girl, coming in at five feet, ten inches in high heels. My shoulder length hair had been layered in a trendy style, thanks to the *Happy Birthday to Me* present. Warm brown eyes, a cute short nose, and a wide smile filled my face. With great rejoicing, I passed, finding no scary 'do or smudgy makeup.

I noted my almost knee-length, charcoal tailored suit remained neatly ironed with only slight wrinkles at the hips from sitting in the car. Passing my hand over the creases, I smoothed the fabric to erase the imperfections. The white blouse with red pin dots perfectly accentuated my outfit. A multi-flowered enameled brooch adorned my left jacket lapel. According to the fashion magazines, pins were *in* this season. The pointy-toed, slingbacks looked stylish, yet comfortable. To complete my ensemble, I carried a red leather handbag, a designer knock-off. I'd crammed a paperback, a historical romance I couldn't set aside, in the bag in case waiting took a while.

A small *ding* signaled the elevator's arrival. With a final glance, I leveled my shoulders, sucked in my tummy, and decided I looked very business-like and positively would leave a good impression at NLB.

As I entered the carriage, I nodded at the woman with enormous bleached blonde hair—*yuck*—standing next to me. The notion smacked me about seeing her somewhere else on another occasion, but I couldn't remember the specifics.

The elevator deposited me on the eighteenth floor. I observed NLB's office doors stained a dark pecan which, upon my slight push, revealed a large reception area. Paneling lined the walls. The hardwood floor had been polished to a high luster. A receptionist sat behind a massive island topped with granite veined in tonalities of white, tan, and pewter. The company logo, an oval shape emblazoned with *NLB* in blue lying over a steel background, hung on the wall behind the lady's head.

"Hi, and welcome to NLB. May I help you?" she asked.

"I'm Hattie Cooks." I rested my forearm on the counter. The coolness of the surface filtered through my coat's fabric to my skin. Even though I lacked enthusiasm for the accounting profession and this particular job, I hoped cheerfulness laced my words. I smiled wider. "I have a nine o'clock interview with Mr. Stuart Steems."

"Let me buzz him for you." The receptionist punched buttons in the phone and briefly spoke to someone. She replaced the handset and pointed to a waiting area.

Removing my arm, I paid attention.

"Mr. Steems will be right out, Ms. Cooks. You can wait over there." She stood and with a gracious demeanor, escorted me to comfy vanilla-colored leather sofas grouped adjacent to the windows.

I murmured the standard "thanks" and took a seat.

She asked, "Coffee or tea?"

I shook my head. "No, thank you."

With a smile, she walked away.

I shifted my gaze to look out the windows which overlooked the streets nearby. An incredible view. Lots of small cars, small roads, small trees, and small people walking around down there.

The loud clop-clop of determined footsteps intruded on my nonsensical musings. Instinctively, I rotated to face the wearer of the noisy, hard-soled shoes.

A slender man entered the reception area and stopped in front of me. Almost so close, he nearly trod on my toes. I looked up to his face.

He said, "Hi. You must be Harriette Cooks."

I rose. "I am."

The stranger shook my proffered hand. "Glad to meetcha, Ms. Cooks. I'm Stuart Steems, Senior Audit Manager of Northside, Lancaster, and Brookside."

I squashed a giggle. *The cleaning firm association still tickled me.*

"I understand you're interviewing for the temporary position as the administrative assistant to Mr. Hiram Northside, our Senior Managing Partner."

"Correct."

"Would you please accompany me to my office where we can begin our talk?" And with a wave of his hand, he indicated a direction, seemingly the way he'd come.

He escorted me through the maze of hallways, which gave me ample opportunity to examine him further. I started at the top and worked my way down. He looked to be about my age, six-feet tall. His coarse black hair had been styled in a crew cut, and he had the unfortunate and dreaded uni-brow.

His clothes told a regrettable tale. A white oxford-cloth shirt with a buttoned-down collar looked slightly frayed around the edges. A solid burgundy tie—*tsk-tsk*—resembled a dinner napkin Mom had once owned during her mauve, forest green, and maroon decorating period. A serviceable, but not outstanding, black suit topped off his outfit. The standard wingtip shoes, buffed to a glossy black, completed his ensemble. The tapping sounds coming from his shoe soles I'd heard earlier were now muffled by the carpet lining the hallway.

Stuart Steems wasn't an ugly guy. He fit the profile

of nerdy accountant to a *T*. If anyone needed my fashion skills, he was my man. I would start the ball rolling by swapping the dinner napkin tie for a conservative striped one and upgrading his shirt style, preferably one with French cuffs and links. His uni-brow could be waxed. Thankfully, no pocket protector crammed with pens and pencils looked to be in sight.

Stopping, he opened the door to an office.

Before stepping inside, I noticed his name etched in the sidelight window.

As he passed, he gestured to a dark blue-patterned wingback chair placed in front of his partner-styled desk. "Please, have a seat."

"Thanks." As I settled in the chair, I studied his office which displayed more stylishness than his clothing, a variation on the hunting theme. Caramel paint colored the walls. Cherry wood bookcases had been placed off to the either side of a window with the desk centered in front.

A navy, green, and beige plaid valance accentuated the upholstered furnishings. A few worn leather-covered books, some accounting awards and certificates, and neatly framed in shiny silver, family pictures, which looked to be from a dance, packed the shelves. *Interesting.* After setting my tote by my feet, I scooted to the chair's edge and waited for him to begin.

Finally, he asked, "Something to drink?"

I shook my head. "No, thank you."

"No coffee, no tea?"

Finding it awkward to interview with a cup in my hand, I deemed it prudent to pass on drinks. The interviewer always asked a question at the precise moment I took a sip. I swallowed too quickly and scalded my tongue or spilled on my clothes, which didn't look pretty or impressive. More like expensive, as in dry cleaning bill. Anyway, unlike the rest of America, I had no coffee or tea addiction.

Now, if Stuart Steems had offered me a warm Krispie Kreme doughnut, the sugary treat would have been inhaled in two secs flat. Bite. Bite. Gone. And sugar crumbs on the clothing—would I care? Didn't most security personnel define sugar crumbs as hazard duty? I'd find some way to discreetly lick them off. "I'm fine. Thank you."

He wiggled in his chair to get comfy and selected a pen from a leather box next to the lamp fashioned from a French horn. "Ms. Cooks, shall we get down to business?"

"Please." I gave him a broad smile and suggested, "Call me Hattie."

His brow lifted in a quizzical expression. "Hattie—which is short for Harriette?"

"It is."

"A good-old fashioned name one doesn't hear any more." Stuart sniffed. Afterwards, he wiped his nose with a hankie, which coordinated with his over-sized tie, and returned it to his pants' pocket.

Obviously, he had a slight cold or allergy problem.

Setting aside the pen, he reached into his inside coat pocket and produced a mini-pad.

My brows rose. I then concluded this device had replaced the pocket protector and pens.

His finger tapped and swiped all over the device's surface. "Northside, Lancaster, and Brookside, Accountants are interested in hiring you to temporarily fill the position as the administrative assistant for Mr.

Hiram Northside, our Senior Managing Partner. His current assistant is on medical leave."

I shifted slightly to my left hip and crossed my legs. "That's my understanding as well."

He flipped open a file folder which contained a printed copy from the email the thorough and efficient Trixie had forwarded to NLB's Human Resources Department. Hopefully, the file contained my resume and other appealing facts.

He perused the folder with a querying eye. "The administrative assistant's job responsibilities include typing, filing, answering the phone, maintaining a calendar, copying, et cetera. I'm assuming the employment agency—ah, let's see. Here it is—Jobs Inc. tested you for the necessary computer skills, and you can work with the latest operating system?"

"I was tested and passed. I'm trained in several systems and have plenty of office experience in filing, copying, and phone." *Oh my!*

"And please, describe your business background in the accounting profession."

Oops. There is none. What do I say? Like the fearless first President of the U.S.A., I couldn't lie. "Mr. Steems—"

"Please, call me Stuart."

"Okay, er…Stuart. I don't quite know how to say this…didn't the temporary agency explain…I don't know a thing about accounting." And with my confession, ladies and gentlemen, this interview had been terminated. Uncrossing my legs, I readied myself for dismissal by inching my hand toward my handbag.

Stuart's eyebrows elevated over this revelation. "Oh?"

Maybe, there's hope. Maybe if I pray to the great money provider in the sky all will be saved? "Is this a problem? If you desire someone more qualified than me in accounting, then I understand."

"No, no, of course not." He stumbled a bit. "Accounting skills aren't a necessary requirement for the job, but a familiarity in accounting would be of benefit to you." He pointed his finger in my direction.

"I did a flyby in Accounting 101 at State Tech. I'm sure my background information is on my resume which was emailed to your office."

"Yes, it's here. I found your degree in Fashion Merchandising to be an interesting choice." He assessed me over the top of the folder. "I didn't know such a degree plan existed."

You and my mother.

For the rest of my life, I would be resigned to always clarifying-slash-backing my selection. Holding my sigh, I wondered if maybe Trixie wouldn't yell at me for blowing this meeting. I took a deep breath and rattled out my oft-repeated explanation. "I took many business courses as well as basic accounting in college as part of the required curriculum, but accounting barely took."

Stuart scrutinized the file some more, and then slapped shut the file folder. He eased back in his chair. "Well, good. We're settled. Do you have any questions?"

I, on the other hand, sat taller. "Settled?"

He nodded.

So quickly? "Settled—as in, you mean, I have the position?"

Again, he nodded.

Amazingly fast interview. None of my others had been finalized this quickly. Of course, Trixie had stated my hiring was a sure thing.

He said, "If you want it, the job's yours."

"Thank you," I said in a drawl while recovering from the dizzying interview daze. "Shall I begin tomorrow?"

Stuart consulted his trusty tablet. "Tomorrow will be fine. I'll meet you at eight-thirty in the lobby and escort you to Mr. Northside's office."

"Are you sure, I mean, about tomorrow? If I'm needed, I could start today." *Not today, not today.* I didn't mean it. *God save me, not today. Not if I want to attend the library's book sale. First in line gets the best stuff for pennies.*

"No-no-no, won't be necessary. Tomorrow's fine."

Woohoo! And great relief. "Thank you...ah...Mr. Steems."

"Remember, Stuart."

"Stuart."

My time had come to an end, so I wrapped my fingers around the handles of my handbag and shifted to the balls of my feet, readying to leave. "I'll let you get back to work. I wouldn't want to intrude any more. See you bright and early."

He had his head in my file again. "Your birthday is almost here. Planning a big party?"

How did he know about my birthday?

I dropped in the chair with reluctance, letting my bag plop to the floor. I hadn't been interviewed for vast quantities of jobs, even though my friends thought I had. My understanding from the few times I had been his questions weren't standard politically correct ones.

"Isn't this questioning…personal?"

"I just wanted to get to know you better." Stuart sniffed and removed the maroon hankie from his pocket for a wipe. "'Choo."

"Gesundheit. Allergies?"

He nodded as he gave a blow. "I'm miserable. This time of year there's so much decaying leaf dust and ragweed. I need a pill." Stuart fished in a drawer, found a bottle, and shook a tablet on his palm.

I watched in rapt fascination as he swallowed it with a chug of water. Catching myself, I decided if pill swallowing looked wholly captivating, I needed to get out in the big wide world more often.

He blew his nose again, making a sound similar to a trumpet. "Let's see, where were we? Ah, yes. Your birthday party." He glanced in my direction, replacing the hanky in his coat pocket. "Sooo…"

"Excuse me?"

"About your birthday…it's this weekend. Happy happy day. Happy happy birthday." He sang off-key, but when noticing my open mouth and stare, he sobered. "Are you having a huge blow-out?"

Blow out? I tried hard not to laugh and set my hand over my lips. Stuart's *happy-happy-happy* stuff sounded like a Duck Dynasty family member. Why was Stuart pressing so hard on the birthday subject? On the other hand, what would it hurt for him to know about my birthday?

All of this politically correct verbiage seemed hard to keep up with anyway. My birthday was just a regular ol' birthday. *Oh hell,* I might as well answer and threw out this bone. "There's a party at my parents' house."

"When?"

Does Stuart ever give up? I repeated, "When?"

"When is your mother throwing you a party?"

Personal again. My brows narrowed in the confused and worried way. All this discussion about my upcoming birthday felt unusually awkward, especially for an interview. "I don't think you're supposed to ask these questions."

He took out the hankie and did a wipe, wipe. His allergy pill hadn't kicked. "I don't mean anything harmful by asking. I'm just curious. Is your birthday party Saturday?"

"Hmm." I twisted my mouth to one side. "In other interviews, I haven't been asked about my birthday."

"I understand. I wanted to get to know you a little better."

"Okay. Fine." *Somebody—anybody—get me out of here.* Exasperated, I threw a look at the ceiling then continued explaining, "My mother's having a birthday barbecue this Saturday. Is that what you wanted to know?"

"Barbecues are fun."

I cut my gaze toward the door. "Yes, they are."

"Will there be dancing?"

"Maybe—"

"Will there be lots of food?"

"For God's sake, it's a *barbecue*."

"And drinks?"

A little warning bell about where our conversation headed dinged in my head. "Yes."

"And presents?

I rolled my eyes to the ceiling. "Yes."

"Will there be a big birthday cake?"

"Yes! Yes! Yes!" I said. "Most birthday parties

have these things."

"Great! What time shall I pick you up?"

"What!?" I jumped to my feet. To hell with this interview. Time to leave Mr. Stuart Steems and his outrageous questioning. "Whatdayamean by pick me up?" I positioned my hands on the rolled edge of his desk. Profound irritation crept into my cheeks and eyes. Leaning closer, I said, "This isn't a—a normal interview. What's with all of these questions about my birthday? Do I have the job or not? If it means you go with me to my birthday party—For. Get. It. I don't even know you. You could be some kind of stalker, murderer, or rapist, and I wouldn't know which one."

Oops. Something slammed me with the comprehension of what I'd said. Talking extremely loud and using profanity weren't good interview skills. And I might want to reconsider a little tiny bit calling a potential employer a stalker, murderer, or rapist. Fortunately, I forgot to mention harassment. Slowly, I slid back into the armchair.

Stuart's shoulders slumped with dejection over my rejection. He twisted toward the window. He snorted then he did another hankie wipe-wipe. "I'm not any of those things you said."

"I'm sooo sorry." Possibly, I could redeem myself by apologizing profusely. "I didn't mean to sound...ugly. Please forgive me for yelling. My anger was talking." I ducked my chin and repeated in a lower voice, "Honestly, I'm sorry I said those things." All I heard was sniff-sniff. He sure took a long time composing himself. "Mr. Steems, are you crying?"

He glared back at me. "Of course not." He shook his head. "Remember, you can call me Stuart."

"Okay, Stuart. Why would you want to go to my birthday party? You don't even know me."

He took a few minutes before answering. "Truthfully? I don't date much. Some girls think I'm a geek. I thought going with you would be fun."

A geek? Amazed at his honesty, I blinked.

"You seem to be the kind of person who knows lots of fun people, particularly women. I bet you have plenty of girlfriends. Maybe you could take me, and I could meet some. Maybe your friends would see me in a new way, not as a geek."

Stuart sounded a little nasally from the not-quite shed tears or allergies. But, he was right. I had lots and lots of girlfriends. *Did I know any who were desperate for a guy like him?*

I searched my brain Rolodex for possible victims. *Let's see, there was Holly, or Hannah, or*—I brushed my hand over my forehead. So far, his assertive inquiries into my birthday appeared to be his most offensive aspect and possibly, the sniffing and hankie wiping. Otherwise, he looked passable, just barely though. He acted polite and in all likelihood, was very brainy.

As I reviewed Stuart's situation further, I felt sorry for him. I remembered what it felt like in high school to not have many dates. Sorta sad, actually. Recently, I'd hit a dry spell after the cop thing didn't develop. My friends and I called a dating dry spell *nundom*.

Nundom meant:

No dates.

No sex.

No fun.

No nothin'.

Since the cop thing had been extra harder emotionally, I took baby steps to prime myself for the dating scene. Using one of *About Moi* magazine's self-evaluation questionnaires as a guide, I'd determined:

I recovered from my stab wounds and the emotional trauma attached to the insane Opal-attacking-me episode.

I'd recovered from the cop using me to solve his big case.

It took me longer to recover from the man.

Nundom.

Chapter Three

The Wellborn family resided three blocks from my family in Sommerville. After school, I'd played at their house with Sarah Ann, and every now and then, I'd noticed her older brother, Allan, staring at me.

Back then, he'd looked so immature. He had a funny boy body, which hadn't fully developed. He wore ugly, black Buddy Holly-style glasses, played the trombone in the high school marching band, and participated in the accounting club, serving as treasurer in both organizations. Undoubtedly, numbers had always been an integral component of him. In Sommerville's yearbook photo, he displayed with pride a pocket protector complete with a yellow highlighter and mechanical pencil, a monument to geekdom and a turn-off to every potential girlfriend.

Naturally, I didn't want to have anything to do with him. I could have caught his cooties.

I'd looked geeky also. In ninth grade, I was too short, wore ugly, rectangular tortoiseshell glasses, and had straight-as-a-board, limp hair. No boobs, no long blonde curls, no big blue eyes, no contact lenses—nothing resembling the pretty popular girls like the cheerleaders who had every male in school sniffing after them.

Sarah Ann and I had stayed super-glued together until we went our separate ways after college. Now, she lived in Denver with handsome husband, Tom, and her newborn baby girl. When Sarah Ann breezed into town for the rare family visits, she called, and we played catch-up.

Allan had improved enormously. He stood six feet, one inch tall. His chocolate hair cut short, and his dark eyes shone almost black. Through running and weight training, he maintained a muscular body a woman—like me—would want to hold onto. I knew firsthand because I'd had an opportunity to test it a few months ago.

But even more desirable were the characteristics he held inside—a good heart, sweet, sincere, loving, and dedicated. He was smart, funny, and sexy, in or out of a suit.

Through the enterprising scheme my boss at Buy Rite Insurance Company had masterminded and the resulting investigation, I'd become better and better acquainted with Allan. We ate pizza and burgers, attended a party, and when long-suppressed sparks flew, I'd awakened to the possibilities of being with him and graduating from nundom.

We came passionately together to have almost-wild, almost-sex. Only our highly anticipated romantic interlude had been interrupted abruptly by his newly adopted cat, Lucky, hitting me on the head just as I was poised for *The Big One*, followed shortly by a poorly timed call on his cell phone.

Extremely frustrated best described my feelings then. Well, so did unfulfilled, unsatisfied—the entire world was clued into the picture.

After Allan had shot the insane administrative assistant holding me hostage at Buy Rite Insurance Company, his real role as detective was revealed. He possessed an unwavering allegiance to his job which kept me in the dark and at risk, and my unspecified one as quasi-informant at Buy Rite had aided in solving his cases.

Upon my disillusioning discovery, I needed time and space away from him. I ordered him to "get out" and "leave me alone," vowing to "never-never, ever-ever" see him again.

He left.

And so began another plunge into nundom.

A couple of weeks had passed and with better perspective, I determined I'd made a huge mistake. The Funsisters and I were celebrating a large wedding order I placed for Button and Bows Stationary Company over dinner at my favorite Italian restaurant, Mamma and Pappa's Italian Bistro. Across the candlelit room, I unwillingly observed Allan had moved on with his life in the company of an over-blown blonde. She was attractive, if you liked her type. They were doing intimate couple things like sitting close, her touching his arm, and him stroking her hair from temple to the tip, just like he'd done me.

Almost sick to my stomach, I exited, stage left.

Buckets full of tears seeped from my eyes while I lay prostrate on my bed. Yet through the waterworks, I determined I hadn't moved on with my *own* life well at all. I drifted through the motions, floating like a leaf in a stream, blindly following every bump and bend.

I wasn't happy.

Not feeling proactive in the direction my life had taken, I gathered my courage to overcome my embarrassing fears and drove to Allan's apartment. I blathered through a personally revealing version of how

I felt and asked him to "choose me" instead of the girl in the restaurant.

Shocked that his answer "no" wasn't the one I'd expected, the newly liberated, brave me, courageously—but not really—fled the scene.

And so life and living continued on.

I pondered Stuart's dating situation and recognized I could be compassionate—just this once—and invite him to my birthday party. When the blinding light summoned me to the great beyond, I might get booster points past the pearly gates.

And yes, Stuart would meet more people, even girls.

He-he-he. Maybe one of the single Funsisters would be interested. For instance, wild sister Tracey could be the first victim.

In all likelihood, I might not be her sister for very long either.

The present returned me to Stuart, my birthday, and taking his word on the stalker, murderer, and rapist thing. If I took him to the party, I could pack pepper spray in case of an emergency…only I had to figure out where to hide the canister in my new swimsuit. The key chain version, one Dad had dropped in my Christmas stocking this past year, could be pinned inside the suit's matching sarong's waistband, the knot disguising it. "You can pick me up at five-thirty."

Ecstasy didn't seem to be a large enough word to describe the look on Stuart's face. He could have been in middle school, celebrating the last final exam. Or he could have been gifted with a Popsicle on a hot, hot day. Stuart looked extraordinarily, close to jumping-up-and-down-happy, thanks to me.

"Great! I'll be there—er, what time? Five? What should I wear?"

Obviously, his hearing wasn't operational.

"I'll be ready at Five. Thirty," I said louder and with strong emphasis on the numbers.

"Super! I'll pick you up at five-thirty."

I sighed. Label me *extraordinarily nice girl*. I shook my finger in warning. "Not one minute earlier."

"Okay."

"We need to cover the ground rules."

"Ground rules?" His brow vee-ed. "Is this normal?"

"Absolutely." I nodded. "The ground rules are: No kissing. No hugging. No whispering lovey-dovey stuff in my ear. No nothing. Understand?"

"I understand, but I thought people in love do this."

"Let's set the record straight right now—we are not in love. And here's another rule: don't speak to anyone."

"Don't talk to anyone—why not?"

Noticing the bizarre look on his face, I relented. "Okay, you can talk. Just say one sentence."

"Is this a weird family thing?"

"Nope. It's a Hattie-who-is-being-nice thing."

"Oh." He slid his mouth from one side to the other before answering, "I'll behave."

Lordy, what have I done?

Chapter Four

With my first week at Northside, Lancaster, and Brookside, I experienced the learning curve all newcomers had in a freshly assigned position. During this time, I familiarized myself with the accounting business as best as I could, the convoluted layout of hallways and offices, and how Mr. Hiram Northside, the Managing Partner, handled his workload.

At first, the job didn't demand a great deal, but I suspected Mr. Northside—who said to call him Hiram, but I couldn't address my boss in this familiar manner—was being nice to The Temporary in a parental way and not loading me down with big accounting projects I probably couldn't handle anyway.

I typed, filed, emailed, copied, scanned, fielded phone calls, and became acquainted with the other employees at the firm. Everyone seemed friendly and introduced themselves, gave helpful hints, and "just call me if you need anything else" instructions.

One morning in the kitchenette as I poured a cuppa Joe for Mr. Northside, I heard a male co-worker say, "You must be the new girl."

This statement floated over my shoulder and startled me so, coffee splashed on the counter. I quickly snatched and smashed a paper napkin over the mess, then swiveled to find a tall, slim, cool, Robert Redford-looking guy with sun-kissed blond hair. My Funsister friends would say "he didn't break mirrors," which translated from girl speak meant "he wasn't an ugly one and to go for it."

"If you mean new as in Mr. Northside's temporary assistant, that's me." I stuck out my hand. "I'm Hattie Cooks."

"William Christiansen, Senior Audit Manager. Call me Will." His firm shake sent warm squiggles up my arm and over my body. I would be overjoyed to call William Christiansen "Greek God" and bow to worship at his feet.

He let go of my hand and passed me a few paper towels. "Need more of these?"

Duh. I sensed a blush creep over my cheeks as I took what he'd offered. "Thanks." As I blotted the spill again, I recollected about how I'd heard on the NLB gossip network he was hot, very single, and always on the prowl. This bit of attention from him had me blazing with special-ness.

He poured himself a cup of coffee. "How's it going for you? Is Hiram working you too hard?"

"No, not too hard." I gave a small laugh as I tossed the wet towels in the trash. *Bingo!* "I'm taking full advantage of being the new girl. Right now, he's being easy in a nice fatherly manner."

"Good to hear. Otherwise, I'd have to go wrestle him on your behalf."

"Thanks to my karate classes, I think I can handle him." I lied about the karate class. However, I did flail my hands in a *chop-chop* anyway. "I appreciate the offer."

"Anytime." Will sipped his coffee. "Did anyone mention—"

"What?"

He glanced out the door. "I'm guessing not. I'll tell you some other time." Narrowing his gaze, he cocked his head. "Would you be interested in joining the gang for happy hour on Friday?"

Stunned would probably describe my look at his from-out-of-left-field offer. I clamped my lips in a firm line so I wouldn't appear overly eager before answering, "Uh, sure. Where and when?"

"We meet at Jack's Bar at six-thirty. Maybe you can stop by."

"I'd love to." A resurgence of the specialness and warmness swept through my insides. "Th-thanks for the invite."

"I'd like to get to know you better."

He bounced his brow in a suggestive manner which scared me *un peu.*

Will picked up his coffee cup and winked over his shoulder as he exited. "Nice to meet you."

"Same here."

My gaze roved around the room, noting nothing in particular.

Oh boy, I'd definitely like to get to know him better.

****

On the very same day, Stuart stopped by my work station. He dug his hankie from his pocket for a sniff-sniff and a wipe. "There you are, Hattie. I've stopped a few other times to speak with you, but you weren't at your desk."

After making a final keystroke, I transferred my attention from the computer to him. "You know, Stuart, bathroom and coffee breaks are allowed."

"You don't drink coffee."

"How did you know that?"

"Someone around here mentioned it."

I was beginning to feel like Stuart was hanging around, hoping for something more. "So what can I do for you?"

"I've been wondering." A puzzled, pensive way took over the goofy expression he usually wore, one with a narrowed and studious brow. He rubbed a finger along the side of his nose. "I need to know what to wear to the barbecue. You forgot to tell me."

"Pretty explanatory. Dress for a barbecue and swim party."

He humpfed. "I know, but what exactly do I wear? I don't really have fun clothes."

I rolled my eyes. *Go take your pill, Stuart.* I should have known I would have to dole out explicit instructions on clothing attire. We were talking Stuart here and no telling what he would conjure up. "Don't you have jeans, shorts, swim trunks, and stuff?"

"Not really. I wear shirts like this"—he pointed to the button-down garment he wore—"nearly every day."

Amazing. But not too surprising. "Every day? Even on weekends?"

His head bobbed. "Even on weekends. I use a permanent marker and write the date of purchase on the inside of the collar. That way, the newest ones are worn to work and the others for every other day."

"How thorough." *And nerdy.*

"It's"—the corners of his mouth drooped into a tiny frown—"it's why I need your help."

I bet he had a hard time admitting that. With a soft sigh, I melted a tiny bit. *Poor baby.*

I'd visited Casey's Sports and Fishing the other day and spotted men's swimwear marked seventy-five percent off with the end-of-summer sale. At the fantastic price, he would be lucky if anything but junky leftovers remained on the clearance tables.

I told him what he needed to know and where to go.

****

The next day, I met Cathy Bartholomew, who I instantly placed as Allan Wellborn's current girlfriend and the blonde I'd seen when waiting for the elevator on the day I interviewed. What a shocker! I didn't know she worked at Northside, Lancaster, and Brookside. But I didn't know anything about her, except what she looked like—glimpsed the one time through water-filled eyes—at Mamma and Pappa's Italian Bistro with Allan. Afterwards, I'd wanted to obliterate the whole incident.

I'd made my way to the supply room to scan a large document and hadn't paid close attention to where I was headed. As Cathy Bartholomew and I rounded our respective corners, we collided. Literally. Like the incidents portrayed in a movie.

After polite apologies, we introduced ourselves and talked about our specific jobs at NLB.

She handed me the documents I'd dropped. "So sorry 'bout that, darlin'. Are you hurt?"

I had no bumps or bruises, but I wasn't comfortable either. "I'm fine. Are you okay?"

"Perfect," she said in her perky voice. "You're Mr. Northside's temp'rary administrative assistant, right?"

I juggled the papers and folders into a manageable pile and set the book on top. "Yes, I'm Hattie Cooks."

"Nice to meet ya. Cathy Bartholomew, administrative assistant to William Christiansen. He's a Senior Audit Manager."

I pasted a faux smile on my face and nodded. "I met him in the kitchen the other day. He seems nice."

"He is. And very handsome." She tilted her head. "Are you settlin' in okay?"

At this point, I prayed she hadn't recognized me as Allan's old girlfriend which could be sticky, especially with both of us working at the same company. Uncomfortable notions clouded my head. Talking with her caused my stomach to clench in a hurtful way. My grip tightened on the papers I held.

Eventually, I found my voice, and because Mom would say *be nice to everyone*, I said, "The NLB staff has been so kind. Your boss helped me clean up a spill I'd made."

"Isn't he a dream?"

Her eyes twinkled when she talked about him and made me wonder if something was going on between them. "He sure is hunky."

"We work so well together."

"How nice." *Nice.* Gag me. *I need a new vocabulary.*

"A good administrative assistant can anticipate her boss' every need," she said.

"I'm sure he appreciates the quality."

Cathy Bartholomew embodied everything I wasn't, nor would ever be. She stood five feet-three inches and looked to weigh a hundred pounds soaking wet. She sported dry, bleached-to-death long locks, a small tight ass, big round baby blues, and most importantly—for all guys' requirements—large imported tatas.

Combined with four-inch heels, though she didn't struggle in them like I did, she appeared to be almost as tall as me.

Without a doubt, I knew all guys ogled in appreciation when Cathy Bartholomew sashayed by, her hips rocking in a seductive sway to mesmerize them. Surely, her admirers bent over backward and forward to peek down her low-cut blouse and catch a hint of the imported tatas. Her voice dripped with the honey-dewed sweetness of the Southern drawl she employed.

Guys loved her kind, and their girlfriends disliked them just…because.

Flummoxed best described what my head experienced while she yakked on and on. For the life of me, I couldn't figure out why Allan dated a girl who looked like her. I mean, his alternative could have been me.

What's so bad about that?

"If you get in a jam, you call me. I've been here for a while and know my way 'round real well," she said with an affirming nod.

I'd call her over my dead body, but I'd never say so. Something false hovered about her, and I couldn't put my nose to it, just a woman's intuitive feeling, and one which rarely led me wrong. "Thanks for the offer. Oh," I held up one finger, "there is one thing—"

"Yes?" She paused by the door.

"People ask me if 'I know' then don't follow up. Is there something I should know?"

Her eyes narrowed to viper-like slits. "I can't imagine what it would be. I can find out, if you'd like."

"Don't go to lots of trouble."

"Darlin'," she tossed a hank of her big hair with a full-powered smile, "trouble is my middle name."

I didn't doubt for a nanosecond *trouble* was her middle name.

Seeing all her bodily perfection, I seriously considered hating her even more—if that was possible.

****

The same day of my run-in with Cathy Bartholomew, Stuart and I had a chance encounter at the stairway door leading to the office suite beneath us. "Hey, Stuart," I said while hurrying past him.

"Hattie." He lightly touched my upper am. "Just the woman I need."

"What can I do for you?" I rested my hips against the railing and looked up where my gaze was assaulted by another napkin-sized tie, this time in Kelly green. My eyelids fluttered rapidly to blot out the blinding color.

"I'm wondering what kind of gift I should bring to your party?"

Oh, surprise me, Stuart. I ground my teeth. Instead, I used a page from Mom's "Be Nice to Other People" little talk. "You don't have to bring a gift."

His eyes and mouth formed a pout, something I'd expect from a little boy, not a grown man.

"But I want to."

"Why don't you make a donation to your favorite charity instead?"

"I don't know. I could but would rather do something else." He looked at his shoes then up at me from the corner of his eye.

What to do, what to do? I tapped my finger to my cheek. Then a terrific suggestion popped in my head.

"How about flowers?"

"Flowers? Just flowers?" His brow creased as his finger stroked the side of his nose. "Are you sure? Doesn't seem expensive enough."

"You can never go wrong with flowers," I said with good authority. "If there is anything women world-wide adore, it's flowers."

"Any kind?"

"Any kind—except sprigs of holly. Save that one for Christmas. Nor poison ivy. Pink is a safe bet, and your recipient's favorite color."

"How many?"

I cocked my head. "Depends on the flower."

"Sometimes, roses come in a dozen."

"True."

His brows crinkled. "Wouldn't a potted plant be more desirous?"

Desirous—*seriously?* My head did a no-no-no. "Cut flowers are the best way to go, wrapped in paper. Your recipient likes to arrange her own."

"Ten-four." After giving me a jaunty farewell salute, he continued down the staircase.

H*as he been watching British television dramas with his mom?* Floating toward me came this one word, "Flowers."

I could have sworn he skipped away like a baby goat. I studied his departing back, praying I'd prevented a catastrophe.

****

The next day, I munched on my tuna sandwich— home-prepared to save cash and without my favorite veggie, onions—in the break room adjacent to the kitchenette. In between bites, I was absorbed in reading

49

the ever-present lurid romance on my e-reader.

"Excuse me," someone said.

Reluctantly, I drew my gaze from my e-book. A cherubic young man stood next to my table, a brown paper bag in one hand.

"Can I sit with you? All the chairs are taken." His wave took in the rest of the room.

I glanced around. He was right; no other places to park his bod were available. "Of course."

As he eased back a chair, he said, "I won't bother you while you read."

I shut my secret indulgence. "I'd rather talk with you."

He took the hand I'd extended.

"I'm Hattie Cooks, Mr. Northside's temporary assistant."

"I know. I heard. Phillip Meadows." A freshly scrubbed, right-out-of-college boy, beginning his professional accounting career with Northside, Lancaster, and Brookside best described Phillip. He stood about five foot-eleven, blond hair cut short to curb the wave, and had grass-green eyes. Pimples dotted his chin and forehead. Healthy, young, energetic.

I munched a barbecue chip, an excellent accompaniment to the tuna sandwich and way more fun than a carrot.

He shook a pbj and a yogurt container from a plastic grocery sack. "I forgot to bring a drink. Excuse me while I get a soda."

"Sure."

Phillip trekked to the drink machine, deposited change into a slot, and retrieved a can. Over his shoulder, he asked, "Want another? My treat."

I lifted my unfinished one. "I'm good."

While we ate, we discussed our first-day jitters, where he'd attended college—State Technological University, like me!—and his career aspirations.

He took a bite of his sandwich, and a plop of grape jelly nearly soiled his shirt. "It's nice to visit with somebody. The hallways are confusing. I tend to get lost when I leave my desk."

"I know exactly what you mean." I leaned in. "I've never worked at such a large firm before. I kinda memorized routes to this room and the copy room. Possibly, taped lines like what you'd find on a hospital floor would help."

"I like that idea." He spooned some yogurt. "So where's the nightlife around Sommerville?"

"There isn't much. Sommerville is a quiet, relatively crime-free town. I'm going to happy hour on Friday at Jack's Bar. You should come, too."

He licked the plastic ware spoon clean. "Sounds good."

I heard anticipation tingeing his response. Looked like I'd adopted another stray. First, Stuart, and now, Phillip.

Does everyone believe I rescued puppies and kitties as well?

I would.

****

Later on while inputting data, I noticed Stuart coming toward my desk. I stopped what I was typing.

"Hattie."

"Yes, Stuart?"

"I forgot to get the address for your apartment."

Be still my heart. I jotted down the full street

address on a memo pad and handed him the slip. "Here you go. My apartment complex is on Boston Avenue."

His smile was larger than a Texas cowboy hat. He slipped the mini-pad from his shirt pocket and inputted the information in his map app. "I'm almost positive I can find it, but to be sure, I'll put the address in my phone's GPS, too. I wouldn't want to get lost or be late." He trotted off, scrutinizing the paper.

The line from a seventies tune about "how to treat a lady" followed him. Heat swathed my head and using my hand, I fanned my face. I began to have regrets about letting Stuart Steems accompany me to my birthday party.

Here's praying he remembers the ground rules.

****

On Friday after filling the Jeep with much-needed gas, which caused me to run a smidge tardy, I met the party-hearty NLB gang for happy hour at Jack's Bar. Their loud cheers of "Hattie!" sounded reassuring to my ears, yet called to mind a sitcom my parents had watched when I was younger about a bar and its regulars. Lots of wood paneling. An assortment of beer pulls. Racks of glasses stored overhead. A light-on-his-feet bartender dispensing drinks and quips.

My watch read six-thirty. I looked around for William Christiansen, but I didn't spot him. I made a few discreet inquiries only to discover he'd already left. *Darn it. Whatever happened to getting to know me better?*

Maybe Will had made other plans. Maybe he'd forgotten he invited me to happy hour. Maybe he had gone back to work.

I convinced myself a million excuses existed and to

not take his early leaving personally.

I noticed Cathy Bartholomew across the room with a dozen swains draped over her. Our gazes intersected, and she gave me a dazzling smile and signaled for me to join her group, but I just shook my head, smiled, and flicked a short wave. *Best to steer clear of her.* She may be nice, but she was still Allan's heartthrob.

By the way… *Why isn't he with her?*

After I visited with other NLB employees, I pushed my way to the counter to place an order only to find Phillip belly-up to the bar with a Lone Star beer bottle in his grasp.

He threw his free arm across my shoulders and gave a slight squeeze. "Hey, Hattie, you're here. Lots of people have asked about you."

"Really?" *How interesting.* My pulse elevated in a flash. *Will Christiansen?* "Who?"

He gave a small frown. "Cathy. Will. Bookie Dave."

I indicated our co-workers with a slant from my head and sat next to him. "It looks as if you're having fun."

"They've been great." He twisted on the bar stool. "I feel lucky to have this job. You helped me feel welcomed."

"Aw." I fluttered my lashes. "It was nothing."

"Nevertheless, I want to buy my new friend a drink. What'll it be?"

"Lemon-lime soda with a lime wedge."

"No booze?"

"Sometimes, I have a glass of champagne, but not tonight." I usually limited myself to one drink because without food, I became an easy drunk. Since Jenny and

I had plans for dinner afterward and the only designated driver of my car was me, a soda was the best alternative.

After my drink had been delivered, he asked, "Did you hear about the…"

I'd heard a variation on this question two other times now. "About the what?"

"You don't know?"

Biting back disappointment, I shook my head. "Nope. Ignorant as a newly birthed babe."

His mouth twisted aside as he rotated his bottle in circles. "If no one else has said anything, I don't think I should say."

I patted his arm. Using my best coaxing skills, which involved a low sexy voice, long slow blinks, and the sure-to-rope-'em leaning in, I drawled, "Come on, Phillip. Tell me."

His hand covered mine. "Hattie, I like to think of you as my pal, but this time, I can't. I shouldn't have opened my big fat mouth. I hope you understand."

I slid my hand from his grasp and lengthened my spine. "Of course. It's okay."

Phillip and I chitchatted with the NLB people for about an hour. I searched the room for Stuart in case I needed to implement my duck-and-cover escape plan. Another auditor asked who I was looking for, and when I said, he told me Stuart drove straight home after work to fix dinner with his mother. *No big surprises there.*

After finishing my drink, I excused myself to meet Jenny for a much-deserved steak dinner with a side order of onion strings at Yahoo! Ranch Steakhouse, because every now and then, we had to eat meat-for-the-week.

Chapter Five

I woke with the euphoria everyone experiences on their birthday. *My day. Nobody else's.*

Special things were coming. As I took another glance out my window, I stretched my arms overhead, and then let them flop to my side. My mouth widened in a pleased grin. *Today is the very best day.*

Outside looked picture perfect, like a Saturday morning cartoon. The blue jays chirped a cheerful song. The bright yellow sun bounced in rhythm while smiling. And the cute and cuddly animal friends seated on the windowsill sang a gleeful "good morning" greeting as they swayed in unison.

"My birthday, my birthday, my happy-happy birthday." I cheerfully sang this little made-up ditty as I laced my fingers and lifted my arms into a second overhead stretch. When my muscles made a relaxing give, I released an *aah*.

I felt the love.

That wasn't what I got.

What I got was Jenny banging on my bedroom door.

"Hattie."

She didn't even wait for me to answer, she barged in.

"Are you up?"

Jenny, short for Jennifer, Arbuthnot settled on the

edge of my bed and bounced the mattress up and down, up and down in a light movement presumably just to annoy me. A mischievous spark fired in her warm brown eyes.

I shook my head. Her pesky efforts would not work, not today of all days. Nothing anyone, absolutely positively anyone, anywhere—including my roommate—could do would ruin my day. My birthday.

After fluffing my pillows, I propped my head against the headboard. Now, I could give her silly game my full attention. Jenny gave a light giggle. "Do you want your present here or at your mother's?"

Why would she be offering my present now?

Oh-oh-oh, I know, I know. Maybe she's bought an extra-special gift. I adored those. Maybe she purchased something from Tuckers Department Store. I would really love something extraordinary—and expensive—to wear.

On a previous birthday, Jenny had given me sexy pink lacey undies and a matching bra. I hoped she would gift me with something like that again—especially considering the panties from the set were missing since the night of almost-wild, almost-sex with Allan.

However, the word "mother" caused my mom-o-meter to tick on. "Mother? Is there something weird about my present? Something I need to know?"

"You know how she is." She examined her fingernails and flicked a hangnail. "She has planned a really great theme party for you. Teasing you beforehand seemed like a good idea."

I extended my arms and rippled my fingers to magically summon the present forth. "Give it to me.

Now."

"N period. O period," Jenny said in a firm voice.

No? I dropped my arms and cocked my head. *What does this mean?* Her joking wasn't a nice manner in which to treat a birthday BFF. I fastened on her a one-eyed frown. "So, you really have no intention of giving me my birthday present?"

"Not really. This one needs to be savored." Bouncey, bouncey. "Besides, your mom would kill me if I told."

Uh-oh. My radar surfaced like a periscope on a D-class nuclear submarine armed with twenty deadly missiles. *This would not do. No siree.* Sometimes, Mom's surprises were incredibly unique. Translated, this meant on occasion her presents were:

—Butt ugly

—Not needed

—Childish

I didn't want to sound completely ungrateful about Mom's gifts. In truth, I very much appreciated everything she gave me. I really struggled with keeping the unusual presents and then donating them to a charity when they weren't used. Most had been stashed on the top shelf of my closet in case she visited and made inquiries about them.

"I know this story. Mom's presents are just…slightly…bizarre. One time when asked what I wanted, I answered a sexy nightie. What I got was pink feet-y pajamas embellished with cute white bunnies, styled like the red long johns old miners wore during the Gold Rush days."

Undoubtedly, this kind of nightmare-wear had been Mom's idea of birth control.

"On another joyous occasion, I received sets of socks embroidered with holiday symbols for every month. Hearts for Valentine's, spring chicks for Easter, pumpkins for Halloween, and candy canes for Christmas. Again, Mom had asked what I wanted for my birthday, and I specified a particular brand of expensive hosiery." I shrugged.

"Unfortunately, she happened to be shopping at the mall and passed a store which specialized in zany gag gifts. Cutely displayed in the window were the holiday socks. Intrigued, Mom entered the establishment and"—I rolled my hand along—"I received socks, not the requested hose, for every freakin' holiday."

This year, Mom didn't ask. I wouldn't be out of line to assume *Days of the Week* panties were probably in my future. I touched my finger to my cheek. Perhaps Days-of-the-Week panties weren't such a bad idea after all. They would be easy to organize and keep track of.

I might need to do pre-damage control. Opening that gift at my party would be mammoth-ly embarrassing. "You should tell me everything. If you're my friend who loves and adores me, you'll tell what Mom has planned."

Jenny's hands flew to cover her chest, conveying the horror of the thought. "Not me. No way. I'm not saying a thing. I know your mom, and she's mean."

After all the years of hearing about each other's mothers, the Funsisters accepted all mothers were mean. Not altogether true, except for Trixie's mother. Maybe Trixie exaggerated. She invited us to accompany her on road trips to her mother's house. We would emphatically say "no" because her mother's scary reputation seemed real to us.

I knew Mrs. Wellborn was mean as well.

"My mother loves you." I hadn't lied. Mom said very complimentary things about Jenny and would converse with her on the phone often, just like she did with her own offspring, like an adopted daughter, or a foreign exchange student.

"True." Jenny pressed her well-manicured hand to her small bosom's valley and feigned adoration. Then she gave me a level-eyed look. "I'm still keeping the secret."

What a tough nut. "I'll phone Tracey. She'll tell me."

"Only when drawing her last breath before she passes to the great beyond."

Darn.

Jenny and I'd been best friends since our Tucker days. She moved into the second bedroom my other roomie had vacated after her wedding. We shared our apartment, our food, and our most intimate secrets like blood sisters. We even shared chocolate.

Bouncey, bouncey went the mattress.

Each squeak caused me to hope her trampoline act wouldn't break my grandmother's old iron bed. *Oh well. Lately, it doesn't get a workout any other way.*

"She came up with a good surprise. Wish I had thought of it."

Her words further intrigued me. Not put off by her tactics, I had a foolproof plan I could fall back on. I knew all the tricks. Later on, Jenny would run an errand. I would thoroughly search the apartment, because I knew her hiding spots.

That's a really good plan. Nonchalantly, I studied my own nails. A manicure before my birthday debut would be a superb idea. "Fine. I can hold out." I flicked my fingers. "You go do whatever you have to."

"It's not here."

Jenny could read minds—a talent. "Damn." I gave my temple a memory-inducing rub. And *presto!* Another plan was called forth. I could phone the other Funsisters and wiggle from them what Jenny's gift was or even better, their gifts, and Mom's master plan.

"They won't tell either. The Funsisters took a secret birthday gift-giving oath." Jenny held up her three fingers in an endorsing pledge. "Your mother made us."

I fisted my hand in the comforter. *What kind of friends are these? There must be some other way.* "Damn."

"No way are we telling you anything. Trust me, you'll be so surprised, you'll laugh your pants off."

Where does Jenny get her bizarre mind-reading capabilities? "This isn't fair," I whined more to myself, "Aren't you my friend?"

"The very best. Don't worry. You'll love it. I told you, trust me." Bouncey, bouncey.

Trust her? I don't know. The same friend who, on occasion, revealed my deepest darkest secrets to all, ultimately embarrassing me?

At that moment, a scary idea passed through my brain. I bet my gift was a newly published copy of Mom's little talks. Instead of good reading, her gift would make good kindling.

****

Darn GPS! Stuart arrived right on time. Couldn't the mapping system be non-operational for once? Why not today?

I opened the door at his ring, but if he spoke, I didn't hear a word. My mouth wouldn't work. My voice didn't come. Hell, my body was close to being paralyzed. I examined Stuart from head-to-toe. He looked, for lack of a better word, out-rage-ous.

I turned my gaze to the heavens and pleaded, *dear God, help!* Guilt planted in my chest as I remembered why I'd invited him in the first place—to be nice. I could only blame myself; I'd known better.

When I had been cornered by Stuart at the office and asked what to wear, I'd given him general dress instructions. I'd supposed everyone knew what to wear to barbecues, but not weirdly clothing-challenged Stuart.

I should commit to memory the phrase "never underestimate Stuart. "

"Here." He shoved a paper sleeve filled with the tiniest blush pink roses in my arms.

Probably more like three dozen. "Oh, Stuart, they are stunning."

"Glad you liked them. Mother has a friend who is a florist. She knew exactly what a man should give his date."

Date? I stiffened. Lordy. I had to remind him about the ground rules. I set the flowers on the coffee table.

Smiling, he lifted his arms and spinned on the ball of his left foot. "How do you like my outfit?"

In one quick instance, my wonderful flower thoughts diverted to his clothing.

Pinching the seams of his red-and-black plaid swim trunks paired with a white, short-sleeved, oxford cloth shirt, he rotated from side-to-side to show off. The tie was missing. Slowly, my gaze swept over the shirt to the shoes to find sandals on his feet—*don't get me started on shoe colors*—which looked new with knee-length tube socks.

His grin stretched across the entire universe. "And how fantastic the socks and shirt match."

I hacked out a choking cough. "G-great."

"After our talk, I ordered this shipped express from an outdoorsman catalog my mom recommended. The customer service lady assured me this would be the perfect ensemble to wear to your party."

Ensemble? *Strangling Ms. Helpful Sales Rep later* swept through my mind. He would have been better off wearing a sweater when the outside temperature was one-hundred degrees.

That wasn't all.

He'd placed on his shirt pocket a fill-in-the-blank "Hi! My Name Is" sticky nametag, inscribed with what appeared to be permanent blue-black ink in large capital letters, "STUART STEEMS."

This pretty much confirmed what I'd been aware of all along: Stuart didn't party. Desperately, I needed divine dating intervention.

With a firm line shaping my lips, I determined not even Stuart could ruin my special day. I didn't have to marry him. Just be nice. To send the bad dating doldrums from my head, I hummed my song: *It's my birthday. My birthday, my birthday, my happy, happy birthday.*

"What to do, what to do" thoughts flooded my entire being. While I tapped my toes, I attempted to decide between a home improvement plan versus an extreme makeover for my escort. I decided to give him a demi-overhaul now and pointed to his legs totally encased in the knee-high lederhosen while smothering a giggle. "Stuart, my advice is to lose the-the socks."

His look dropped to where I'd gestured. "But they match my shirt."

"Socks match shoes, not shirts."

"Oh." He paused for a long, long, long time. "I have ugly legs."

Once again, Stuart managed to stun me. I'd never heard a guy admit he had ugly legs. *Aren't most guys' legs hairy?* Just visualizing them could lead to picturing other furry parts of his body. I didn't have nor want that kind of imagination.

Allan Wellborn's were—*change the subject, Hattie.*

I prayed again and even though my family didn't practice Catholicism, I crossed my chest.

After a reluctant peek, even from my side, I could see he was right. His legs were kinda knobby in knee socks. What could be underneath? He was sorta on the thin side. So maybe, they were skinny?

However, if he wanted to meet girls, his geeky socks had to go. "Stuart, the look you're sporting is from the fifties. I'm telling you girls don't go for guys wearing socks with sandals."

Stuart scratched the side of his nose while considering what I'd said. "Okay." He sat on the threshold step and took off the sandals, then the socks.

I leaned over to watch.

He was right—Stuart had ugly legs. Ugly. Scrawny. Very gorilla-hairy legs. Yet firm calves. I shuddered. If his legs were like this, what…

Don't go there. Don't go there.

Wasn't it interesting teenage boys want man hair?

And later on when they reached the old man time of their life, when hair sprouted from ears and noses and eyebrows, growing stiff and poky, that same hair could be too much?

I checked again and couldn't decide if Stuart's legs were improved with or without the socks. Perhaps tonight at the party, evening would come quickly, and under the cloak of darkness, his legs would be hidden.

Or maybe I could suggest weight workouts to improve the skinny aspect. I glanced at my watch. Not nearly enough time.

Or we could stop at the convenience store and load up on junk food. With a lotta luck, possibly Stuart could put on a few pounds and plump up the legs by the time we got to Mom's.

Or Stuart could sit at the head of the table for the whole entire party, and I would wait on him hand and foot. I would convince him the Cooks' family treated every special guest in this manner. He would believe me.

I rubbed a circle on my temple. *None of these schemes will work.* Inevitably, he would have to use the bathroom, and everyone would catch a glimpse of his lower limbs.

I had to lay on him a good pep talk. Straightening, I towered over him, and when the name tag caught my eye a second time, I said, "Stuart, we're leaving the accounting profession at work. Tonight is all about fun."

With a serious intensity, Stuart's gaze directed on me like a cat readying to make a gecko his lunch.

I extended my hand, palm up. "Give me your calculator."

When he stood, he cut his eyes to the holly bushes by the front steps. "I don't have a calculator."

"Don't lie to me." I patted swim shorts pocket on his right side and felt something small, about credit card size. From his pocket, I seized the computing device. "Gotcha."

Stuart's cheeks bloomed red.

"Hand over the pen, pencils, and whatever else you stashed in your left pocket unless you want me to frisk you."

With slow moves, he passed over the requested items.

"I'll give them back later." After I'd tossed them into the open apartment, I rippled my fingers. "Your phone."

His mouth dropped open. "My phone? Seriously, you can't take my phone. What if my mother calls?"

Lordy. "Why don't you text her my cell number?"

"I can't do that. She wouldn't answer. You two haven't been properly introduced."

Lordy-lordy. "Fine. But you better not use it. And I mean don't use the calculator app either. Nothing. *Capiche*?"

"Yes, ma'am."

I'd done the best I could. A quick check of my watch said five-forty-five. Time to go. I gave Stuart one last once-over.

He bobbed over and under my arm to peek inside my place.

With a quick pull, I shut the door.

"Aren't you going to invite me in?" he asked.

"Nope. Why would you want to go in my apartment?"

"I just want to see how the other half lives."

The other half? I rolled my eyes. You'd think we were already engaged. For the second time, I swiftly made The Sign of the Cross. "We don't have time for a guided tour of my apartment. I have to help Mom. Do you remember the ground rules?"

"No kissing. No hugging. No whispering in your ear." He ticked off each item on his left hand.

"Good. Don't forget hand-holding."

"Is there a ground rule for having fun?"

Smarty pants. Setting my hands on his shoulders, I turned his body and gave him a push toward the parking lot. I chanted under my breath, "It's my birthday, my birthday, my happy, happy birthday…"

Stuart's face was smeared with exuberance like someone who'd just won an over-sized stuffed animal at the State Fair's Midway. I hadn't seen him slobber, but the possibility could still occur, just as long as he didn't sniff crotches like a lot of doggies did.

Sniffing reminded me. "Stuart, you aren't sneezing or wiping today."

"I planned ahead and took the allergy medication. I didn't want to blow snot over any prospective babes."

Babes.

Look out, girls, here he comes. I closed my eyes and breathed to find my zen. *I'll need lots of it tonight.* Again, I sent my gaze to the heavens above. How in the wide world of ducks did Stuart get promoted to Senior Audit Manager? His talent in accounting must outweigh his social ineptness.

I could only hope his allergy pill was the twenty-four-hour variety.

****

I had better hopes for Stuart than the burnt sienna 1998 4-door sedan he owned. At least his Grandma-mobile didn't look rusty, wasn't dotted with dings, and hopefully, polluting smoke didn't cloud the atmosphere. I took a deep lungful of air. The upholstery smelled and looked clean with no visible signs of out-of-body experiences on the back seat. The car hadn't been lined with aluminum foil to channel aliens from outer space. Nope, Stuart's ride looked to be dirt-free, highly polished, and with shiny chrome.

Just prehistoric.

Stuart drove with capable skill to Mom's and Dad's.

Visibly relieved, I sat with my hip hugging the door. My companion's vibes undulated across the front seat to my side. He acted so excited about the party, he was about to jump out of *my* skin.

It's my birthday, my birthday, my happy, happy birthday...

"Interesting car," I said. According to a recent article in *About Moi* magazine, this line always bought a girl a lot of mileage with men. Guys loved to dish the dirt about their cars.

Stuart beamed and patted his ride's dash with affection. "I like it. I saved a lot of money buying from Mom when she purchased a new one."

I guess he wasn't into hot cars to impress the babes. *Wonder what she drove?* "Oh?"

"And with the savings, I invested in mutual funds."

Practical Stuart invested in his future, an admirable quality. Time to discover, uncover—*oh, whatever*—more. "Stuart, what do you do for fun besides investing in mutual funds?"

He blushed and ducked his chin. "It's sorta embarrassing."

"Tell me. I want to know more about you."

"Promise not to laugh?"

This must be really good. "I promise."

"For fun, my mom and I take ballroom dancing lessons."

Maybe my hearing was non-operational. I swallowed deep, the kind one does for corroboration. "Stuart, did you say you dance with your mother?"

"Yes." He bobbed his head so vigorously, he nearly chinned the steering wheel. "Mother's a fantastic ballroom dancer. We've even waltzed in competitions and won several local contests. We hope to go to Nationals one day."

This explained the photos sitting on his office bookshelves of the couple on a dance floor. I wondered what his mother looked like and envisioned a stout female, resembling him with a crew cut. Hopefully, she didn't have the hairy—I shook my head. My imagination didn't need to go there either. "Can you tell me about your family?"

"Well, I mentioned my mom. My dad died when I was five." He lifted his left shoulder. "I don't have any brothers or sisters, just me and my mom."

"I'm sorry."

"That's all right. He died a long time ago. When we lived in the small West Texas town where I mostly grew up, I took dancing lessons at the local recreation center. Mother decided I should take them as part of my developmental curriculum, along with the etiquette and deportment classes."

Most guys I knew from my adolescent days would

go kicking and screaming to those classes. My sister and I had participated in something similar which focused on:

Proper posture: Shoulders back, chin up.

Sitting: Legs crossed at ankles.

Conversing: It's all about them.

Dancing: No smelly arm pits.

Hygiene: Combed eyebrows.

Was it possible he'd been absent for some sessions? I stared out the window and recited another prayer.

Stuart could be a regular guy, but he sounded more like a mama's boy.

****

Stuart and I were the first arrivals at the birthday party. I had the esteemed privilege to introduce him to Mom and Dad. I rarely introduced dates to my parents and with good reason—the guys would have to endure Mom's scrutiny and possible little talks, and Mom would have to tolerate their oddities. I probably blew this out-of-proportion. My parents were just being parents.

After presenting Stuart to them, I saw a little wiggle of shock course over Mom's body when her gaze hit the "Hi, I'm Stuart Steems" nametag.

Knowing her Mom Code, she would never intentionally embarrass him. First, her lips pressed in a stiff line and her eyes squinted to read the tag better. After a while, she composed herself and extended her hand, saying, "How nice to meet you, Stuart. The nametag is an excellent idea." Here she used a page from the "Say Something Nice about Everyone" little talk.

But my body froze with an *uh-oh*. If Mom really liked the nametag idea, she would dig up some for the rest of the partygoers, which would be bad. But on the other hand, *he-he-he*, I could stick one on Tracey's butt which read "Follow Me." Sure, the idea was juvenile, but weren't birthdays all about fun?

Hastily, I diverted attention from the nametag scheme by introducing Stuart to Dad.

Dad took Stuart's hand and gave a firm shake. "So, you work with Hattie?"

"Yes, sir," Stuart said. "Hattie's a breath of fresh air at the office. We really enjoy having her. She's so helpful and kind. We really are grateful for—"

"Well, Stuart, that's nice to hear." Dad interrupted Stuart's overenthusiastic accolades about his darling daughter. He slung his arm around new friend's shoulder. As he propelled Stuart toward the drinks area, Dad asked, "How about a beer?"

Stuart nodded. "I like beer."

"Great."

In Dad's hands, Stuart would be helping with bartending and talking sports in a matter of minutes—if he knew what sports were. Maybe Stuart would succumb to our family motto: A beer leads to dancing. And if my plan worked, Stuart would find another victim besides this date for the dancing part.

A brush of my hands rid me of Stuart for the time being. I followed Mom's beckoning—read, demanding—finger to the burger station located by the pool.

Mom. *What more can one say?*

Most mothers were unique unto themselves, and mine fell into the upper echelon of the category. Known as Elaine, my mom was a very pretty woman, about five feet-seven inches tall, her brown hair cut short and highlighted with dark blonde streaks. From her, I inherited my brown eyes and wide smile.

She was a highly creative person and worked in multiple volunteer capacities in our schools when we were younger. The library, church, and other organized groups of ladies involved in projects to better the world benefited as well. Her food contributions for potluck church dinners were scarfed down. She cleaned like a hospital worker and competently drove her darling daughters everywhere.

Most mothers dispensed moral advice to their children, and ours was no exception. My mother's most outstanding characteristic was instructing her young girls on proper behavior through "little talks," causing her to sound like a Nag-A-Matic. She delivered her speeches with grace and charm. Truths were instilled in us, and thus, we were armed for life.

We'd always hoped Mom would take on other benevolent causes like Save the Whales or World Peace. But no. Raising her children to perfection with proper ethics would be her path to perpetuity.

Aside from the little lectures, Mom was tons of fun, filled to the top with hugs and kisses. She packed picnics, even though we had to sit on the kitchen floor because of rain. To our everlasting embarrassment, she shook her tushy when she chaperoned school dances. When watching timeless musicals on the classic movie channel, she sang along with all of the songs. Presumably under the guise to save our teeth, she ate our chocolate candy treats collected on Halloween.

From the grilling station, she signaled even more

furiously with a fiercely whispered, "Hattie!"

With a sigh, I joined Mom only to be assigned the job of flipping burgers. After all these years, I knew to arrive early to my own birthday party in order to help— a daughter requirement.

Mom had decorated the backyard patio areas with twinkling party lights. Red-and-white checkered plastic tablecloths covered the wrought iron tables. Centered on each had been placed a sizeable flower arrangement...

I studied the flowers. They looked...

I tilted closer.

I could have sworn...

I scrunched my eyes. It couldn't be...

I smiled. *How original!*

I fingered the petals. "Mom, are the flowers made with little treat packages of M&Ms?"

Mom giggled. "They are."

"Unbelievable. Where did you find them?"

"I made them. I asked your guests to gift you with your favorite chocolate for your birthday. This"—she pointed with pride to the arrangement—"is my contribution. Yellow packages are hot-glued in a circle with a black one in the middle. Then I wrapped them on a stiff wire and covered the stem with floral tape, slipping in random leaves. I arranged them in a pot with green ivy and tied with a bow. Voila!"

I was surprised. I was floored. I was speechless.

Jenny was right. I had to hand it to Mom, her out-of-this-world gift was really, really good and amazingly, not weird at all. I'd learned from my mom chocolate possessed restorative and curative powers. And she'd given me the ultimate birthday gift of all time—a large supply.

No way would these be seeing the garbage can or the lofty stratum of my closet. While squeezing her shoulders, I said, "This is the most excellent gift ever."

Her head modestly dipped to the side as she twerked her hip against mine. "I know. Bet you were expecting Days-of-the-Week undies." She brandished her finger at me, primed with a little talk. "Don't eat all the chocolate at once."

I understood her implication: I'd get an upset stomach, or constipation, or diabetes from too much sugar.

The arrival of the Funsisters, some of whom had dates, interrupted our conversation. Collectively, the Funsisters were Jenny; Trixie, owner of Jobs, Inc.; Maggie, our physician; Kella, aka Killer or Keller, the sensible financial planner; and Tracey, my younger sister.

After greeting the girls, I turned to welcome the next guests and froze like a stalagmite. Mom's best friend, Shirley Wellborn accompanied by her husband, Ken, had arrived.

Spying her grocery cohort, Mrs. Wellborn waved and weaved her way toward us. "I missed you at this week's Library Board meeting, Elaine. We worked on the art show." She gave Mom a hug and then turned to me. "Why hello, Harriette, and Happy Birthday!"

After all these years, Mrs. Wellborn continued to call me Harriette. She stood slightly shorter than Mom, her white hair bobbed, dressed impeccably in fresh-from-the-cleaners sky blue capris with a matching floral print top, knotted at her trim waist. Overall, she carried an air of intimidation.

"Hi, Mrs. Wellborn. So nice to see you." I hoped lightning wouldn't strike me over the falsehood I'd just told and suppressed the urge to make a run for the Grand Canyon.

Mom took my spatula and flipped a pattie. "Oh, I know. I hated to miss the planning. I wanted to work on Hattie's party."

Mr. Wellborn pushed between them and crushed me to his chest. He pecked the top of my head. "I hope all your wishes come true on your special day, Hattie."

"Thank you, Mr. Wellborn. I'm happy you could party with us."

"Wouldn't miss it."

From over his shoulder, I saw the biggest shock of all time: Allan Wellborn coming through the garden gate with the woman who just happened to be my new co-worker, Cathy Bartholomew. She was affixed to his arm like a burr in a sock, like superglue stuck to my finger, like duct tape sealing a tear on a car's rag top.

Sweat coated my forehead while my stomach clenched. My gaze swung to Mr. Wellborn which threw me a little as I realized Allan resembled his dad so much, they could be identical twins. The same height. The dark hair. The long nose. I extricated myself from Mr. Wellborn and stepped back.

I watched Mr. Wellborn wave a small "hey" to his son and make his way to the drinks station to shake Dad's hand and take a beer from Stuart.

After Allan and I'd parted, I'd kept our breakup a secret from Mom. I didn't want our relationship failure to affect her long-time friendship with Mrs. Wellborn. Every Monday, she and Mrs. Wellborn convened over eggplant, or zucchini, or radicchio in the grocery store's produce section and discussed their respective families.

With Mom noticing Allan coming toward me with his date, she wouldn't have a hard time determining he and I were kaput.

To my relief, she didn't look up. Instead, she sent me to retrieve more burger patties from the fridge. With replenished platter in hand, I made my way through the breezeway only to pause at the fourth step down to the patio.

Allan stood at the bottom, looking up.

His face wore the uncomfortable look one had when lost like a baby lamb. We'd not spoken in a couple of months, and as a result, a huge knot took up residence in my belly. I tried backing my way out, but he'd already caught my eye. Being the polite birthday girl, I took the initiative and pasted on a bright smile.

"Why are you here?" I'd said a rude opening line, but sometimes my thoughts hurled forth all by themselves.

Apparently happy to be talking to someone—even me—Allan leaned over and kissed my cheek. My face flushed at the graze of his soft mouth against my skin which tingled better than my memory of other times.

"Happy birthday, Hattie. Your mom saw my mom at the grocery store on Monday."

Big surprise.

"They started talking—like they always do. Eventually, their conversation turned to your party, et cetera. She kindly invited the whole family."

I bet a newly acquired M&M pounder taking up residence in my sock drawer, she'd phoned Mrs. Wellborn to meet her at the grocery store. Over Brussels sprouts, she conducted her mission: Make judicious inquiries about Allan and invite the entire family to the party just to torture the birthday girl.

The complete cosmos knew she desired Allan for a son-in-law. She'd recited tomes on the topic. When she'd discovered through her co-conspirator we were dating, she trotted out her special, yet oft-repeated "What a Nice Boy Allan Wellborn Is" little talk, a particular favorite of hers during my high school years.

Neither Allan nor I knew where to begin conversing, so we just stood there. After a bit, he looked me over with an alluring twinkle in his eyes—one I had a hard time resisting.

His finger playfully plucked my swimsuit's shoulder strap. "I like this color."

Juusst great. Once, Allan had made this very same comment in regard to my lacey pink underwear which he peeled off me the night we engaged in almost-wild, almost-sex.

His remark had been directed to my new turquoise, cut high-on-the-thigh, tank-styled swimsuit with matching floral sarong, wrapped low around my hips. After all, my duty was to look exceptional on my birthday. Tonight was another one of those times when I felt my skinniest to be presentable in public, particularly in a swimsuit. No tummy bulging allowed.

To complete the ensemble, white flat sandals with a little flower between the first two toes shod my feet. My freshly manicured toenails had been painted Beautifully Pink. I opted out of high-heels because of my poor track record in falling off them. I would have looked supermodel good, but ruined the effect when I walked.

My cheeks flared to hot. I called on everything I

possessed to not make a smart retort. "So I've heard before."

His black eyes penetrated deep into my heart and soul. His grin guaranteed my body would dissolve into a puddle all over the floor.

I did a man-up thingy and stared in that I'm-not-backing-down way. God Almighty, he looked so beautiful. Swaying, I grasped the doorway to aid in gaining equilibrium while shifting the platter balanced on my other hand.

He said, "Let me help you. I wouldn't want to be responsible for ruining good food."

Me neither. I'd never hear the living end from Mom.

Allan supported my elbow and guided me carefully down the pavestone steps to the patio.

I sidestepped away. Again, we stood looking at each other, still unable to resume our conversation.

"So, how are you?" he asked. Before I could answer, he said, "Hattie, I've been meaning"—his voice trailed off as his head turned away. His finger rubbed across his chin—"I've been wanting…to talk to you about…"

Sucking in a breath, I braced myself for what was coming.

"About no."

Holy hell! I can't talk about that!

The shock and mortification caused me to flame and flush all over. My cheeks had to have turned an unattractive red. I used all the nerves I possessed while standing here, chatting with him now. My gaze circled the whole back yard as I searched for a direction I could gracefully exit.

Then off to my left, I heard an unexpected, high-pitched call, "Oh, All-llaaann."

Thank God. But when I turned to see who approached, my insides cried "not her.*" Anyone but her.*

Coming to his side, Cathy Bartholomew twined her arm with his and tugged him cozily in a possessive fashion. Cheerfully, she chirped with a cute nose scrunch, "Here you are, darlin'. Happy birthday, Hattie. How does it feel to be so old?"

The nerve. Bashing her pert face just topped my hit parade.

My dismay transformed into rage. If Allan had to bring a date to my birthday party, *why bring her?* First, I would strangle her, then him. Fortunately for them, my hands were occupied as I continued to hold the platter of uncooked meat.

"You know, she's very well-preserved."

Cathy Bartholomew whispered this newsflash loud enough for me to overhear while she batted an eye my way.

"I didn't know your birthday was today. You should have said something. I'd have baked a cake, and am guessin'"—she giggled—"Tee-hee-hee chocolate's your fav. I could've put M&Ms on top, too."

I would never-never, ever-ever eat anything she'd concocted. I would rather be poisoned or stabbed or even drawn-and-quartered first.

Allan put a serious look on each of us. "I didn't know you two worked together. When did this happen?"

"Not long ago, however, we're not technically together-together." Cathy Bartholomew gestured between our bodies. "Hattie's filling in for Mr. Northside's assistant who's on medical leave over the next few weeks."

"I know him and the firm well. I interned at NLB one summer before senior year."

"She's doing a fantastic job. Everyone at the office just loves her. She's so competent and efficient, kind and helpful—"

He nodded. "That's good."

Allan was man of few words. However, I could get a weird complex with the way Dad and now, he had cut-off my—well deserved, I might add—accolades. All their nixing any affirmation could give me a self-esteem complex.

"Didn't I tell you how Hattie and I met, darlin'?" Cathy Bartholomew continued babbling in her lazy drawl.

Darlin' again? She moved fast. And I never called Allan "darlin'." A. Wellborn—yes. Darlin'?—icky.

Allan's body cringed a tiny bit at her use of the endearment. He shook his head.

"It's sooo funny." She continued like a locomotive on the express track. "I was on my way to the copier, and she was on her way to the copier and *bo-ing!* We ran into each other." Cathy Bartholomew's hands clapped together, emphasizing the *bo-ing*.

During her mindless chattering, Allan and I gazed at each other over her head. Laughter danced in his eyes as he parroted, "Bo-ing?"

I clamped my lips in a level line to conceal the small giggle bubbling in my throat. With a straight face, I mouthed "*bo-ing*," too.

"I was surprised I didn't have a bump on my head,"

she finished.

Too bad she wasn't unconscious right now. While I studied the two-some, I teethed my lower lip. I could understand him scoring action with a NFL cheerleader, but not an over-aged wannabe.

She tossed and whipped her big hair like she stood in front of a mammoth fan. The long blonde—what looked to be badly dyed and crispy fried—locks smacked him in the face and settled across his mouth. With his gaze converged with mine, he politely peeled her hair over and over again as her flinging continued.

Did she think her flings were sexy? Did she know the word haircut? Should I offer him anti-bacterial soap?

In a smooth motion, his attention diverted back to Cathy Bartholomew. "Isn't that funny."

"I thought so too. Well, right on the spot, we introduced ourselves. I already knew who Hattie was"—she patted my forearm—"and that she worked for Mr. Northside. So the polite Southern girl thing to do was to officially introduce oneself."

"I see." Once again, he stripped away her hair from his lips.

This whole conversation seemed way too surreal—like a Salvador Dali painting labeled the *Birthday Party from Hell* complete with melting candles and disintegrating cake.

"Hattie!"

My unspoken prayers were answered when I heard Mom's call. Soon she would be screaming my whole name which wasn't music to anyone's ears. "Gotta go." I gestured with a nod toward the platter and took two steps in her direction. "I need to deliver this food.

Excuse me."

"First, tell me. Where should I put this?" He gripped my upper arm in a light clasp which halted my Bonnie and Clyde-style getaway. He took a slight step to his left and picked up something from the seat of a nearby chair.

This was a plain brown bag with "Hattie" written in pen and tied with a Get Well Mylar balloon shaped like a flower pot filled with colorful daisy-like blooms.

The nucleus of my whole being squeezed until an intense coil formed. He'd brought me this gift on purpose. And like before, this gesture gripped my heartstrings. He'd heard me pontificate about the curative qualities of chocolate and figured by replenishing my supply, he'd be in my good graces and forgiven.

Gobbling some right now seemed like an excellent idea. A noisy exhale escaped my lips. "You shouldn't have." I planned my escape. If I delivered the burgers to Mom and made for the restroom, then grabbed a gift bag and passed through the breezeway gate around the garage to the alley...freedom. I nodded; my plan would work.

But I wouldn't. I couldn't.

Stuffing the ache, I indicated with a tilt of my head toward the side table which was loaded with lots of candy in various gift bags and balloons. "Over there."

He laid his contribution with the others and laughed. "Guess I'm not so original after all. You must be saving for additional restorative times."

How well he knew me.

Forget the cholesterol and unwanted carbohydrates. I could mainline the pounder right now. I expressed a faint smile and then frowned when my attention was captured for the bazillionth time by Mom who motioned with frantic hands then tapped her watch. Heaven forbid the burgers weren't cooked in a timely fashion. Her whole agenda would be ruined. I repeated, "Gotta go," and hurried to Mom.

Behind my back, I overheard Cathy Bartholomew say, "She'll just get fat. There are two-hundred and fifty cal'reez in a vendor-sized bag. Just look at the table loaded with more cand-ee than a superstore. From my experience, the carbs go straight to the thighs. Can you 'magine Hattie with fat thighs? She should give some of them away…"

I shook my head and tuned her out. Bimbos knew nothing.

No chocolate would ever be fattening. My birthday decree.

Chapter Six

My family's backyard was ideal for hosting parties. Under the covered breezeway, two buffet tables had been arranged for the food. Dad's bar had been set up there as well.

Tables and matching chairs, cushioned with comfy pads, had been grouped on the large pavestone patio. For tonight's event, additional seating and tables, probably borrowed from the Wellborn's, were scattered around. A walkway connected this patio to another larger one located next to the pool. Off to one side of this patio was where Mom reigned over the gas grill.

Sister Tracey had been drafted to help our dear mama at the burger station, too. Tracey threw me a quick, conspiratorial look.

She knew birthday parties were no exception either.

Mom saw me approaching and dispatched Tracey with her typical so-so task so she could speak to me in private.

I recognized Mom's modus operandi. Without a doubt, she was gearing up for another one of her famous little talks, for example, "Are You Entertaining Your Guests Properly?" Or the ever popular "Respect, Respect, Respect."

These dialogues were interrelated and could sound similar with some even snowballing into another. What differentiated amongst them was the title Mom selected when starting her sermon.

Birthdays should be the one day of the year when all heavy discourse had been banned. I wondered which one she would select from her repertoire. I still had time to implement the-hiding-away-in-the-Alley-with-vast-quantities-of-chocolate plan.

"What Are You Doing?" Mom demanded.

Oops, silly me. I guessed wrong. She'd picked "What You Are Doing Wrong," an awful, long one, similar in length to "What Mothers Want for Their Daughters."

"Who me?" My sarcastic answer guaranteed commotion. And on that note, nearby guests faded away. I put on a defensive look and shoved the platter into her hands. "I'm helping you?"

"Don't be sassy."

I flinched. "Isn't sassy a virtue?"

"Some say yes. I say no." She laid the uncooked patties on the flaming grill.

Instantly, an appetizing aroma rose. My nose wriggled like a rabbit's. My tummy gurgled in anticipation.

"I mean, what are you doing to Allan Wellborn?" Mom zeroed in like a stinger missile on its target.

Time to face the music.

With a sigh heavy in capitulation, I let my chin drop toward my chest. Ignoring the rumbling in my stomach, I combed my hair away from my face. With a slow, slightly exasperated tone, I said, "Mom. He said hello first, and I was being polite—just like you taught me—and said hello back. That's all. I promise. I didn't hit him. I didn't yell at him. Nothing."

Mom nodded in the direction of Blonde Bimbo standing next to the Man of the Hour. "And who is that?"

My gaze followed hers. "That's his date, Cathy Barf-thol-omew." *Who could resist?*

"What did you say her last name was?"

I knew very well what I'd said, and Mom knew, too. I correctly answered, "Bartholomew."

"Huh." She smacked a pattie, letting the meat juices drip on the grill, and then threw her arms skyward, nearly flinging the spatula into the pool. "What's Allan thinking? I didn't invite him to bring a date to your party. I can't believe it. And what's with her hair?"

Mom punctuated the air with the grilling tool. "Shirley knows how I feel. I can't imagine her having anything to do with this arrangement. I'll have a long talk with her later."

That sounded...unfun.

"All my plans will be ruined. Ruined."

I had no words.

From the time I'd become interested in boys, she pointed out Allan's merits. All of them added up to perfect, almost saintliness. Except for the few itty bitty lies he'd told. That was when I'd uncovered his flaws.

Mom laid her spatula on the platter and then turned to face me, giving me a long hard look. "It should've been you."

A scrunch took over my face. Feeling clueless in America, I stared at Mom. "Me?"

"You."

"What are you talking about?"

"You should be Allan's date tonight. You should

still be dating him."

Amazing. I crooked an inquiring eye. "Is this the 'What Mother's Always Want for Their Daughters' speech?" No way did I want to hear a rerun of that particular talk ever again. In truth, a little was boring, and I tended to tune her out.

Her smile was generous but short-lived. "No, you know that one by heart, but I'll repeat if necessary." Her body softened. "All I'm saying is you should be dating him."

"Why?" I knew my thoughts, but I was curious about hers.

"Lately, when I meet Shirley at the grocery store, she would say you two had pizza or had gone to a party—"

"Mother." My huffed breath lifted stray bangs from my forehead. Her interference in my dating life could best be described as...annoying. "This is what single people do."

Mom shook her spatula. "Harriette Lee Cooks."

For a long time, I'd hated my whole name until I discovered Harriette could be shortened to Hattie. Hattie had sass linked within it, although according to Mom, sass wasn't a virtue in her day. "Mom—"

"Hattie, please let me finish explaining."

"Sorry."

"You know how private Allan is. He wouldn't have talked freely with Shirley about you unless you meant something to him." She tilted her head a tad to the right, a questioning expression passed across her face. "Perhaps, my darling, somehow you messed things up?"

Moi? I messed things up? Surely, my hearing was

on the fritz. The only thing I ever did to Mr. Saintly-ness was throw him out of my apartment when he'd acted stupid.

I'd had enough of her interference. I shoved my hands on my hips, tucked my chin, and fought to keep my tone in a lower register. "Mother. In case you've forgotten, he nearly got me killed. Remember, he didn't tell me about the danger I could be in? Remember insane Opal at Buy Rite Insurance Company? Remember the stab wounds she gave me and all the blood?"

Even months later, nightmares about the day haunted me. I knew Mom hadn't forgotten; she just needed reminding. At the hospital and later at my apartment, she'd fretted excessively over me. She even made her famous German chocolate cake to "restore me back to health." Her baked goods had helped me gain unwanted poundage.

"Certainly, I remember. You're my daughter. I love you, and I always remember important things involving you." Mom adjusted a knob on the grill. "Yes, yes, you're right. Allan should have done things differently. However, you were angry and overwrought. And when time passed and your anger had cooled, you could have gone and explained—"

"I did." Finally, she knew the truth. My hands fell to my sides.

When gobsmacked with the whole enchilada, Mom's eyes bugged to the size of a large platter.

I affirmed my comment with a nod. "I really did."

"Well"—she swallowed hard—"th-that's good. What did you say?"

I looked to the ground hoping to find courage, but

knew the courage I needed was found within me. I faced her. "I drove to his apartment and asked him to choose me over who I now know is Cathy Barftholomew. The End." I let my finger punctuate a period in the air.

"When did you do this?"

"A few months ago."

"And he said?"

"He said…no."

"No? Why would he say no?" One side of her mouth screwed up. "Choosing that Blonde Bimbo over you. His brains must look like two week-old fettuccini. Look at her hair. And don't get me started on how skinny she is. What is he thinking? Not thinking is more like it."

Now, Mom jammed her tool under the cooked meat and smacked the burger on an etched aluminum tray which had once belonged to Grammie, her frustration showed and could be heard with each wallop. She added a few uncooked ones to the grill. When she'd finished her task, she turned a hard look toward me. "You did the right thing. I'm proud of you. And, pardon my French, but he's a stupid ass."

I liked the way my mom thought, how she defended me. The corner of my mouth crooked. We rotated and stared in Allan's direction. He hadn't moved from the spot where I'd left him on the breezeway, only now, he was conversing with Jenny. Cathy Bartholomew had intimately curled her arm with his.

Sensing our penetrating stares, he glanced our way and did a tentative finger wave back.

My mother's foreign language and mine were on

the same page. I said, "Yep, he's a stupid ass."

We looked at each other and laughed over the shared moment. Like most mothers and daughters, we agreed upon very little. But nothing in the world was like mothers and daughters bonding over "stupid ass" stupidity.

Mom wrapped me in a hug. "That's my girl." She released me and then hooked her arms gently over my shoulders to gaze into my eyes. "I had hopes."

I heard a shade of wistfulness in her voice. Comprehending her statement, I let my mouth fall into a flat line. "I know. Sorry."

"Hattie, in all of these years, we've only met one young man you were serious about. Don't get me wrong; College Boy was fine. Your dad and I really liked him. He was—*is*—a nice, upstanding, hardworking person. But, he wasn't the right one for you. You needed more than he could have given."

I'd underestimated how well she understood me.

In high school, I'd considered myself to be a member of geekdom and dated rarely, mainly because no one asked me. In college with a mature body, contact lenses, and better clothes and hairdo, I'd improved. I settled into a nice, sweet relationship with whom my sister had named College Boy.

After a couple of years, I'd discovered I had more wild oats to sow, and as painful as a breakup was, I'd made the right choice. After him, I'd dated other guys on occasion, and I'd been involved in a few short-term relationships. But none coupled with me in the right way until I'd been reacquainted with Allan. With him, I connected onto a higher level of friendship and a deeper, intimate relationship.

I, too, had harbored the same high hopes. A seed of disappointment lodged in my throat.

With grand melodrama, Mom pressed her right hand to her heart. "He's the kind of man a mother wants her daughter to find. I always knew he would grow up to be a fine specimen, and look"—she pointed the spatula in his direction—"he's fine."

I looked his way and nodded. "Migh-tee fine."

"He has a good job even if it's dangerous. He's big and strong. He's handsome. He's—"

Traits I knew all too well. "I get the idea, Mother."

"Can't you do something to fix things between you?"

So this was where I found myself at the crossroads of truth, to be truthful not only to her, but to myself. "No, and honestly, I'm not happy about it. But he has moved on as you can see. I have to also."

"Oh, my darling daughter, things always work out for the best." Still holding the grilling tool and with all the love she possessed, Mom circled my shoulders for a tight clinch. "There's always a reason, and sometimes, we don't know why at the time."

Mom was, indeed, a very wise woman.

Chapter Seven

Mom returned to grilling food, and Tracey returned from running her fictitious errand.

Thank God for good timing. No telling what Mom would do to me next or how long she would lecture. And I could confess only so much.

"The buffet table was perfectly arranged," Tracey informed our mom. Under her breath, she added, "As you know." Louder, she said, "And the guests seemed happy, snacking on dips and chips and your special version of trail mix. Adding Hattie's favorite candy to the nuts was…inspired."

Tracey and I were working side-by-side, readying more cooked food on a platter, when she glanced over my shoulder.

A deafening scream hit my ear. Automatically, I covered it.

My sister shook my arm. "OhmyGod, I think I'm in love. Who is that gorgeous hunk?"

I peeked over my shoulder in the direction her pointing finger indicated to search for any hunk I might have missed earlier.

Not there.

I should know if an unidentified gorgeous guy was at my birthday party. With Allan spoken for, I was on the prowl just like Tracey. *It's my birthday and any available man belonged to me*—a special birthday edict

I'd just fabricated.

With a twist to my mouth, I scanned the guests again. *No one.* "I don't know who you're talking about. I don't see any available hunk."

Tracey stabbed her finger toward the other patio. "Over there. That guy. Who is he?"

I followed the line of her thrusting finger and only saw Stuart seated at the other patio table, eating a tortilla scoop liberally dunked in what looked like cream cheese picante dip and chasing it with a swallow of beer. "I don't see anybody."

"Yes, you do." Tracey palmed each side of my face and rotated my head precisely in the direction she'd indicated. "There. The guy over there, the one eating the chips. Who is that delicious specimen?"

I blinked to bring into better focus the object of her desire. *It can't be...can it?* Could Tracey be pointing to Stuart Steems? Could Tracey be smitten with him? "You mean the guy in the white shirt and red plaid swim trunks?" Disbelief swamped my question.

Tracey nodded with more vigor than she'd ever shown before.

I fastened a prying look on her. "Are you sure we're talking about the geeky-looking guy in the red-and-black plaid swim trunks and white button-down collared shirt, eating chips and dip?"

"Yes." The single word whooshed out.

Wow, her yes came out incredibly fast. I looked at her. "The guy wearing the name tag?"

"Yes. Yes. Yes."

I tilted my head in the age-old wise way. "Have you suffered a recent head injury I don't know about? A concussion? Hairline fracture?"

"You know I haven't." Tracey grabbed my swimsuit straps and tugged me closer until we were almost nose-to-nose. "Cut the crap, sister dear, and tell me now."

"Hey." I brushed away her hands and stepped away. "You'll ruin my new suit."

"Sorry."

"Can't you read his nametag?"

"Not from here."

"That's Stuart Steems." I giggled one bit, then sobered, "He's my…date."

"Oh." Tracey's gaze revolved to the ground. Her whole posture collapsed.

My comment had squelched the light in her eyes and her lips had gone flat. If there was an expression worse than dejected, her face wore it.

Tracey and my Funsisters loved to see me embarrassed. And I could use this perfect opportunity to let my sister suffer as payback.

But she looked pitiful, similar to a little dog who lost his bone. Or horrors upon horrors, a woman whose worst nightmare came true—she could no longer buy chocolate.

Well, damn. *With her pathetic face, I can't let her suffer…for long.* "You're way off track."

Tracey's gaze shifted to my face. "About what?"

I grinned and shook my head. "Stuart."

Her countenance brightened just a smidgen. "You're not involved with him?"

"He's just a guy I work with at NLB. He thinks he's a geek and asked me to bring him to my birthday party so he could make new friend or two—"

"No one that cute could be a geek. Can I please

meet him? Please, please, pretty-please?" She bounced on her toes.

You're sounding real desperate, ma soeur. "Sure."

"You're telling the truth. You really aren't interested in him?" Tracey asked.

I gave her a *Get Real* face.

Tracey, my younger sister by five years, didn't resemble me in most respects. She was born with blonde hair and blue eyes. One day, she reached her full height potential of five-feet-four inches which didn't match my giant height of five-feet-eight inches. Possibly, with golden highlights in my hair, I'd grow closer to looking like my sibling.

During our younger years, Tracey and I'd shared a bedroom with twin beds. She always complained how my stuff ended up on her side. I'd put up with her yelling and complaining for years. I solved the problem by erecting a sheet barrier between us, building my version of the Great Wall of China. Amazingly, I didn't have a complex either.

Wow, talk about a missed opportunity. A psychotic condition to saddle on my parents would be hysterical.

My free-spirited sister looked at life in her own way. She expressed her creativity in the jewelry she designed. She dressed artsy-fartsy, wearing colorful flowing scarves and unusually outrageous shoes. And not surprisingly, she had looked at a different Stuart. They had something in common already as they shared the same profession.

"I'm not involved with Stuart. Actually, I'd considered introducing him to someone else."

I started to explain more of the how and why Stuart accompanied me to my birthday party when Tracey and

I were interrupted.

"Burgers are ready," Mom called, as she banged her spatulas together. "Everyone grab a plate."

Tracey and I shifted our attention from the grill to the breezeway where we arranged the serving dish and aided our guests with the fixings and drinks. During a lull, I whispered in Tracey's ear, "Later."

She looked beyond pleased, more like love struck. Her face glowed with a rose pink and her eyes took on a dreamy cast. Just imagine Tracey Steems. And the biggest surprise of all—a babe for Stuart.

Fairy tales do come true. *Ladadee, ladeeda, dada...*

****

After the partygoers finished their food, Jenny presented my birthday cake which had been decorated with the girl M&M figurine surrounded with red candies.

I didn't realize I was such a fanatic about candy-coated nuts, and everyone knew of my obsession. Could any other food be more perfect? The chocolate was tasty. The peanuts were a nutritional added bonus. They lived up to their advertisement about not melting in your hands. And they could be purchased in portable packages.

My idea of heaven was the specialty stores located in Las Vegas and New York. Giant tubes in every color lined the walls and were mine for the picking. The whole concept was jawdroppingly brilliant, awesomely fantastic. Now, if only one tube could be installed in my room with an unlimited supply...

Before I blew out the candles with the hot wax streaming down the sides, Tracey carried the Birthday Queen—aka BQ—tiara on a pink velveteen pillow.

For Tracey's birthday, we'd traveled to San Francisco for a Funsister weekend. I'd made Tracey wear the BQ tiara from the moment we departed until our return. Strangers threw fun remarks her way like, "Are you really the Queen?" which she played up by waving in a royal manner.

Tracey smashed the pink rhinestone headpiece on my scalp, the teeth from the comb bit into the skin. I squeaked out a smile after she stepped away, made an adjustment while everyone clapped with enthusiasm.

Across the table, my gaze locked with Allan's. He winked. My glare said *he had better not be enjoying this too much*.

I curtsied prettily and waved in a proper queenly fashion to the masses. Camera flashes popped to capture the perfect Kodak moment. However, the resulting photos would undoubtedly be wretched because my eyes would be shut. I never could figure out the deal with cameras. My eyes were always closed, especially now with the ones taken by a cell phone. Worse would be breaking them like Tracey does.

The guests chomped down their cake and ice cream. My sister and I gathered dirty plates, cups, and plastic silverware and tossed all in a bag-lined trash can. Mom encouraged me to initiate the dancing on the patio.

In addition to dispensing the beer, Dad had been relegated to choosing the music. His style of music happened to be mine. We preferred the nice, easy oldies like the timeless Nat King Cole, Frank Sinatra, some Rosemary Clooney, the Beatles, and my personal disco hit, YMCA, with arms shaping the letters. The music of today didn't sound great to the previous generation. I had yet to decode hip-hop lyrics. All I heard were curse words.

After dinner, Dad would put on his favorite tunes and dance around the kitchen with us. Some of my best steps were taken from those times.

To promote the dancing, I paired the Funsisters with their respective beaus. I looked over my quasi-date to assess his—*oh, what was a good word?*—capabilities. My finger tapped my lips. He couldn't be too bad. The ballroom dancing hobby was a positive marker. He snapped in time to the tempo which indicated his musicality.

I flung my hands in the air, surrendering once again to do the right thing. Anyway, Mom would remind me how rude I was to consider someone else. Besides, all the other guys were with dates, except for Trixie. *Sorry, Trixie.*

With no other choice, I snagged Stuart's hand and tugged him toward the patio. "Come on."

Stuart danced competently for an accounting nerd. No toe stomping or sweaty hands. No weird monkey moves. With a delicate hold, he clasped my right hand in his left, placed his other arm around my body, circling my waist, and led me around the patio with sure steps.

Looking over his shoulder, I focused on following him and not my friends' nor my family's reactions. I had the ideal opportunity to put on my creative thinking cap to plot how to match Stuart and Tracey.

With no time like the present, I asked, "Stuart?"

"Hmm?" He pressed the side of his head against mine.

I caught a whiff of beer off his breath. "Did you

meet my sister, Tracey?"

"I think I did. It's so confusing 'cause you have a sister and the Funsisters. Is she the one with the spiky hair?"

Oh, goody. He did remember. "Yes, the one with spiky hair."

"Then I met her."

"Isn't she nice?"

"She's okay. She isn't you." Stuart pulled my waist closer to his.

Not a good sign. I'd hoped by now he'd dropped his *other half* thoughts. And I did not want his man junk anywhere near my thigh.

For the sake of my sissie, I persevered. Using a womanly tactic I stockpiled in case of dire emergencies, I employed the antiquated ploy guys always fell for. "No, she isn't me." I lowered my voice to the sexiest tone I possessed, "She's interested in you."

Stuart's eyes flashed multiple times. "Really?" He tilted his head and studied me. "But, she isn't tall like you. I say the taller the woman, the better."

I rolled my eyes to the bead board ceiling. *Sigh.* Most guys responded positively to the *Girls Interested in Them* strategy. So, I fished out another tactic from my woman bag, also known in highly educated circles as reverse psychology. "You know, Tracey isn't too short. I'm too long-legged."

Stuart absorbed my comment with a swallow.

"And when she wears high heels, she towers. Don't you think high heels are sexy?"

His eyes flickered multiple times while taking in the image. He stared at Tracey, who stood off to the side talking to Jenny.

"And she has such pretty gray-blue eyes and fun blonde hair," I said.

He continued to think while we circled the dance floor. I leaned in to whisper in his ear, "You have so much in common. She's a number cruncher, too." While I watched Stuart process this revelation, which told me the girly psychology had worked, I went for the big close. "Why don't you ask her to dance and get to know her better?"

Halting, he lifted and dropped his shoulders. "Oh, I don't know. Sometimes, I get nervous asking strange girls to dance."

Yes! He took the bait; so I reeled him in. "But Stuart, you dance like a dream." Stuart did boogie extraordinarily well because of the ballroom dancing lessons. Without a doubt, he'd invited girls to pair with him at those classes. Perhaps, he had a comfort zone issue, and I could solve that problem in a jiffy. "I'm surprised to hear you're nervous asking girls to dance. Tracey hasn't bitten me in years. Let's go."

Anticipating he might make a speedy getaway, I dragged him by the arm to where Tracey stood.

Jenny's eyes widened when she saw our approach. Before the party, I'd clued her in to my plan to match Stuart with someone. She checked her left for a possible escape route and evaporated into the shadows.

I reintroduced Stuart to Tracey. Then I told a big, fat white lie, figuring I wouldn't go to hell for this particular one. "You two would be doing me a humongous favor by keeping the dancing going while I run inside for a moment. Okay?"

They barely looked at each other, afraid to say or do anything.

Unbelievable. "Please. It's important. Girl stuff."

Stuart took a deep confidence-building breath and turned to Tracey, extending his hand, palm up. "I'd be honored."

My sister's face glowed with happiness. Her irises deepened to blueberry and were circled by a wide band of black. Joy and gratitude bounded in her eyes. She let her hand creep onto his.

She finally had Stuart right where she wanted him.

Maybe the planets would be aligned, and Stuart and Tracey would be occupied for hours.

****

With the mission-impossible situation under control, I felt free to stroll around and converse with my guests. I made a small modification to the lopsided tiara, and then joked with each of the Funsisters who happily called attention to their gifts.

"You should have informed me what Mom had planned."

They shook their heads and chorused, "No way."

"Not telling me was mean."

"Hattie," Trixie said, "our intent was to dodge a bullet."

"Cowards. See if I share any with you."

The Funsisters locked the *I'm not believing that* attitude on their faces.

I caved. I'd share my newly acquired stockpile. Besides, they knew where to go in case of an emergency. We had an understanding which read *Funsisters supported each other with chocolate.*

Anyway, they knew all my hiding spots.

I turned from them to spy Mom and Dad chatting with Mr. and Mrs. Wellborn who sat in the glider on the breezeway. *Better avoid that area.* Mrs. Wellborn hadn't made me squirm—yet.

As I continued to walk around the patio, I attempted to evade Allan.

But he was quick. He grabbed my arm, though not very hard. "Hattie."

He said my name in a low voice, the one which made me want to melt in a puddle.

"You've been avoiding me tonight."

No kidding. I would be insane not to.

He glanced at Stuart and Tracey. "Who's the guy you were dancing with?"

I could feel the warmth in his grasp and saw the hard look he'd pinned on me. *Maybe...* Only one way to find out. "Jealous?"

Allan's eyebrows lifted.

Okay, nooo comment. Maybe I didn't want to hear his comment anyway. However, my business wasn't his business. Not anymore. Not since he dumped me. He stroked my arm which sent a nice tingling racing through my blood.

"Why would I be jealous?" he said.

That stung. I squashed a retort on the tip of my tongue, thinking, *be nice, be nice, Hattie. It's my birthday, my birthday, my happy, happy birthday...*

Oh crap.

I leveled my shoulders and answered him in a proper and polite tone. "My date, who isn't really a date, just a friend thing, is Stuart Steems, a Senior Audit Manager at the accounting firm for which I'm temping."

"Another new job? Already?"

I bobbed my head. "Making my way up the food

chain."

"What happened to the one at the stationary store? Weren't you ideally placed there with your extensive retail background?"

"How…did you…know…" I bet the Moms Always Know Network told on me, the one which always knew everything you did—good or bad. Then, realizing the lengthy, unsavory explanation, I said instead, "Oh, never mind."

"And this is the same accounting firm where Cathy works." He returned to caressing my upper arm.

My insides grabbed. I loved his touch and flushed. I loved any move he made on me. "Yes, the same place—Northside, Lancaster, and Brookside, Accountants."

Allan moved his gaze to Stuart. "Your date looks like an accounting nerd."

"You would know."

Once, accounting nerd Allan had taken a job with a big name firm after college. After a few years of moving up the corporate ladder, he felt accounting would never be a fulfilling profession. Pencil and paper-pushing weren't dangerous enough. He changed careers and took a job with the Sommerville Police Department where he'd made detective the year prior.

Secretly, I believed he'd yearned for the boys and their toys thing.

"I was never that nerdy, not even as a bean counter," he said.

At that moment, the accounting club picture I'd uncovered in our Sommerville High School yearbook resurrected in my thoughts. *Wrong.* He *was* pretty nerdy back then.

Allan locked a lengthier look on Stuart who twirled Tracey around the patio with great flourish. "He's wearing an interesting outfit."

"Really? I hadn't noticed. Yours"—Allan's Hawaiian shirt of red vintage cars and mileage signs imprinted between blue swirls definitely spelled tacky —"is remarkable, too."

Catching my tell-all glance, he patted his shirt. "What's wrong with what I'm wearing?"

What was the deal with pool party attire anyway? People latched onto the dress down and tacky or glammed it up. I'd played safe and had gone with the glam it up. I grinned and fibbed, calling on the Big Guy upstairs once again. Maybe lightning wouldn't strike. "Nothing."

He directed his finger at Stuart. "Does he wear a nametag at work?"

"Not that I've seen." I giggled. "Tracey's infatuated with him."

"They're perfect," he said in delighted amazement.

He was right. Stuart had geeky clothes and my sister had her fun, spiky hairdo.

At this point, Stuart displayed his ballroom steps by grasping Tracey's trim waist and lifting her in the air, whirling her around and around the dance floor. All the guests stepped away to make room and enthusiastically applauded their act. He returned her to her feet, and both blushed and bowed with unexpected finesse.

"At least he dances well. No weird monkey moves," I said.

"We were better."

Allan resumed massaging my upper arm when he

said this innuendo.

Unsettling feelings captured my tummy, like fresh salt had been rubbed in my old wounds. Painful and irritating ones. Frustrated. Deeply hurt. I yanked away my arm. "Allan, cut-it-out."

"Give me some scissors."

"That's so juvenile."

"I'm sorry, Hattie. I don't mean to hurt you."

"Yea? If you're so sorry, you'd be more sensitive. How about remembering you're at my birthday party with a date? What's with that?" I stalked off, increasingly annoyed with him.

It's my birthday, my birthday, my happy happy birthday...

Shit. Would this night ever end?

Chapter Eight

As the party wound down around midnight, the guests collected their belongings.

I thanked each and every friend for coming by using a page from the *I'm so Glad You Came*, Mom's polite hostess little talk. I hugged my Funsisters and promised a chocolate party soon so they could get a portion of the sweets. I surveyed the national disaster left in the backyard, grabbed a trash bag, and began picking up the mess.

Stuart approached me while I worked. "Hattie? Need some help?"

"Oh, hey, Stuart. I'm good. Thanks for dancing with Tracey."

"My pleasure." He stubbed the toe of his sandal in the grass. "Hattie, I, uh, I have a question."

My brows shot sky-high. *He better not be hinting for a kiss.* I'd covered that territory in the original ground rules. I let the trash bag drop on the grass. "Ask away."

"Would you mind if I took your sister—er, Tracey—home?"

Now, my birthday date had officially dropped me. Yet, his request didn't bother me. My intent all along had been for Stuart to connect with a girl, and apparently, he had with Tracey.

Not all that angry, I had to tease one last time. I put

on a faux irritated pose—hands on hips and slanted my head with 'tude. "Didn't you say something to me about her short height a while ago?"

"Mmm." Stuart flexed his woven fingers away from his torso. Obviously, he had changed his mind about my sister. Stuart and Tracey danced every song, displaying incredible steps which were the hit of the party. During breaks, they chatted and shared quite well. Their coming together was pretty cute, and in doing so, they took the pressure away from me, the Birthday Queen. Great relief!

"Perhaps," he said, "I was wrong."

"Go for it." My blessing. His face displayed more puppy ecstasy.

"Really? Gee, thanks! I didn't want to seem rude by bringing you and then leaving you…She's so nice and—"

"It's okay, Stuart, have fun. Tracey's a great gal, even if she is my sister. I'll catch another ride. Maybe Jenny's still here, and she can take me. I'll see you at the office on Monday."

"I had a really great time, and I like your family."

Unexpectedly, he wrapped his arms around my shoulders and gave me a big hug. Good news he liked the family because I bet he would be seeing more of us.

He departed with the *Have a Happy Birthday* phrase trailing over his shoulder.

Picking up the garbage bag, I watched Stuart rush with jubilation to my sister's side. Tracey gave me an appreciative look and then blew a kiss.

Maybe when she did some smooching with Stuart, he'd transform from a frog into Prince Charming. He already looked to be on his way with the name tag removed and the top shirt button undone. As they walked toward the house, he looped his arm around her waist. She nuzzled next to his side.

Presenting my sister with a boyfriend on my birthday was a good gift.

"I heard that."

I cringed when this comment glided over my shoulder, and I knew very well who'd said it. Swiveling, I found Allan standing behind me, his mouth attempting to suppress a grin teasing the corners of his lips.

He passed me a wayward napkin. "Your date dumped you for your sister."

I wanted to ignore everything about him, but noticing Mom watching, I decided on the *Be Nice* plan. I stuffed the balled napkin in the bag. "Aren't you funny."

"I'm glad."

Glad about what? Why should he be? Was he glad I wasn't dating Stuart? And why did he seem to have a problem remembering his own date?

"I heard him say he was taking Tracey home." A lively glimmer shimmered in his eyes. "Do you need a ride?"

No way would I ask Mr. Ready-to-be-Canonized for a lift with his own date plastered to his side—*where is she anyway?*

I checked out the few remaining guests. No Cathy Bartholomew in sight.

"She's freshening up."

A "freshening up" wouldn't be long enough.

I scanned again, praying someone else could help me out. The other Funsisters had already departed. No one left but him, and I'd rather walk the five miles home in the dark with sure-to-hurt-me shoes than be a part of his two-some.

"No, but thank you kindly for the offer," I said prettily.

"It's not a problem, sweetheart."

"Don't call me that."

"What?"

"You know what. That-that sweetheart thing. I'm not, nor will I ever be."

"Sorry. It just comes out." His mouth crooked to one side. "So no ride?"

I locked on him with my best haughty look. "I'll be fine. I can take care of myself." Then I latched my gaze on the best possibility of all—Dad. He'd rescued his daughters on many an occasion to maintain a *We Need You, Daddy* link. At least this kind of rescue was easier than changing tires like he'd done a few months ago. "I'll ask Dad."

"Suit yourself. Seems unnecessary as I go right by your place."

I crossed my arms, tucking the trash bag against my side. "And why would you be driving by my apartment? Miss me?"

The corner of his mouth quirked up. "It's on the way to the station, sweetheart."

Right. Now, I felt stupid. "You called me that name A. Gain."

He laughed like I'd made a big deal over nothing. "I'd be happy to help out." He leaned over and kissed my cheek good-bye.

I caught a whiff of my favorite soapy scent, pine trees. *Mmm.*

His husky voice touched my outer ear, "Happy birthday, Hattie. I had a nice time."

My big day would have been happier if you hadn't brought a date. You. Me. Champagne. Roses. Chocolate. Bed.

Rats. I emerged from my sensory overload. "Thanks for coming and the offer. Quite magnanimous." Watching him stroll away, I fingered the damp spot on my cheek. It was moist and delicious and sank deep into my marrow.

After I watched him disappear in the shadows cast by the trees lining the drive, I gathered the rest of the garbage and hauled my bag to the bin in the garage. Then I gave Dad the go-ahead, who stood ready by the door to hit the close button.

In response to my asking, he said he would be pleased to help his oldest daughter with a lift home, especially after I explained my date left with his new girlfriend, my sister. He chuckled. "You kids are so funny."

Kids. Today, I'd rounded a birthday bend, but I would always be a kid. How ironic. When he turned ninety and was a great-grand pop, and I turned sixty, and a grandmother, I would still be his kid.

Dad and I loaded all the M&M gifts and table decorations into several of Mom's laundry baskets. We tied the balloons to the baskets' rims. We carried the stuff to the driveway and stopped as soon as we realized *Houston, we have a conundrum.*

Mom's small SUV blocked his truck.

"I'll get my keys, and we can shuffle the cars around." Dad and I placed the baskets at my feet. He took a step toward the house.

He didn't get far when we heard, "I can take Hattie home."

Like the Terminator, Allan turned up exactly when I didn't want him to. I swore to God Almighty Mr. Superstar was placed on Earth to raise my ire and squashed the impulse to stomp my foot like a four year old. I really, really, really did not want to ride with Cathy Bartholomew.

I turned on him. In a voice which clipped each word, I said, "Stop. Following. Me."

"Hattie!"

Oops. I knew Dad's tone of voice all too well.

"No need to be rude to Allan."

"I'm not being rude, Dad. Thanks to Mother, I'm never impolite. He's been pestering me." The look on *ma pere* said *I don't care and apologize.* Rolling my eyes, I sighed with an attitude adjustment and twitched my shoulders. "Sorry I said rude things, Allan. Thanks again for the offer. Dad and I have everything under control."

"Allan"—Dad retrieved a basket and passed it to my nemesis—"if you don't mind, would you take her, please? Save everyone some time."

I raised my palms, not believing my own father had betrayed me. Staring his way, hoping I'd bore sense into his brains, did no good. He shrugged, smiled, then took another basket to the rear of Allan's 4-Runner. With a shake of my head, I let my hands fall. I gathered up one and followed him to what I now named the Ride of Doom.

"I got it." Allan took the last basket from my arms.

I resented how they'd decided everything without my input and stuck out my tongue—at his back.

Dad noticed and shook a warning finger in my face.

They placed the containers in the backend, batted the balloons inside, and then closed the hatch.

I walked over to my pop and hugged him. "I appreciate your taking care of Stuart and the good music for dancing."

"Yea"—he squeezed me back—"beer leads to dancing, the family motto."

We shared a conspiring look. "Stuart turned out to be an interesting guy," he said. "He's possessed with football, is pretty good on his feet, and helped me with drink orders. I like him."

"Apparently, Tracey does, too."

We laughed again. I kissed his cheek. "Thanks, Dad. You're the best."

"You're welcome. I hope you had a happy birthday."

With my arms still wrapped around his waist, I drew away slightly to look him in the face. "Did Mom leave you plenty of cake?"

"I'll survive."

Dad had a midnight snack craving, usually for chocolate sandwich cookies and milk, but if cake or pie were available… "Feel older?" I asked.

His mouth shaped a bare grin. "Every time you girls have a birthday, I have one, too."

Dad escorted me toward Allan's truck. He stood by an open back door, waiting for me to get inside.

I slid in the seat and buckled up. The door was slammed shut, and Allan took off.

Undoubtedly, a great conspiracy had just taken place.

****

"Oh, Hattie." Cathy Bartholomew slung her arm over the back of the seat to look at me as Allan drove toward my apartment. "I'm so sorry Stuart dumped you. The disrespect of some people. He has deplorable manners."

"They hit it off. He asked, and I said okay. No biggie." I brushed invisible lint from my nose. "I apologize for intruding on your"—I choked for a nanosecond—"date."

She reached over the seatback and patted my forearm in a consoling manner. "A small inconvenience is not inconvenience."

However, a dark nasty look crossed her face, and I knew differently.

She pinched me hard.

I jerked my arm to my chest and stared at her. Cathy Bartholomew faced the windshield and scooted as close as she could to the console between the seats to lean her head on his shoulder. I rubbed the spot screaming with pain. Confusion enveloped me. *Why did she act nice at work then mean right now?*

A moldy pea-green sickness rooted in my belly. I forced myself to stare out the window and not to puke. No one said anything on the drive. I could hardly focus my gaze on the passing scenery.

At my apartment, Allan parked his truck and assisted my exit. He gathered a basket from the rear end and placed the container in my arms. He scooped up the others and followed me to my door. The balloons bobbled in an air ballet over his head. Cathy Bartholomew took the rear.

Not surprising she didn't offer to help us. *Can*

there be any one more disingenuous?

Inside, we put the bins on the kitchen table. "Thanks for helping," I said to Allan, all the while thinking *please hurry and leave.* I didn't want his date to assault me a second time.

"My pleasure."

The look he gave me said more than I needed to know at that moment. "And thanks again for the ride. Sorry to have intruded on your evening."

"Not a problem."

However, the malicious glare Cathy Bartholomew pasted on me as she passed expressed something different. If an expression could make someone vanish, hers would have taken me out.

As I closed the door behind them, I blew out a relieved breath while resting my back against the portal.

OhmyGod. What is he doing?

****

On Sunday morning, I woke to find Jenny pushing on my arm in a *time to wake you* way. Was this a repeat of yesterday?

Jenny must have noticed my one half-mast eye because she said, "Get up."

"No. I didn't fall asleep until three A.M.—"

"Poor baby—"

"And stop invading my room. Doesn't privacy mean anything to you?"

My mind had rewound multiple times the whole party, the drive home, the nasty looks Cathy Bartholomew had given me, and how she pinched my arm. I looked at the spot which had turned a blue-black, remembering the hurt. I never wanted to cross her path again and wondered how I would accomplish that at work. I rolled to my back and rubbed the owie. "Go away. To quote Garbo, 'I vant to be alone.' "

"I don't think that's what she said."

"Don't care."

She heaved her body in a determined flounce. "I'm not leaving. I want you to get up and open all the birthday presents."

She deserved something wicked to happen to her for not informing me about the big birthday surprise Mom had cooked up. "Why should I? You know what kind of gifts they are. Hungry? Go. Eat—with my blessing."

"I don't know. Some are still wrapped. One gift is very intriguing, and IMHO, you should open that one first."

I didn't recollect an *intriguing* present. I'd deliberately *avoided* opening one, and knowing Jenny, the very one she wanted to see. "The packaging's a dead giveaway—the gifts are all chocolate."

She flung aside my covers, her hand seized my arm with an aggressive hold, and then she attempted to drag me from my comfy bed.

My free arm scrambled to hang on to the duvet life raft. "I don't want to go. Can't I sleep some more? It's only"—I glanced at my clock radio and gasped—"six-thirty? On a weekend? Are you insane?"

"Stop your whining. Every other day you're up by now."

Jenny's hold was strong. Since I didn't want to tear up the pretty picture toile bedcovering because it was fairly new and expensive, I released the fabric and grudgingly let her help me to my feet. She led me to the kitchen table where I'd piled the laundry baskets last night.

With a smug grin, Jenny picked up the brown bag inscribed with my name, tied with a balloon, and waved the package gently in my face. "I've seen one…like this…on other…occasions," she singsonged.

"You need voice lessons." I'd knowingly avoided opening this one. I snatched the bag from her hand and shook it. "This is the intriguing one?"

Jenny nodded.

"Hold out your hands, palms up."

She gave me a *what are you doing* squint and held up her hands.

I slapped all two pounds in her hands. "Enjoy."

Dismay curved her mouth, and within a heartbeat, she returned the bag. "I don't want your presents."

"Could have fooled me."

"Why won't you open it?"

I tossed the bag back onto the pile of gifts. "What are you doing to me?"

"Nuh-thin'."

"Liar. Quit driving me crazy. You know who the gift's from."

"Chick-en." Then she flapped her wing-configured arms and strutted around the room. "Bro-ock, brock, brock, brr-rock."

Chicken Little—that was me. Sadly, she resembled a cocky strutting rooster which didn't look particularly attractive this early in the morning. With a *humpf*, I overlapped my arms. "I don't want to."

Jenny stopped doing her version of the chicken dance. "I talked to Allan and the she-devil at the party."

"Lucky you."

"She's such a bimbo."

"You've got that right."

"I overheard her say to Allan peanut M&Ms are fattening. Only bimbos make stupid statements like that." Jenny mimicked Cathy Bartholomew as she drawled, "Thay haf two hunnerd and fif-tee calrees in eech bahg."

"You just might make a true Southerner with that drawl."

She trailed her finger along the table edge. "I grew up down there, but I don't speak like her. I can't decide if she's a phony or not."

I pointed at her chest, right about the boob line. "Thanks to my dad, they gave me a ride home."

Her mouth fell open. "Un-be-lieve-able. What did Blonde Bimbo say?"

"Something about my inconveniencing them wasn't a problem, but the look she gave me was real nasty. And she hurt me." I showed Jenny the damage on my forearm.

She touched the spot with one finger. "Need ice?"

I shook my head no. "I'll wear this proudly and remember why I should avoid her and more importantly, avoid Allan."

Her mouth twitched. "She does not like you."

"So I learned."

"Let's get this over with."

Oh well. Sorta like the game Truth or Dare. Jenny would push, push, push me into doing what I didn't want to. I plucked the objectionable bag from the pile and tore it open. From inside spilled two one-pounder packages of my adored candy. He'd enclosed a crisp, white notecard with a hand-painted pink heart.

I passed Jenny the treats. Long ago, the Funsisters

had deemed eating this candy for breakfast was a good thing. Tons and tons of proteins were in the peanuts. And who could forget the chocolate contained anti-oxidants. With a greedy gleam in her eye, she ripped a corner off the bag.

I flipped back the card's front cover. The card said:
Hattie,

I hope you have a nice birthday. Since this one is extra special, I would like to take you to dinner sometime soon and really celebrate.

Love, Allan

"Nooo!" My blood boiled to epic proportions. Enraged, I split the note card into two pieces and then four. Like the bubonic plague had infested it, I flung the missive on the floor and then stomped on the sections multiple times. I stopped when pain shot up my ankle and tears formed. Bending, I rubbed the joint. "How could he do this to me? He had a date last night on my birthday, my birthday, my happy, happy birthday, and he had the audacity to bring Blonde Bimbo to my party. I hate him."

Again, I jumped on the pieces hoping they would squash into nothingness, exactly the same place I wanted him to go. "What am I missing here? Why does he make overtly suggestive comments? Why's he doing this to me? He told me 'no.' Why?"

Jenny touched my arm and flipped over her hand. "Give me the note or what's left."

I picked up the bits and, with an angry swoop, slapped them in her palm.

"Ow." Jenny flapped her stinging hand. "I'm thinking Allan's still a masochist. And I am, too." She walked to the living area and sat on the sofa. Then she laid the pieces on the coffee table and began assembling them like a jigsaw puzzle. "When you're mad at a guy, you're really mad."

I paced the room. "Not funny."

Raising her hand, palm up, she rippled her fingers. "I need tape."

"Get it yourself."

"Harriette Lee Cooks."

She had some nerve mimicking Mom's stern tone of voice. I stalked to the kitchen where I retrieved the tape from the junk drawer. I tossed the dispenser in her direction.

She caught it one-handed. "I know this isn't funny…to you." She applied sticky segments to the pieces. When finished, she smoothed her hand over the bumps and read the note. Once done, she waved around the reassembled card. "If I am reading this correctly this implies Allan still has feelings for you."

"That's what he implied last night, too. He said we danced better, was relieved Stuart and I weren't involved, and how he—quote—*knew me so well* about my favorite indulgence—unquote."

Sighing, I slung my weary body next to hers on the couch. The back of my head rested against the cushion and my gaze studied the popcorn ceiling, only to find no answers there. "I thought I'd been dealing exceptionally well with his rejection, only to discover I'm not dealing well at all. I hate him sending mixed signals."

I dropped my hand in a pathetic flap. "What am I supposed to do? Aren't I supposed to have a life, especially when Allan said 'no' after I practically crawled on my hands and knees and begged him to choose me? And now, he says things which have stirred up my insides."

I touched a finger to the corner of my eye to stop a lone tear from inching its way down my cheek. "I don't understand anything anymore."

"You're tired. You got up early—"

"Thanks to my so-called friend—"

"Your scowl isn't one bit intimidating. You had a bad night." Jenny patted my shoulder. "Hang in there. Everything happens for a reason. You haven't had enough time."

"I think if I don't see him, I'll feel better."

"Won't work." She flipped her hand in an inconsequential way. "Your families are close, and we live in a sorta small town where mostly everybody knows mostly everyone. Sooner or later, you'll run into him."

She was right. Sooner or later, I'd run into him. Maybe by then, I could do something without wanting to escape to Guadalajara.

She cradled my hand in hers. Colorful candies trickled on my palm. "We're great believers in restorative and curative powers of chocolate. Let's eat."

I popped a couple in my mouth and crunched. The treats tasted good. So good, I ate a few more.

I always said Jenny was wise.

Chapter Nine

On the Monday morning of my second week with Northside, Lancaster, and Brookside, I made my way to the kitchenette to retrieve coffee for Mr. Northside. There, I discovered hunky Greek God, Will Christiansen, pouring himself a cup as well.

Yumm. Here's someone who could send away a former lover. I straightened my spine, sucked in my gut, and stuck on an adoring smile. "Hi, Will. Sorry I missed you at happy hour."

"Hattie, o gorgeous one, you're looking the epitome of professionalism, as usual. Settling in okay?"

Boy, does he have a line, and even through his compliment, I'd fallen. The temp of my cheeks escalated to feverish. I filled Mr. Northside's mug and checked my watch, deciding I could spare a few minutes to chitchat. Placing the coffee cup on the counter, I rested my hip against the lower cabinets.

Will took my subtly signaled cue and settled next to me. His coat sleeve brushed my arm. His citrusy cologne wafted my way and teased my nose. "I had a good time," I said, "and got to know more of NLB's happy staff. Spent about twenty minutes with Philip. He's pretty nice."

"I heard from others you were there. I had another…engagement and couldn't stay long. I also heard your birthday was Saturday. Happy Birthday! Did you have a party?"

Oh my! Where did Greek God Will hear about my birthday? Remind me to thank whoever had told him. "I did. Mom threw a barbecue and swim party, only there wasn't any swimming, just dancing."

"Sorry I missed the big event. Maybe you can invite me for another time."

"Sure." I bumped his shoulder with mine. "You'll be on next year's guest list."

"You don't look too old. I'd say pretty well-preserved."

Smiling, I patted my cheeks. "It's in the genes."

"Lucky you." He dipped his head. "Would you want to go to dinner on Friday and celebrate in style?"

I was stunned. Surely, my chin had whacked the floor. What mattered was he said something outstanding and even better offered a dinner invitation. I predicted nundom was on its way out the door.

"What a marvelous idea. I say yes," I said eagerly, but not too eagerly.

"Great. I'll call you Thursday, and we'll finalize plans."

Elation filled my soul. "I look forward to it."

He pushed off the counter and took a sip before saying, "Think of somewhere special. Sky's the limit."

I pendulumed my finger. "Uh-oh. I might go wild."

He grinned. "I can handle it. Mañana."

After Will left, I picked up my melting body, Mr. Northside's coffee, and managed to drag my feet with sluggish awkward steps to the doorway.

Will Christiansen. Hunky Greek God and dinner. *Maybe a new love?*

****

On Tuesday after lunch, unforeseen news circulated like wildfire. Bookie Dave, a short, balding, semi-senior auditor who worked under Stuart, found Phil Meadows slumped over his sandwich in the employee's break room. Dave checked Phil's pulse. There wasn't one. He called 9-1-1 and notified Mr. Northside.

Word flashed like a thunderbolt through the office and said the paramedics had arrived. They summoned the medical examiner. He didn't like what he found— young man dead for no apparent reason—and phoned the police. When the police arrived, they cordoned off the break room and other areas to conduct their investigation.

Seemed young people rarely keeled over like Phil had.

Not a normal day at NLB.

I sat at my desk and took in the news. Employees expiring at the workplace were shocking. Even considering my prior, yet limited, experience with death, I felt ill-prepared for anyone else's, but especially for young Phil Meadows'. The only deceased people in my lifetime should have been elderly relatives who quietly passed with old age or possibly, someone with a rare or incurable disease like cancer. Instead, a sweet young man died with his face smashed in his peanut butter and grape jelly sandwich at my place of employment.

Mr. Northside stood nearby when the paramedics and the police came. The investigators turned up and searched for evidence.

On my way to the restroom, I observed the staff grouped around Bookie Dave's cubicle. As I returned, I joined them, and we saw something on each other's faces which told we knew nothing would ever be the same.

The techs measured, took photos, and dusted for fingerprints. After a long while, the coroner had Phil's body taken to the morgue.

The detectives started their questioning by interviewing Mr. Northside in the small conference room they'd commandeered. Afterwards, he returned to his office and asked me to get Phil's contact information from HR. I copied the phone number on a yellow sticky and gave it to him, closing the door behind me so he could make his call in private.

The detectives fanned out and began groundwork interviews with the Senior Audit Managers which included Stuart and Will.

Later the same day, I flicked my foot in an agitated tap, tap, tapping under my desk. My thoughts hadn't strayed far from the incident at hand. Anxiety had rooted in all of the NLB employees, and I found I had a difficult time resuming my work. My fingers and my brain had a disconnect.

Allan Wellborn silently materialized in my office.

I shouldn't have been too surprised he'd been called to aid in the investigation, considering he was a police detective and all. I gave him another long glance. Yet again, Allan looked migh-tee fine—navy slacks, black belt and shoes, white shirt with pale blue pinstripes and a navy tie with matching blue dots.

Concentrate, Hattie. Banish handsome policeman thoughts. Remember you have a date with Will Christiansen. A nice attractive man. A nice attractive and available man.

Allan wouldn't go away until I said something in response to his presence. I bypassed formalities and asked the question inquiring minds wanted to know, "Why are you here?"

He rested his perfect derrière on the edge of my desk. I had to crook my head way back to look at his face. Flapping his tie playfully, he said, "Aren't you glad to see me?" He tipped closer. "You know why. I've been assigned to the Phil Meadows' case. Preliminary interviews."

I did my best to ignore him by staring at my pencil jar and tweaking the yellow mechanical ones I favored to the same height. Any feelings I had, even the *overwhelmingly delighted to see him* kind, had been stuffed and strangled with the proverbial pantyhose. With an attitude of nonchalance, I plucked a writing instrument from the container. I rubbed my finger across the tip. The lead hadn't been rolled into play. "Have you begun your interviews?"

"Not yet. I just arrived."

"I heard some of the other detectives have already talked with the Senior Audit Managers."

"Standard procedure. They're working their way through the executive team first."

I dropped the pencil in the jar and picked up the stapler. I opened and closed it. Click-click. Still didn't meet his gaze. "So, why are you here?"

"Just checking on you."

"I'm fine, thank you very much." A part of me wanted to yell and scream my frustration. My nagging subconscious reminded me to stay focused with my *hunky Greek God* plan.

Shoving the stapler in the left drawer, I turned my

attention to the computer cords fed into the hole in the desk top. A skim of my finger along them told me dusting was called for. From the right-hand drawer, I dug for the microfiber dust cloth. Trying for a laid-back face, I ran the cloth over my desk lamp. "Going to see your girlfriend?" I bit the bullet and looked up. The questioning gaze he flicked my way looked note-worthy.

He asked, "Am I making you nervous?"

"No. Why do you ask?"

"You're fiddling with the stuff on your desk."

"It's messy." *Liar, liar, pants on fire.*

"Your idea of messy and mine are different." Long pause. "I had a nice time at your party."

"So you said. Thanks again for the ride home." I gave him the scary eyeball my fifth grade teacher had perfected because I was still mad about the gift bag, the note card, the innuendos flung my way, and insisting I ride with him and his date who had pinched me. "Mom does a good job."

"You got a lot of gifts."

"I did. I'm positive all the calories will go straight to my thighs. Can you imagine me with fat thighs?"

Allan must have realized I'd overheard Blonde Bimbo's remark as he turned his head aside to disguise the red staining his cheeks.

Could he be distracted and disclose something interesting about the new case? "There's something funny about Phil Meadows' death," I said.

Perfect cop face.

Which didn't surprise me.

Allan was a by-the-book kind of policeman, the primary reason I'd chucked him from my life after my problems at Buy Rite; so why would he disclose anything now? He'd withheld information which could have prevented me from working there and getting hurt, but because *of that*, I was stabbed and slashed.

The great detective shifted to a more comfortable hip position for further conversation. "Why do you say funny?"

I leaned back in my chair and swiveled on my toes. "You know what I mean, not ha-ha funny, rather odd funny. Why would a young man die while eating his pbj?" Letting my thoughts flow, I continued to rotate. "Was he sick? He didn't look sick to me."

He shrugged and opened his notebook. "They'll do an autopsy."

I steepled my fingers. "Makes sense."

"Tell me what you think."

I plucked my lower lip. "Truly, I didn't know Phil well. He was a fresh-from-college kid. We briefly visited yesterday. I had lunch with him for the first time earlier last week. Bookie Dave—"

"Who's Bookie Dave?" he asked, holding his pen above the pad.

"Dave is a semi-senior auditor reporting to Stuart Steems. He found Phil and wondered if he'd had a heart attack. Is that true? Normally, young men of his age don't keel over unless they have a congenital heart disease or defect. So how did he die, and if he was murdered, who would do such a thing?"

He stared, not moving an iota.

"Or what if he had been poisoned? What do you think?" I got the regulation policeman look which screamed squat. Naturally, Allan's cell phone rang with the excellent timing the device possessed.

"Wellborn." He stood and stepped six feet away. "Hey, Cathy."

Cathy Bartholomew's feeling free to ring him whenever she wanted was a revelation. I sensed a bit of jealousy root in my chest and grimaced. Since I only knew of one *Cathy* who would call him, I tuned in to eavesdrop.

Ever-so-subtly, he rotated his body even more. "Fine, thanks for asking." He lowered his voice to just above a whisper.

Another pause. He strolled even farther down the hall, making overhearing more difficult. "No, don't have a cold. Just respecting the workplace environment. Sorry, can't do lunch. Call later and we'll talk dinner." He disconnected, automatically sliding the phone in his inside coat pocket. Allan pivoted back to me. "Gotta go."

My least favorite of his phrases. *She must have whined and twined him around her little finger to get a dinner invite.* I bestowed on him another eye squinch. "So go."

"We've done this dance before."

Which seemed to be the story of my life with this man.

I never had the opportunity to finish almost-wild, almost-sex, or dinner, or anything else when his damn cell phone rang. If Allan and I were together, I would gladly throw his down the sewer. On second thought, his phone had the ability to resurrect. I'd stomp on it first, and then hurl it down the sewer. "I heard you the first time."

He leaned within a breath of my hair. "I fell for your routine before and won't fall for it again, sweetheart."

"Who me?" Acting—my second career. "I don't know what you're talking about."

"Remember? You got me to confess you're the only woman in my life."

Wide-eyed, I touched my chest. "Wow. I did that? I had no idea I possessed such powers."

"Smart aleck."

"And?"

Allan made his way to the hallway, halted, and turned halfway back. His mouth crooked up sideways.

I was pretty sure something unfathomable percolated in his eyes. Zings zigzagged throughout my body.

"You're the only woman in my life."

****

Feeling shell-shocked at his pronouncement, I sat in my chair unable to move. I couldn't believe he'd said "you're the only woman in my life."

You screwed up again, nagged my subconscious.

Oops. Me and my forgetfulness. I drummed my fingers on the desktop. I needed to remember Will Christiansen and my refrain, *Greek God and dinner, Greek God and dinner*.

And remember, Allan's dating Cathy Bartholomew.

I had too many distractions. *Greek God and dinner.*

No one else employed at NLB accomplished anything for the remainder of the day. I would never become used to pointless death, and without a doubt, Phil's screamed pointless to me. Just beginning his career in accounting—why would someone want to take him away so brutally?

If he was poisoned, why? Was deliberately

poisoning someone murder? Maybe even premeditated murder? If he'd had a heart attack, why? He looked way too young to have had one.

Parents worked hard to get their children grown and self-sufficient. When someone young did pass, everyone knew the time was too early for the loved one to go.

Bearing in mind the depressing atmosphere, I decided a workout would be the perfect diversion. A good round of aerobics changed my outlook and reduced body fat which I supposed I needed after consuming two hundred fifty calories multiple times.

I can't believe I thought about Cathy Bartholomew's comment on calories.

A while back, I'd found an affordable gym, and another visit seemed in order. I alternated between running and walking on the treadmill. I held high hopes of achieving a two-mile run...someday. Anyway, for a chocoholic, I should consider banking a few fat-burning cardios. If I didn't, I would probably eat too many of the birthday presents while thinking about Phil and those fat thighs could morph into reality.

I called Jenny who liked dance aerobics because she couldn't run two miles either. On the treadmill, we would do our sisterly gossip thing while walking and motivate each other.

****

Meat market best described the gym. Instead of meeting people in bars, my generation hooked up at the muscle club. All available eyeballed, flirted, and scored. The guys hoisted big weights and flexed humongous biceps, wore tank tops or torn-up t-shirts, flaunting their massive broad shoulders and well-toned thighs. The girls arched their backs and exhibited their imported tatas, flat tummies, and tight bums, while garbed in their skimpiest Lycra outfits which emphasized their perfectly sculpted bodies.

Unlike the other females, I didn't show off my figure, which wasn't bad. I decided on comfort—cropped black pants and a white V-neck T-shirt. My workout clothing didn't fit into the wardrobe coordinated thing I did with business attire—which surprised my friends. My interest lay in exercising instead of posturing. I told everyone I wanted "to be fit" which could explain why icky, sweaty me never caught the interest of the hunky guys.

Jenny and I stood in the lounge off the women's dressing room, inspecting the faultless physiques passing in front of us. We glanced at our practical outfits and shrugged. Maybe their outfits were skimpy because the girls were hot—not to be confused with hotties.

After an hour and thirty-minute turn on the treadmill, exhaustion ruled. A cool shower provided relief. Wrapped in a light terry towel, I returned to the locker I shared with Jenny, opened the door, and looked.

There must be a gigantic mistake. Confused, I stepped back and checked the locker number again. *Seriously?* I riffled through our clothing.

Our underwear was missing. Gone! Vanished! Poof!

A frantic feeling whirled in my chest. This was not normal.

Like a crazy woman, I searched the locker's interior, throwing gym bags and outer clothing with wild, chaotic flings until everything had been dumped on the floor. When I didn't find anything, I turned my search to the bench area behind me.

In desperation, I stopped to ask the other girls sitting on the dressing area benches who watched me racing around, "Have you seen anyone hanging around my locker?" I pointed to number 108.

The girls giggled behind their hands. "No."

This situation seemed weird, surreal-ly weird. I knew I wasn't careless. I'd heard the lock click when I turned my key. Someone else might be forgetful. But not me. At least, not this time. Sure, people sometimes opened the wrong lockers by accident with an old key. Afterwards, they'd realized they had picked up someone else's belongings and returned the stuff to the reception desk for lost and found.

I returned to locker number 108, the number I always chose because this specific numeral sequence reminded me of my old dorm room number at State Technological University. I tapped the plate attached at the bottom of the door, knowing I was correct and thought about what to do next.

I had to tell Jenny.

As I jogged toward the shower hall, I called her name. Nobody answered. Finally, I set hands to hips and said, "Jenny, come out right now."

"I gotta rinse off." A moment later, she peeked around a drawn white curtain at the far end of the hallway, a towel cupped against her chest. She snatched a daisy-embellished shower cap off her head. "What's up?"

I fast-tracked toward her. "Our underwear is missing. I've looked and looked and can't find anything anywhere."

Jenny transformed into action-girl mode. She did a fast towel wrap around her torso, then slapped shut the faucet. She dogged me to the dressing area, trailing drips as she traversed the hall. We checked number 108 a third time, asked our neighbors still parked on the bench—who giggled another no—and then checked the wicker towel bins. Again, we found nothing. Slowly, we surveyed the dressing area with the hopes the missing underwear would magically manifest.

I dressed in my few items left. Since I carried no spare underwear, I had no other alternative, but to go commando.

Jenny shook out her hair and combed her fingers through her mostly dry locks. "This isn't good."

"Nope. I'll check lost and found."

According to the receptionist, no underwear had been turned in. She, too, turned her head aside and snickered in her palm.

I reported my conversation to Jenny who'd donned the little bits she had.

Jenny had no other choice either. We just stared at each other, knowing this could be the most awkward moment in our lives. "Like they say, what happens in…"

Solemnly, I crossed my chest in the age-old expression. "Stays in Sommerville."

Chapter Ten

Northside, Lancaster, and Brookside, Accountants operated as quietly as possible for the rest of the week, especially considering how the police carried on their investigation around us. We were banned from the employee's break room where Phil's body had been found for an indeterminate period. Yellow tape emblazoned with *Crime Scene* in large black letters, exactly like what anyone would expect to see in movies and cops and robbers shows, barred the entrance. Which was okay. Who would want to eat in there until the room had been sanitized—literally, with full-strength bleach.

And mentally.

One of the stairwells was cordoned off with the same tape and blocked by Mr. Beefy Policeman. I heard the cops had requested the video from the security cameras. Phil's cubicle was inaccessible; in fact, the whole section was. Police watched and catalogued each employee as they packed their work and personal items, ferrying the boxes and carts to another floor of the firm's offices.

From what I could tell and heard via office gossip, everyone was fingerprinted, making me feel guilty about *something*, and making matches would take time. Analyzing the evidence would take time. Unsettled employees would take time.

Most of the first floor was off-limits, which included the main break room. NLB employees now congregated in the smaller area on the second floor. Two bistro tables and four chairs had been crammed in, but were still usable. No one minded considering the circumstances. Coffeepots appeared in odd places throughout the office, bringing to reality caffeine addicts had to have their morning fix one way or another.

With the arrival of fall came football season, and NLB shifted into high alert as the game ruled. Monday morning discussions at the water cooler deliberated the various wins and losses which had taken place over the weekend.

A weekly betting game had been organized by Bookie Dave for the employees. Most everyone knew about this pastime and had played before—except for me. I just knew it existed. However, the format looked simple. And Bookie Dave provided the expertise.

A piece of paper had been folded and divided into one hundred squares. The numbers zero through nine were written along the grid on the left side and likewise, across the top. Participants would write their initials in their respective selected spots. We could select up to three. The winner's numbers matched to the winning game score.

The betting game followed us into our new break room and had been taped on the refrigerator along with a nine-by-twelve interoffice envelope to place each five-dollar bet in.

At lunchtime, several of us had gathered around the refrigerator in the squishy wishy kitchenette. I saw something new had been stuck next to the game envelope.

One down and one to go.
That's what you get
When you play with a 'ho.

"Pretty bad poem," commented someone from over my shoulder.

"Who would write this crap? Is this a joke?"

"I can't figure out the meaning."

"I think this refers to Miller, the new quarterback for the Dragons." Several employees surrounding me nodded their agreement.

"Could be."

"Maybe his exorbitant contract is like buying a high-priced 'ho."

Heads bobbed again. "Could be."

"And maybe the part about 'one down' and 'one to go' refers to the game played last week and another game coming up this Sunday."

An auditor shrugged. "Makes sense."

And further discussion ensued regarding the quarterback's selling out for a record-breaking salary.

I knew very, very little, meaning really nothing at all, about football. Nada. Zip. Not a thing. I attended a few games in high school and college. I knew the basics like the oddly shaped ball moved from here to there through passing, running, or kicking. And whoever ran through the goal posts at the end of the field scored the big points. A lot of rough shoving of players by really big guys whose size resembled a major appliance dominated. But not any intricacies or nuances. That was what I knew.

Well, sorta.

As a youngster, my family and I had visited my

aunt and uncle on weekends. Naturally, the cousins played games. My one boy cousin, a year older than me, worshiped football. He organized his younger sisters, my sister, and me into two teams. We set up in the back alley and executed his plays. We were supposed to "take out the opponents." Only I heard my cousin, who took the glamour spot as quarterback, speak a foreign language. I never did catch on.

Whatever.

I was a lousy player. Besides, from the time Tracey and I were little bitty, Mom had taught us not to fight or hurt each other. This included rough-and-tumble football. My tomboy cousins trampled all over us— obviously used to shoving, thanks to having an older brother. My idea of high adventure had been playing treasure hunt or climbing a tree house.

When in college, I didn't like sitting nor watching a four-hour game in sub-zero weather, especially considering I didn't tolerate the cold well. Layered clothing made one look fatter, a big fashion no-no. Hats messed with hairdos. Super thick sweaters plumped the chest and tummy unattractively.

I would rather spend my time in a more productive manner like shopping, baking cookies, watching a movie, or reading. Anyway, State Tech had always lost their games; so we weren't inspired to attend them except to drink Gatorade margaritas and applaud the band. The drumline performed a cool circle thingy after halftime.

Understandably, the employee rumor mill's discussion turned from football to Phil Meadows. Very little had been determined, except once I'd dined with him over lunch and visited with him on another occasion in the break room.

This statement was interesting and, yet, worried me. I couldn't be the only person connected with Phil. Surely other NLB employees ate lunch or dinner with him. He had supervisors—Bookie Dave and Stuart—and was acquainted with other auditors at the firm. Perhaps, I'd been remembered because I was a new employee as well. Considering the short time Phil had been employed at NLB, he appeared to be admired and worked hard.

Because my name had been bandied about, I wanted to know more. Since learning Bookie Dave was the one who had found Phil, I cornered him in the small break room after the football nuts had returned to their desks. I poured Dave a cuppa high-octane. "Tell me about finding Phil."

"Not you, too." He blew out a forceful huff. "I wish I could be assigned to an out-of-town audit just to escape all the interrogations."

"Wow, that sounds...desperate."

"I am."

"You know," I said, "I have every right to ask. I had lunch with him, and everyone thinks that's suspicious."

His head tilted toward the football game taped on the fridge. "If I talk, will you play?"

"I'll consider it."

"Consider?"

I tossed my hands skyward. "I'm the last gamester you'd want, but if you insist, then yes."

"Great." As he sighed, he scrubbed his hand down his face. He stared at the ground for a long while before saying anything. Resting his hands on his hips, he stared at me.

I patiently waited, yet screams threatened to erupt from my inside.

"I found Phil slumped over the table," he said. "Peanut butter and jelly was smeared on his face. I touched him, and his body felt stiff, and then I took in a strong odor of pee, and…"

Bookie Dave seemed helpful, but I wanted to hear something different than what he'd told everyone else. "Was he bleeding?"

He shook his head. "Didn't see any."

"Did his face look funny?"

"Dead."

I rolled my eyes. "Not amusing."

"Sorry, Hattie, I'm tired of telling the same story over and over. I've been interviewed multiple times by the detectives, and although they don't seem to think I did it, I still feel…weird."

Yea, I know that feeling. "Which is understandable."

Bookie Dave leaned closer, cupping his hand around his mouth and my ear. "Don't spread this, but I was scared."

I would have been too. I'd been too close to a dead body once, which wasn't pretty physically or emotionally. "Anything else?"

"They took away his coffee away."

Coffee? "I didn't know Phil drank coffee. I've only seen him with a soda. And at happy hour, a beer."

He shrugged. "A mug at his right hand had dark liquid inside. The contents looked like coffee."

"Thanks, Dave." I turned to leave, wondering if the police knew what he'd told me.

"Hey"—he pointed to the fridge—"what about the football game?"

As I moved toward the door, I gave him a playful look.

****

To make matters more intriguing, the police called me for an official interview for nine A.M. on the following day.

The last time a detective had interviewed me had been after the insane Opal of Buy Rite fame attacking and slashing me episode. Then, the whole process appeared to be conducted in a no-nonsense, straight-forward approach.

However, how many people were interviewed by the police twice in their lifetime?

I prepared myself to handle this one with some trepidation due to the interviewer, Detective Wellborn.

The detectives had conducted their discussions with the NLB's employees in the small conference room located next to Mr. Northside's office. From my desk, I observed all the action. The designated people were ushered in and out, in and out during those sessions.

I didn't bother to greet Allan. Instead, I took great pains to study him as he passed while barely lifting my lashes.

He appeared to be involved in his work with his trademark true dedication. Sometimes, he would glance my way and catch me doing the same thing. In a flash, we'd stare at something else. Truthfully, our eye contact made my heart flutter a pitter patter.

I did my best to ignore him, but doing so was difficult. His constant presence caused anxious feelings to bubble in my stomach. And uncharacteristically, I couldn't eat, which might be a good diet tool, but more likely, would cause an ulcer. Like I told Jenny, I needed distance.

With great relief, I worked hard, thanks to Mr. Northside.

****

Prompt and pretty at nine, I arrived for my interview with Detective Wellborn. Standing inside the small conference room doorway, I paused to casually assess my surroundings. The drapes were closed, and the room had been cleared of all special decorative items, like bowls, plants, etc.

Was this done to keep objects from being pitched at the police if someone became upset?

Detective Wellborn sat in an executive chair covered in brown leather at the highly polished square table. A casual movement I'd made caused him to look up, and he stood, leaving the paperwork he'd been reviewing. "Hey."

I showed some sass to cover my nervousness as I slid back the chair opposite of his and sat down, setting a water bottle on a napkin in front of me. "Howdy."

Dressed in a white shirt with fine maroon stripes, over which he wore a charcoal suit and a matching tie, he looked migh-tee fine. Distractingly fine. I would have a hard time concentrating with such perfection front and center.

He returned to his chair and arranged the paper piles on the table. Once satisfied, he sat as well. "Thanks for coming. Shall we begin?"

At my nod, he found his paper and pen for note-taking, turned on a recording device, and then stated the date, time, his name, and the interviewee's name, Harriette Lee Cooks.

"Ms. Cooks, let's start at the beginning. How long have you been employed at Northside, Lancaster, and Brookside?"

I wiggled in my chair for a comfortable spot. "I've been working here for approximately two weeks."

"It's my understanding you are assigned temporarily to Mr. Hiram Northside, the Senior Managing Partner, whose administrative assistant is on medical leave."

"I was hired to temporarily replace Mr. Northside's administrative assistant."

"How did you come to be employed here?"

"My friend, Trixie, owns the employment agency, Jobs Inc. which also places people in temporary positions. She was contacted about the job opportunity and suggested me as a candidate."

"So, currently, you're saying you are not permanently employed and while unemployed, you're working temporary jobs?"

"That's right." Somehow, the *unemployed* term he used roughed up my ire.

"Please continue."

"Mr. Stuart Steems, Senior Audit Manager for NLB, interviewed me for the position. Since my skill levels were more than adequate, he deemed me qualified for the admin job. Everyone I've met at the firm has been very cordial, helpful, and considerately included me in their social life."

"How well did you know auditor Philip Meadows?"

"Not very well. He was brand new to the firm. I

met him for the first time last week."

"Last Tuesday"—Detective Wellborn rummaged through his notebook and consulted a sheet—"last Tuesday, you ate lunch with Phil Meadows."

"That's right. He stood in the break room doorway looking like Mary's little lost lamb and asked if he could sit with me. I had been reading a book."

"What's the book's title?"

I stretched my legs in front of me, glanced at the ceiling, and then to stare at my palms. I so didn't want to say. *And why does he need to know?* "Fiction."

"Fiction is the title of the book?"

Me thinketh he wanted me to squirm-eth. "Of course not."

"So what's the title?"

Again, I lengthened my legs. I so didn't want to say. I'd be embarrassed.

"Ms. Cooks?" He sipped from his bottle of water.

Fine. I knew him, and he'd hammer at me all day long until I'd answer. "*The Taking of Arabella.*"

A dip of his chin should have hid the look on his face; however, I saw him squish his mouth into hard lines.

Finally, he sobered and asked, "*The Taking*—"

"*Of Arabella.* A highly complex gothic romance." Crossing my arms, I huffed. "A work of fiction. Okay?"

His eyes twinkled when he asked, "Love life in the toilet?"

I squeezed my eyes into reptilian slits. "I'm fine, De. Tect. Tive. Wellborn. Can we get on with it?" *Rats, did I really say that?*

"Phil came into the break room and interrupted your reading of...*The Taking...of*, er, *Arabella*. He asked if he could sit with you."

"Yes." I shifted slightly in my chair and rested my forearms on the table. "It's like this… I understand how a person feels when they are new to a job. It's a comfort-level thing. As a newbie, one looks for someone harmless to talk to or sit with. I've had several temporary jobs recently and have felt the same way."

Allan knew everything about my multiple jobs.

I felt positive my cheeks had pinked a bit when I sensed them bloom with heat. Eyeing my water bottle, I stifled the desire to empty the entire contents over my face. "When Phil walked in the break room, he wore his newness like his new shoes hurt his feet. He looked around, finding no unoccupied chairs except for the one at my table. So he asked if he could sit in that place and made a comment about not bothering me, which of course, he didn't. I offered him a seat and started the conversation ball rolling. We ate our sandwiches and discussed several topics."

"What specifically did you talk about?"

"I asked him about his education and how he obtained a job at NLB."

"Where did he go to college?"

My gaze shifted to the ceiling to recollect the information. Once gathered, I returned my attention to the detective. "Phil attended State Technological University which is the same one I graduated from. The coincidence bonded us. We talked about his accounting degree background and how NLB recruited him at the on-campus job fair."

Detective Wellborn knew I'd graduated from State Tech just like I knew he'd graduated from Southern U. And I was betting in one of his piles he'd assembled notes about Phil's childhood and education. "We talked about his family, where he's living, and the single lifestyle in Sommerville."

"Okay." He scribbled for a bit.

Afterwards, he looked at me with a narrowed brow, the *wearing his business hat* one, the very one which told of his supreme dedication to the job.

"Can you recall what he ate for lunch that day?"

This question sounded odd. *Whatever happened to the heart attack theory?* The rumor trickling to my ears mentioned Phil could have been poisoned, which in my opinion was pretty diabolical and planned. Maybe the food question was related to poison?

My nose scrunched while my thoughts reverted to the meal. "Phil brown-bagged a peanut butter and grape jelly sandwich. He bought a canned drink from the machine."

"Is that all?"

I looked at the window for help. Several days had passed and my memory sometimes needed jarring. "He ate chips, mini carrots, and"—my nose scrunched some more—"vanilla yogurt with colorful sprinkles." I shifted my gaze back to him and nodded. I had nothing more to add. "Normal lunch fare."

Detective Wellborn head tilted in a confusing manner with the same confusion reaching his contracted brow. "How do you remember yogurt and sprinkles?"

"That's easy. Not many grown men eat that particular brand topped with sprinkles. Kids do. College boys might. I remembered, because I haven't seen anyone eat it in a while, and I like sprinkles, too. Nowadays, I prefer the new whipped variety, strawberry flavored."

Allan scribbled on his ruled pad. "No coffee?"

"No, not while I was there. Maybe the pot was empty. Since I'm not a coffee drinker, nor do I tend to the pot, nor do I ask anyone if they're interested in any. Occasionally, Mr. Northside asks me to get him some, which is the closest I've been to the coffee maker."

"You're quite sure he didn't have any coffee while you were in the room?"

Why is a great deal of emphasis put on what Phil drank? "Positive. He didn't drink any while I was there. He had a soft drink. If he drank coffee, he must have after I left. I heard the police found a mug which looked like it contained coffee. Was there poison in it?"

"You said you don't drink coffee."

"No, I don't." I shot my brows skyward and asked in a perky, yet annoyed tone, "Anything else? I do have work to get to."

"One more thing, what time were you eating lunch with Phil?"

I glanced at my watch to find this interview was dragging on and on. "We were there from approximately noon until one."

"And have you talked with Mr. Meadows on any other occasion?"

"Yes. I visited with him in the break room the day he died. We talked at happy hour last Friday. He bought me a soda."

"Was he drinking coffee?"

"At Happy. Hour," I said with a clipped tone, "he sipped a beer. I didn't notice any coffee then."

"And did you see anyone else with Mr. Meadows?"

"No—" I drew a blank on whatever memory had

145

been stuck way back in my head. I scrunched my forehead and frowned.

Allan shifted forward. "What is it? Is there something else?"

I couldn't recall. Disappointed, I shook my head. "Darn it. I can't remember. Senior moment." *More like fatigue-from-this-stupid interview moment.*

He consulted his notebook. "Let's go back. You said you ate lunch with Phil, visited with him in the break room, and had seen him at happy hour drinking a beer."

"Yess—"

"What kind of beer?"

I envisioned him picking up the bottle and the label came into view. "Lone Star longneck."

"Are you sure? Not some gourmet brand?"

"I'm positive. Maybe that was the kind he could afford."

He nodded. "I asked if you'd seen anyone else with Mr. Meadows."

"The lunchroom was full; so our co-workers undoubtedly did. Many NLB employees, especially the single ones, attended happy hour, but I don't know everyone's name. Bookie Dave spoke to him..." I paused, then shook my head a second time. "I'm sorry. I know he spoke to someone else, but I just can't remember right now."

"Okay." He wrote something down, terminated the recording device, and then stood. "Thank you, Ms. Cooks. Should you have anything further to add to your statement, like what you couldn't remember, please call me at one of these numbers." After he handed me his business card, he ushered me to the door.

I stood in the doorway and for a brief moment, peeked at him from under my lashes.

He'd returned to his notes, ignoring me.

So, this was how Detective Wellborn interrogated.

****

How the rest of the day passed—I hadn't a clue. Being interviewed was quite troublesome, which caused me to review the questions Detective Wellborn had posed. And reflected and deliberated over some of my own.

Why did they want to know what Phil Meadows ate? Why did he ask about me about Phil's coffee? And what is the lack of memory thing?

Not remembering really nagged me. I wasn't old enough to be incredibly forgetful. I tossed my head to shake the recollection loose, followed by wringing my hands and pacing—none of which helped. I needed to work out my nervousness; so I called Jenny to meet me at the club. I would hate to think situations like this were good for my health.

Almost every machine had a power player using it. Weights were hefted. The spin class instructor shouted instructions, and the bikes ratcheted to a higher whirr. Jenny and I felt fortunate to find side-by-side treadmills. We discussed our upcoming book club selection, a funny mystery set in Ireland involving a policeman with a cast of wacky secondary characters.

Jenny whispered inside info regarding Bob Jon Clifton, the WSFO weatherman who had set his elliptical to high. A year ago, they'd met at the local animal shelter fundraiser, and he'd fallen for a friend of a friend. The Funsisters and I pretty much had decided the couple was in love at first bark. We waited with baited breath for the rumor he'd proposed.

"So what about your guy? The one you keep bringing home and who wastes all the hot water in the mornings?" Letting go of the support bars, I swung an imaginary bat. "Is this the real thing?"

Jenny ducked her chin and blushed. "Yes. He asked me to go to his grandmother's eightieth birthday party to meet his extended family."

Wow. Very interesting news. Meeting the family was an important rung up the wedding cake tiers. "Should I be picking out a bridesmaid dress?" I held a laugh inside. "You know yellow is not my color. I'm all about pink."

"It's too soon to say. Yet, who hasn't thought about marriage?" She sighed wistfully. "Most girls do."

Jenny was right. In the past, I'd imagined marrying someone as well, although I would never, ever confess to it, not even in Mom's wildest dreams.

"Hattie." She stopped running and tapped my machine. When the guy behind her cleared his throat, she gave him a staredown which caused him to vanish. "Tell me about your interview with Allan. I've never been grilled by the police except when you were hurt. Did you feel stupid-like, especially when he's the one you're involved with?"

I shook my head, hoping to dispel any of those notions. "We're not involved."

"Yea, right. He has seen you naked."

While I contemplated her zany theory—Allan had seen me naked; therefore, we were involved—I looked at her like she'd lost her sensibility marbles.

She lifted her palms. "You know what I mean."

I knew what she meant. "Weird. I felt weird. I was

afraid I'd say the wrong thing. He kept asking me peculiar questions about what Phil Meadows ate."

"So are they following a poison angle, not a heart attack one?"

"Guess so. He asked if Phil drank coffee."

She puckered her lips into a bow. "Did he?"

I smudged a sweat drip off my upper lip. "Not from what I saw. When I was with him, he bought a soda. Bookie Dave said they took a cup of coffee from the scene. Crazy. I wonder if the taste of coffee disguises poison."

"But if the sample is analyzed and matched something found in Phil's system—"

"Then it would be the same. Cups with coffee remains are always lying around. Someone could have easily left theirs."

"The buying office has crap sitting around, too." She cranked the treadmill's setting to fast walk. Setting her hands back on the handle bars, she picked up her pace. "I think the police bag everything they find as evidence."

"I guess so. And all the processing at the lab takes a long time."

"How do you know this police stuff?"

"I just put two and two together when they made parts of the company off limits." At this point, I punched up the speed on the treadmill and started my run.

Jenny dialed hers even higher. "Wait for me."

Exercise felt good, and like I'd expected, no repercussions from the interview occupied my mind. While I lathered my sweaty body in the shower, I inhaled deep, cleansing breaths. The liquid cascaded down my tired and sore back, massaging the kinky muscles in my shoulders and along my spine. A moan released with the exhilarating feeling induced by the intense pinpoints of hot water. "Ooh. Aah."

Oops. Quickly, I threw my hand over my mouth with the hope no one overheard my groaning. After peeling back the shower curtain in tiny increments, I peeked cautiously around the edge to ascertain if anyone was looking my way. No one. My reputation was spared. Sometimes, a good, hot shower would be the closest thing to having an orgasm.

Mother would be shocked over the orgasm part.

A little later, bundled in a white fluffy towel, I shuffled my way to locker number 108 which, once again, Jenny and I shared. I opened the door to retrieve my clothing, only to find nothing was exactly as we'd left it.

I flung my hand all over the space, thinking I would latch onto what I needed. Like before, our outer clothes hung on the side hooks and our gym bags had been placed on the lowest shelf. But like before, our underwear had vanished.

This cannot be happening.

I slammed my fist against locker number 109. The hard bang had drawn the attention of the women seated on the benches nearby. Rubbing my hand, which now pounded with an intense hurt, I stared at the locker's innards. Finally, I thrust my hand inside and sifted through the leftover clothing. I didn't have really fantastic-looking underwear anyone else would covet. I used to have a matching lacey pink bra and panty set, but I'd misplaced those panties. Naught. My underwear had vanished.

Dammitohell. What is going on here?

I stomped to the showers where I easily located Jenny by her moaning and groaning. A wash of relief passed through my head as I realized I wasn't the only one who'd experienced joy while showering. I bit on my lower lip as I waited until Jenny shut off the water and took the towel she'd thrown over the rod.

She exited, towel secured under her armpits, and I snatched her hand. "You won't believe this."

"Goddammit, Hattie, you scared me. This had better be good," she said smartly. "I'm not used to being grabbed and dragged through a women's locker room."

Once I'd shown her and explained, we methodically searched the floor, benches, and the adjacent empty lockers, only to find no panties or bras. Like the previous time, we asked the other girls, who resembled the ones I'd queried before, if they had noticed anyone near our stuff, but they said no.

"We just sat down," one said with a choked giggle and a smirk. "We didn't see a thing."

Sensing a possibility of bribery in there somewhere, I didn't believe them. Jenny and I stared back, our arms over-lapped. I said, "Right."

Needless to say, annoyed best described our feelings when our underwear didn't turn up. Dressed in our remaining clothes, we marched with fast purposeful steps over to the receptionist chatting on her cell phone.

Standing at the desk, we looked at her, waiting for her to observe us. Her index finger twisted and twirled a magenta-dyed hair strand. Finally, Jenny's patience had worn to the thickness of a page of school notepaper. She rapped the counter and said in a very loud voice, "Excuse me."

"Just a minute," the receptionist said this to whomever she was occupied with and covered the phone with her hand. She turned in our direction. She slanted our way a *why are you bothering me* kind of look. The gum she chewed popped. "Can I help you?"

Not a polite *may* anywhere in her question.

Jenny asked, "Has any clothing been turned in, specifically women's underwear?"

The girl sighed. "This will take a minute. Hold on." She placed the phone on the counter. Rotating away from us, she opened a lower cabinet door and removed a cardboard box which she shoved across the counter in our direction. "Look in here."

Jenny's and my mouth curved downward with disgust as we looked in the box. Jock straps, men's briefs, some with holes, crusty socks. Too bad she hadn't provided tongs to use. We fished through with a rogue pen but didn't find the undies.

I pushed the carton in the receptionist's direction. "There's nothing in here belonging to us. Where's the women's stuff?"

Another sigh. Another "Just a minute." Another smack and pop. She punched in a couple of numbers and spoke in a very soft voice, "Is there another lost and found other than the one at the front desk? No? Thanks, man."

Their brief conversation did not rouse good karma in me.

She palmed the handset. "I don't know about any other returned items."

"This is the second time we're going commando."

Her palm covered her mouth as she made a little *ha*

sound. I curbed a huge urge to smack her. Jenny and I fixed on her best nastiest stares.

The girl sobered and resumed a stance which would never be called professional. "You wanna fill out a complaint form?"

Hell. A draft hit my upper thighs. Commando was creepy. I tugged my black linen skirt's side seam downward. *How do guys do it, especially in pants?* I mean, parts could get caught in zippers. "Yes."

She rummaged in a drawer, passed us a creased pad, and slammed a pencil on top. The pencil rolled across the granite counter and stopped inches in front of my breasts.

I wrote down the pertinent info, but all the while, my hopes weren't high. Once done, I thrust everything toward her. "Thank you."

"No problemo."

Shoulders back, chins up, Jenny and I walked with a cool confidence to the club elevators. No one would ever know about commando, unless the wind flurried.

As we settled ourselves in the elevator cab for the ride to the parking garage floor, she said, "You were right. Unbelievable."

****

Jenny arrived at our apartment before I did. Something unforeseen had diverted my route, a road block, leaving me irritated because all I wanted was to get home and put on *all* my clothing. Ten minutes made a huge difference. I raced to my bedroom, flung my handbag with bamboo handles on the bed, and slipped on clean undies. Then I returned to the kitchen where I threw wide the pantry doors to rummage for food.

From the corner of my eye, I saw Jenny had

followed me and caught her watching.

"You sure are making a lot of racket," she said.

"Yup." I poured a not-even-a-pinch of fish food on my palm and dropped the bits to feed Two Fish, my new green-and-blue Beta. One Fish had gone belly-up a few weeks ago and, considering the life expectancy of a fish, was probably normal. Feeling compelled to have something to nurture, my pet choice had been limited to fish, because my apartment complex didn't allow furry, four-legged felines. Hard for me because I adored kitties.

"Why?"

"I feel like it." I yanked open the fridge door and poked my head inside. *There has to be something edible in here.* "Weren't you listening to the news on your radio when you drove home?"

"Classical. I was in a highly agitated state after the gym."

"Gotcha. They talked about Phil Meadows. All so senseless." I did a bend and stare at the near-empty shelves.

"You never did say how Allan looked."

What? Pulling back from the cold depths, I shot her my best quizzical face. For someone so smart, she could ask dumb questions. Did she *mean* to ask me about The Great Interrogator? "Allan and I didn't talk about his appearance. I told you, he interviewed me about Phil Meadows."

"I know. He's such a…hottie."

I scanned Jenny over, thinking she had probably left all her brain cells at the treadmill. I traipsed over to the sink and stuck my hands under the tap to wash away any particles of fish food.

She rested her forearm on the counter top. "I'm still wondering why someone would steal our underwear."

"I don't know. This is my second time for commando. Not something I like doing."

"I don't get"—she scratched a spot in her hairline —"how men go without underwear."

Hysterical didn't begin to describe how hard Jenny laughed over her brainwave. *Without underwear* did sound more ladylike, but *commando* really drove the point.

Jenny sobered. "Commando. Which could be too much information."

"My hands itched to smack the receptionist."

She flipped her hands and feet into a self-defense stance. "Me, too. We could have taken her."

I contemplated The Case of the Missing Underwear some more. Then, *bing!* a light bulb moment flashed in my head. "There could be a bright side to this. I'm going to have to go…*shopping*."

Shopping. I sensed my whole being glow with the idea, as if a white light aura circled my head and radiated beams to the ground. I rubbed my palms together—what was best described as eagerly—while rejoicing over the bonus opportunity. I needed underwear. And pro-shoppers never turned down prime shopping opportunities, especially when dropped without warning in their laps. *Nirvana*. Using my most excellent pro-shopper ideas, I formulated a plan for replacing my underwear.

"I don't mean to sound insensitive." Jenny peeked in the fridge and then closed the door. "I'm sorry the undies were stolen. But let's get back to something more important than underwear and shopping—your interview with Allan. Is he still with the Blonde Bimbo?"

Finally, some sympathy for me, yet all negated when Jenny asked about the Bimbo. I eyed her, wondering from what planet she'd originated. "Detective Wellborn and I didn't talk about her."

"Why not?"

"Look, who he wants to date, i.e., Blonde Bimbo, is fine by me. None of my business."

"Whom."

"Yes, O Grammar Queen, whom." I put my finger to my temple and rubbed a slow circle. "He has to feel odd, knowing both of us are working at the same firm."

"It's a strange coincidence."

Since the pinching episode, I steered clear of Cathy Bartholomew. "She doesn't exactly have a nice reputation around the office, sort of artificial. I evade her as much as possible."

"I know the type. You remember Cee-Cee?"

Jenny and I had worked with a girl like Cathy Bartholomew at Tucker's, named Cecilia, but everyone called her Cee-Cee. The artificial type was someone who posed as being better than everyone, usually through lying, cheating, and stealing, and then, when all was revealed, ended up being a momentous bust. Most people took on the attitude to prop up their self-esteem.

According to the NLB employee rumor mill, Cathy Bartholomew had been caught in several whoppers—specifically about her employment background—which turned off people big-time and could possibly get her terminated. Several said they'd heard conflicting stories about her family and where she hailed from. Yet, her employment continued at NLB, thanks to Mr. Northside who declared she'd proven herself invaluable, even awarding her employee of the month on several occasions.

I'd seen her photo in the break room and had to squash every desire to throw rotten tomatoes at her face. I slid a finger along the divot below my lower lip. "She chatters on and on incessantly. She's such an expert on everything, pontificating all the time. She isn't Allan's style."

"I agree. He shouldn't be dating someone who behaves the way she does. Yet, the almighty act to procreate which inhabits all men makes them think in odd ways."

"Yup." Allan and her having sex roused a sickening feeling in my belly. "Sex. Sex. And more sex."

"What does his mom tell your mom?"

"Mom hasn't said anything. You remember our big discussion at my birthday? Since then, she's maintained a low profile on the Allan Wellborn subject—Praise the Lord. And I don't think she's sharing much with Mrs. Wellborn either, which is hard to believe considering what good friends they are."

Jenny set her elbows on the island counter and rested her chin in her palms. "Your mother did say he was a stupid ass for dating Cathy Bartholomew. You know, the phrase *stupid ass* isn't used enough."

"At first, some guys just don't see girls for what they really are."

She bestowed some of the little wisdom she had remaining. *Hmm.* "By the way, I picked up the mail. We got the electric bill, the cable bill, and…here."

I studied the envelope she passed me.

She tapped the spot above the recipient's name. "Looks like the return address is New York City."

After my stint at Buy Rite and Button and Bows Stationary Company, I felt, perhaps, I was meant to stay with my original career path—retail. So, based on my determination, I'd instigated a new plan.

A friend who was an area sales representative for a world-wide men's shirt company had called me after reading about my unfortunate exploit at Buy Rite in the *Sommerville Express*. He mentioned a buyer friend at an upscale department store in New York had been interviewing potential assistants. The rep recommended me for the job.

I'd emailed the buyer, highlighting my retail experience at Tucker's Department Store and my educational background. I mentioned our mutual friend's recommendation and attached my resume.

Disgusted with my employment situation right before I took the temporary job with NLB, I'd found myself at the post office. I'd stood in front of the mailbox for what seemed like hours, deliberating the pros and cons for the gazillionth time. I'd twisted my follow-up letter over and over in my hands, waiting…hoping for divine intervention about the right path to take.

Simply put—I wanted an easy decision. But we all know the real world didn't operate this way. With an unknown impulse, I'd thrust the letter in the drop slot. Then, I hopped in my Jeep.

I didn't confide in anyone about what I'd done. Not Mom, not Jenny, not the Funsisters—no one at all. I didn't want their opinions. Taking this job would prove to be a real challenge. I would have to relocate to New York City and start over. The leaving part caused mixed feelings.

Secrets could be hard to keep. This one might be the hardest. "Huh."

Snatching the envelope from my hands, Jenny rotated the letter to read the addressor's name. "Peter Redmond. Who's he?"

God, she could be sooo nosy. I grabbed my mail.

Her eyes were super-glued on me when she repeated, "Who is Peter Redmond?"

Maybe a light improvisation would distract her. "Oh, he's someone I knew from Tuckers."

She tilted her head. "Funny, I don't remember him."

"He didn't work at Tuckers."

Liar, liar, pants on fire.

Chapter Eleven

Today, I received the most unusual telephone call from Allan. He phoned while I was at work and asked if I could take care of Lucky, his lovable huge gray cat, while he traveled for business. He'd found lost Lucky at a McDonalds and the nurturing instinct encompassed him, which resulted in him adopting the furry feline.

I knew he wouldn't answer me if I'd asked where he was going. I assumed he would be gone for police business. Nevertheless, I could try and ask—*Okay,* I was nosy. Maybe the stars would be in the right hemisphere and he would—unknowingly—divulge more.

"Sure." His cat was the closest to owning one of my own. "I'll gladly take care of Lucky. How's my pal? Found any more super-sized water bugs?"

Allan chuckled. "If I ever have another cat, I'm naming him Eating Machine because all Lucky does is eat. Eat, eat, eat."

And poop, poop, poop. I would have to change the litter box as well. "Maybe he felt starved while homeless and munches to compensate."

"Maybe."

"Is he getting fat? Lazy? Cats consume more when they're bored. Are you giving him the right kind of kibble? Could you be giving him too much? Are you playing with string and stuff with him?"

"He isn't fat. He isn't bored. The variety of cat food I buy is supposed to keep him from gaining weight. According to the label, meat is the first ingredient. I don't over feed him. And yes, we play with cat toys." He paused for a sec and then asked, "So…is it okay?"

Of course, I would help because I did have an ulterior motive for agreeing to baby, er, cat sit. I'd been toying with the idea—if the opportunity ever presented itself—of poking around his apartment to discover what he and Blonde Bimbo had been up to. I had to know the answer to the big question—Were Allan Wellborn and Cathy Bartholomew having sex?

"No snooping, no searching, no looking, no nothing."

His statement surprised me. So surprising, I knocked over my pencil can. I'd forgotten he could read my mind. I scrambled to gather the scattered writing instruments.

"Who—me? Why would I do that?" Better lock up the valuables, and hide the unmentionables because Allan should be very worried. His *no nothing* statement wouldn't dissuade me. No taking the fun out of fun.

Changing the topic under discussion seemed prudent. "Where are you going?" When I didn't get a response, I knew I'd predicted the right answer—police business. He never, ever talked about work. "Will you call?"

"I'll call."

Feeling miffed, I set my mouth in a determined twist. I would show him. From now on, I would check caller ID and decide if *his* calls were worthy of answering.

"I'm not leaving until late this afternoon. When I go home to collect my bag, I'll hide the front door key under the mat. Come after work. I appreciate it."

"Okay, but you wiilll ooowe me." I singsonged the phrase I couldn't resist adding.

"I possess all kinds of ways to pay my debts. Besides, didn't I do you a big favor a while back when I took you to your friend's engagement party? I'm thinking you owe me."

I'd left a *desperate, but hopefully, didn't sound like one,* message on Allan's voice mail, nearly on my hands and knees begging and pleading, asking him to escort me to an engagement party. I didn't actually sink to those subterranean depths, but I did make my message sound as if I assumed he would accompany me to the party. Afterward was when we engaged in almost-wild, almost-sex. His *owe me* comment seemed more like unsettling innuendos.

"Later." He'd hung up before hearing my response.

I set my cell phone by the computer and wondered why Allan hadn't asked his mother or Cathy Bartholomew to care for Lucky, which made more sense than asking me, the old girlfriend.

He-he-he. I scrubbed my palms in a sinister fashion. I couldn't wait to execute my version of Pink Panther.

****

Like a crazed woman intent on a mission, I drove straight to his apartment after five. And I located the key under the door mat, just like he'd outlined. You would think a cop would be more security conscious. Anybody like, burglars…creeps…Cathy Bartholomew, could have found the opener there.

I unlocked the door and stepped over the threshold, softly closing the portal behind me. Lucky pounced on my feet. He followed this with bumping my legs none-too-gently with his head. I heard the click of our bones. *What a great cat.*

The tags dangling from his collar clinked as he shadowed me to the kitchen. I poured dry cat food in his bowl and sat cross-legged on the floor by him. After eating, he drank some water and climbed in my lap, first, to wash his face, then proceeded to groom the rest of his body.

Cat purring had a unique way of calming a person. While stroking the soft fur on his head, I collected my wits. I had to fix on a decision—*now* or *never.* My plan seemed insanely stupid, stupid like the antics of a bond enforcement character from a popular mystery series. The heroine nose-dived right in and always ended up in a big fat muddle, only her muddles weren't for real.

After eyeballing Allan's apartment to map out a doable plan, I established the kitchen looked like the best room in which to begin. Move to the living area, his desk, and leave upstairs until last. That part of his townhouse, the part where the bedroom lay, was the most unsettling. My stomach did a queasy-greasy flip-flop.

My feline friend stayed curled complacently in my lap, watching my every thought like an actual movement. Lifting him under his front legs to eye level, I buzzed his nose. After standing, I dumped kitty to the floor where he landed with a padded thump. "It's now or never. Let's go explore."

I employed a technique plagiarized from television—just a hoist here or there with my little finger—not really stirring anything around. I opened drawers, cupboards, and then the refrigerator. Mostly, my efforts were confined to looking since I didn't possess any tweezers for bagging and tagging like forensic experts.

Overall, the kitchen appeared clean. Dirty dishes relegated to the dishwasher. Placed on the bottom rack were two plates, stained with tomato sauce and bits of pasta which led me to conclude two someones had probably dined on spaghetti.

And I wasn't one of them.

Once upon a time, you had tried.

Two inexpensive wine glasses—thanks to Mom, I could identify high-quality crystal—rested on the top rack. Either Allan was a closet drinker, or he'd had vino with the pasta dinner à deux. A glass, with what resembled an opaque milky residue on the rim and in the bottom, sat in the stainless sink. A blue-and-white striped cup towel had been wound neatly through the fridge handles.

With my fists on my hips, I circled the room, scrutinizing his kitchen. Guys were never this tidy. Mrs. Wellborn must have beat cleanliness into her kids at a very young age. I released a long exhale.

Found nothing.

Except for suspicious-looking dirty dishes.

In the original dining area, I seated myself at Allan's computer desk. His laptop would have been placed dead center...if it had been there. The supply bins contained pens, pencils, and other standard office notions. On a nearby bookcase, I did find another crisp parchment note card exactly like the one in my birthday gift bag. He'd written *Dear Hattie* and crossed out some mistakes. My heart experienced the classic beating-harder stuff. Lost in a dreamland, I heaved a heavy breath while stroking the words.

Stop it, Hattie, my subconscious said. *Have you forgotten about your dinner plans with hunky Greek God?*

Undoubtedly, I had because I'd hardly seen Will Christiansen all week since he'd been assigned to an out-of-town audit. I replaced the card, repeating my mantra aloud for emphasis, "Greek God and Dinner. Greek God and Dinner."

I didn't go to the next level and open the mail which lay on the desktop. However, I pondered taking a gander. Would the spy technique acquired from old black-and-white movies where the perp held the letter to the light to view the contents actually work?

Taking the envelope to the window and holding the letter *juusst so*, I squinted as the last bit of sunlight dropping below the horizon filtered through the paper and shone in my eyes. No, the spy thingy didn't work. *Rats.*

Found nothing.

Except for an old note intended for me.

Turning my attention to the living area, I opened the coffee table's drawer. Inside were drink coasters and bottle tops. Nothing in the end table drawers either. Underneath the couch cushions, I unearthed dust and change. Dusty pretzels and a pen stuck in the corner. I picked up the pen—monogrammed with his initials, ACW—and then returned it to the original spot, thinking with a giggle, *let him figure this out.*

I walked to the entertainment center, searching through his video selection. "The Longest Day," a

World War Two film, caught my eye. I decided to borrow the DVD, pitching the box toward my handbag where I'd tossed it on the chair which complemented the sofa.

The DVD's power button glowed green. I punched eject and the tray opened, revealing a chick-lit movie circa 2000. The selection surprised me. I'd enjoyed this one, although I adored almost every movie with hunky English guys. I also liked James Bond, Indiana Jones, Star Wars, and Bugs Bunny films.

The DVD case lay on a shelf. I flipped to the backside, discovering the receipt slipped inside the plastic cover. Two days prior, he had rented this movie from the neighborhood video kiosk. *Why would Allan watch a chick flick? Maybe he'd had a date—Cathy Bartholomew? Maybe they watched after eating spaghetti?*

Shaking my head, I returned the case to the shelf. Some mysteries couldn't be solved.

Found nothing.

Except for a fishy movie selection.

I stepped to the stairs and slipped off my high heels. I didn't want to leave any trace of my having been here. First, I bypassed the bedroom—too many memories—and fast-walked to the bathroom. My snooping expedition began in Allan's medicine cabinet. He'd stashed the usual stuff: toothpaste, shaving cream, razor, tampons—

Tampons? In his medicine cabinet? And I hadn't put them there, which could only mean the Blonde Bimbo had. *Oh. My. God.* My heart sank. If there was any irrefutable evidence, then a ladies' sanitary product would be it.

Half-heartedly, I rummaged through the drawers and finally, the cupboards underneath the sink. He appeared to be a real low-maintenance guy, having the necessities of shampoo, deodorant, owie medicine, and bandages, the superhero variety pack.

The clean sheets and towels had been placed on a shelf in the linen cupboard located behind the door. The towels smelled spring meadow fresh. I didn't sniff the sheets. A plastic laundry basket sat in the bottom of the same cupboard, presumably for collecting the dirty clothing. Extra toilet paper and two spare boxes of tissues were stockpiled next to the basket.

I let my index finger graze over the additional bars of soap, which had been stacked next to the white bath towels. Closing my eyes, I took a deep sniff. *Mmm,* pine scented. I took another whiff and pictured the spot on Allan's neck which carried this same bouquet after he'd showered—a clean crisp, fragrance. The place where I felt drawn to place a kiss. The warmth of his skin. The softness—

I jumped, startled with the intensity of my memory. I could almost reach out and touch him. Peeking out the bath's doorway, I half-expected him to pop out and say, "boo."

I skimmed my finger over the soap again and caught his presence. The memory of him felt so real. His arms held me tight...my cheek pressed to his shoulder...my head tilted...my lips touched his soft spot, puckering to leave a kiss...a pulsing grew deep and low below my belly—

Oops. My body froze, and my eyes opened wide while realizing what I nearly had experienced...an orgasm. The sense of smell was the strongest sense of all. With a long deep gulp, I swallowed and shook my head, freeing the sensory overload. When I returned the soap to its spot by the towels, I saw my hand quaked.

Found nothing.

Except for great-smelling soap which almost brought me to a peak.

I returned to the bedroom and spread wide the closet doors. His clothing hung tidily on hangers, sorted from left to right—pants, then shirts, suits, and other odds and ends which included Sommerville Police Department's uniforms in the far right corner. Another dirty clothes basket had been placed under the shirts on the floor. One uniform appeared neatly creased from a fresh cleaning and had been stored inside a filmy sleeve. I ran my finger over the nameplate on the navy regulation shirt, fingering the letters in his name—A. Wellborn. I fiddled with his Star of Excellence pin.

With deliberate care, I passed my hand down a stripe on one of his beautiful dress shirts, noting the crisp starch. Colorful ties hung on a pegged rack, and I toyed with them. The silk's delicate texture rippled through my fingers.

Found nothing.

I stepped back to close the closet doors.

Wait a minute. Something on the top shelf caught my eye. Curiosity aroused, I danced on my tippie toes for a better look. Something white and plastic like a grocery bag. *Why would a store bag be sitting on the top shelf of his closet?*

I gave a little jump and snagged the bag's corner. As I tugged, two large packages of M&Ms—the three pounder size only available at the wholesale club store—spilled on the floor. I squatted to examine the remaining contents and found brown sacks. A thin clear sleeve contained flattened foil balloons, and the label featured one shaped like a flower pot full of colorful daisies with a *Get Well* banner flourished across the body.

I knew this stuff too well.

He'd gifted me these things several times, even recently on my birthday. Evidently, he'd kept a supply of gifts intended for me—which I found interesting. And every time I'd opened the bag and read the card, little fluttery *oh, he's so great* sentiments overwhelmed my head and heart.

Does he think he'll have other opportunities to use them? My mouth twitched, letting wistful feelings and regret swamp me. *Oh dear.*

Then my mouth drooped into a frown. What did Allan Wellborn give Cathy Bartholomew? *Diamonds? Orchids? A cast aluminum grill?*

He would be so wrong to gift her with the same things as me. Chocolate candy was my domain.

After I stuffed everything in the grocery bag, I shoved it all on the shelf, giving an extra pat or two to set it into place. Hopefully, he wouldn't notice the bag hadn't been perfectly stored.

I paused to inventory his bedroom. A wooden chair had been angled in front of the window. A music stand sat within a readable reach, and a long black case, which undeniably contained his trombone, lay on the rug by the chair legs. As a geek in high school, Allan had performed in the marching band. His practice sessions at the Wellborn home caused Sarah Ann and me to shield our ears from the squawks and screeches. Eventually, like a billion years later, he'd improved.

Truthfully, the trombone would never be a sexy instrument.

Truthfully, it would make a better lamp.

I turned my attention to the rest of his bedroom, meaning mainly, the bed. Mission style in design, stained ebony, and topped with a navy blue and dove gray plaid comforter and matching shams. Two throw pillows in stripes of olive green and navy had been placed in front of the shams as was a paisley one.

Most guys rarely assembled a designer look without help. Mrs. Wellborn excelled at decorating and had, without a doubt, assisted in selecting his bed linens. In all probability, she had forced Bed-making 101 onto him, too.

Dropping to my knees, I examined the space under the bed frame. Large dust bunnies killed the overly neat theory. Mom would be appalled if any were under her beds. And I stumbled on Lucky's hiding spot, who chewed and tugged contentedly on an old sock.

I smiled at the big cat and wiggled a finger near his nose. "Hi, kitty."

Nothing found.

Unless dust bunnies counted.

I rose and brushed my skirt. With my finger touching my lips, I looked at the bed and wondered about what had almost taken place between us. My fist drove deep into the mattress to test its firmness—soft on the uppermost surface, harder underneath. Before I could change my mind, I lay on top, stretching my legs and rocking my shoulders into its comfort. My hips shaped tight figure eights, rocking the bed in an up-and-down, up-and-down motion.

As the surges subsided, I closed my eyes and

crossed my arms low on my stomach while summoning up our interrupted interlude the night of the engagement party, the interrupted almost-wild, almost-sex. The soapy scent right below his ear which teased all man, all him...the feel of his hands caressing and manipulating me wholly...my skin taking in his warmth which could only come from his naked body on top of mine—

Whoa! Instantly, my eyes popped open. I had to focus on my mission—to go where no old girlfriend has gone before and search for clues about Allan Wellborn and Cathy Bartholomew's relationship. Not rehash ours.

I wasn't doing very well.

Glancing from side-to-side, with an awareness of where I lay crept in my head, I had The Worst, The Most Horrible, The Grossest Thought of all Humankind. They could have done IT on this bed. Cathy Bartholomew and Allan Wellborn could have been sexually intimate on his bed. And now, I lay on top!

Yuck. Yuck. Yuck.

I catapulted to my feet faster than fast and turned, staring at the piece of furniture, half-hoping to find evidence to confirm my suspicions. But my other half found all of that too...repulsive. Something awful, like a fur ball, clogged my throat.

After regrouping, I grasped a knob on the nightstand drawer and yanked, only to find what I'd been searching for, the irrefutable evidence which confirmed every suspicion—a box of condoms.

To be precise, the drawer contained three boxes, and according to the package, twelve condoms in each box for a total of thirty-six. I read the descriptive writing on the side panel which said the box contained sealed foil packages *ribbed for her pleasure and satisfaction.*

Thirty-six condoms? Ribbed for pleasure? And orgasm? *Wow.* As an embarrassing heat flushed over me, I fanned my hot face with my other hand.

Reality stepped in. The bad news could be bigger boxes of condoms containing seventy-five or a variety pack with assorted colors, ribs, and delectable fruit flavors, dedicated to multiple ecstasies.

I had little experience with the latter.

In today's time, most relationships were consummated fairly quickly. Did the unopened boxes mean Allan and Cathy Bartholomew weren't consummated? A tiny butterfly of hope danced in my chest.

Could the boxes be brand new because they'd finished others? When my heart sank, the butterfly of hope dropped dead in the pit of doom.

Allan and I didn't get to use a condom. He'd ripped and rolled and retracted. If I was still involved with him, I would have made sure we had withdrawn a large deposit.

I delicately pried open a box and grasped a sealed foil package. But as I lifted, the whole container disintegrated in my hand, causing the contents to scatter. I gasped then dropped to my knees, gathering and organizing them in my palm so I could restore them perfectly in their box. I counted eleven—one short. *Crap, Crap, Crap. Where could it be?*

"This sooo is not my day." I searched high and low, behind the nightstand and then under the bed. But I didn't find the missing one. I returned the boxes to the drawer and then shut it, thinking maybe he wouldn't notice.

Found nothing.

Which wasn't true.

I found more questions and this part of my search left me feeling nauseous.

Lastly, I checked the chest of drawers which mirrored the style of his bed. He'd stacked a couple of mysteries by a popular author and a biography about John Adams, second president of the U.S., on top. Placed in a leather tray were a flashy watch and a pocket-sized container of breath lozenges from The Brew Spot, the local coffee shop.

His kisses had been wintergreen fresh.

Neatly folded and stacked inside the first drawer lay piles of silky boxers, the everyday whitey tighties, and undershirts. The drawer below held printed pajama bottoms and socks. In the unit underneath, I found solid and novelty T-shirts, like his favorite ratty one inscribed with *Accountants Rule*.

I flipped through his neat pile of clothing and made my way to the top drawer which held his underwear. Secret stuff might have been stored here. At least, I stored my valuables like my pearl bracelet and earrings in my undies and assumed Allan might have stashed something in a similar spot.

As I ruffled my hand through the underwear, a flash of pink caught my eye. Intrigued, I slowly flipped the stack again and then broke off. My heart stopped. In the drawer next to his underwear lay my pink panties, the very same ones of the lacey underwear set Jenny had given me for my birthday which had gone missing the night of almost-wild, almost-sex.

So, this was where they disappeared to. He'd had them all this time. I sent my gaze around his room. "Why?"

I stepped backward until my legs hit the bed and sank automatically to the edge. I remembered searching like a deranged woman several times around the bed and the bathroom and not finding the undergarment.

Why would he hide my underwear?

I folded the panties with care and stuffed them in my slacks' back pocket. This bothered me a lot. In a way, this revelation seemed...perverted. We hadn't been on the best of speaking terms lately, but he could have returned my lacey brief, instead of leaving me wondering. Or he could have thrown them away. A burst of unease tore through my body.

The most outrageous, the most hilarious, the most shocking idea of all time smacked me. *He-he-he.* What if Cathy Bartholomew had snooped in Allan's drawers and found my panties? Would she think he was a closet cross-dresser? *He-he-he*—which would be really funny. She'd examined the undies, knowing they weren't hers while wondering who they belonged to.

With a lighter note in my head, I set my hand to close the chest of drawers. I surveyed the bedroom one last time and determined all looked undisturbed and tidy; he would never know what I'd done.

Found nothing.

Besides my underwear.

I discovered Mr. Perfect to be very neat. Maybe the Boy Scout motto—he certainly utilized the salute—covered this code of cleanliness. *Preparedness* flashed in my mind.

I should be ashamed, but I wasn't, not really. My mother would kill me if she knew what had transpired, trotting out her three R's lecture—"Respect, Respect, Respect. R for yourself, R for where you are, R for others."

But I would never tell.

I'd been curious about his relationship with Cathy Bartholomew and now, I knew. I joggled my head still not comprehending anything. At one time, Allan and I'd had chemistry. I didn't understand why he would say "no" when I asked him to choose me, and instead, be with her—especially when I didn't find any overwhelming evidence of a sexual connection. He still rocked my world.

But I had to move on.

So what kind of relationship do they have? I knew Cathy Bartholomew clung to him annoyingly when I saw them at my birthday party, and he appeared not to be bothered. I shivered from the creepy high school mental picture. Clueless me.

For the most part, I extrapolated Allan as:

1) Low maintenance
2) Ate spaghetti and drank milk
3) Way too neat
4) Had several boxes of unused condoms
5) Continued to have an interest in the trombone
6) Read presidential biographies

And… I tugged my lower lip and added:

7) Carefully put away my underwear

On the other hand, I didn't uncover anything new regarding his relationship with Cathy Bartholomew. With a shrug, I accepted his affairs weren't my business. I needed to pull together my act and fixate intently on my upcoming date with Hunky Greek God and Dinner.

As I descended the stairs, I heard his home phone ring. I paused in icicle mode, wondering *who the hell*, wondering if he knew what I'd done. The answering machine—*who had those nowadays?*—picked up, and I overheard the way-too-distinctive voice of Cathy Bartholomew saying:

"Hi, Allan. I hoped I'd catch you on your cell 'fore you left. Anyway, miss you already, hon. Have a safe trip and call me as soon as you can. Love you. Oh, by the way, who's feedin' Lucky?"

I looked over my shoulder at the machine, disgusted with the *love you* part. She was not meant for him. Maybe I wasn't either. But she definitely wasn't.

Nothing else to do but go home and watch the DVD I'd appropriated.

Chapter Twelve

Thank God for Friday. Mr. Northside had me hopping here and there because he needed this and that. As a result of being zigzagged in too many directions, all life force had been zapped from my body.

However, I had *game on* for my date with Will Christiansen—after I'd freshened my makeup and fluffed my hair.

Will and I had agreed to meet at Jack's Bar for the regular NLB happy hour. Coincidentally, we entered together and were greeted with loud cheers from the already joyous gang. We joined the merrymaking.

After two margaritas, he looked better than Hunky Greek God. He looked exceptional, like Hercules. After three margaritas, I could barely concentrate on what he said. Instead, I focused on his mouth and anticipated his kisses.

Around seven, Will touched my forearm. "Hungry?"

I bobbed my head and set my almost-empty glass on the counter. "Ravenous."

After saying our goodbyes to our colleagues, he whisked very spirited me off in his pristine black BMW to my favorite Italian restaurant, Mamma and Pappa's Italian Bistro, for my birthday dinner.

For a brief second, I held my breath just before entering. I'd hoped my last memory, the one where I saw Allan Wellborn with Blonde Bimbo, would be purged from my recollection. It sorta was—*sorta* being the operative word.

The hostess moved us to a table.

I liked Will Christiansen a lot. He easily distracted me. While becoming better acquainted, we laughed over inane things. We came from different backgrounds which I found intriguing. Him—wealthy. Me—middle class. Him—private education. Me—local high. Him—fair-haired. Me—dark. Him—no siblings. Me—one.

Leaning closer, I rested my chin on my propped hand. "Tell me more."

"I'm from California and studied accounting at Stanford. NLB hired me after graduation."

"I've a friend who was hired from college like you were. Never knew accountants would be in high demand."

"Me, neither, but we are. In the age of cyber theft, forensic accounting is on the rise."

"What about your family?"

"My dad's a lawyer and lives in San Francisco—"

"Ooh, how glamorous."

"It's beautiful."

I sipped from my glass of Chianti and managed not to spill a drop and appear alluring at the same time. "A trip there is on my bucket list with a detour to Napa."

"Shouldn't be missed." He tipped his head. "I always wanted a sister."

"Many a time, I'd have given mine away."

"Lucky you."

"You'd think differently if you had to share a bathroom. Slob doesn't begin to define her."

He grinned, then something swept over his face

and his eyes darkened. "My mom died from cancer when I was twelve."

"I'm sorry." I never liked hearing this kind of news and patted his hand. "How sad for you."

His turned to one side. He inhaled, then exhaled a deep breath, and refocused on me. "Sorry. Her loss wasn't fun." He held up the wine bottle. "More?"

I nodded and tilted back in my chair, watching him pour.

Will would best be described as engaging, traveled, and easy to look at. His body—lean and hard. He kept his bright blue gaze on me while he talked. His sun-streaked hair, cut long on top, short on the sides, compelled me to stroke right above the ear with a light touch, but I didn't. Now wasn't the right time.

"Lived in Sommerville all your life?" he asked.

"Yes. Love it. I never want to leave, not unless I have to." My reference to leaving caused the potential New York job to cross my mind. "Do you like living here?"

"I do. The standard of living is economical, and the women are pretty." His mouth shaped a wicked smile as he toyed with the ends of my hair.

Will told me he had been employed by NLB for eight years, rising through the ranks to Senior Audit Manager. He didn't monopolize our conversation and asked polite questions. Interestingly, he'd had a long-term relationship in college which didn't pan out, just like me. All I cared about was him being unmarried and very a-vail-a-ble.

No dieting tonight. We mooned over a large serving of mile-high lasagna, thick slices of toasted bread liberally spread with garlic butter, a crisp green salad, and more Chianti. After we'd done all the damage we could, he took the menu from the waiter. "How about dessert?"

Never one to turn down my favorite part of mealtime, I selected a slice of cherry chocolate fudge cake, asking for two forks. The treat covered my chocolate addiction and was a good alternative to the large supply of my favorite candy which awaited me at home. Also, a garlic breath eliminator.

With several glasses of wine on top of the margaritas, I grew more than loopy, more like Happyland, similar to Candyland.

Will helped me in his BMW and drove me back to my car still parked outside Jack's Bar. Through the window, I saw the sky had turned an inky black blue. A sliver of the moon was shaped like a shallow bowl. The stars winked and twinkled.

In fact, he looked twinkly, and I felt twinkly.

We reached Jack's bar, and he parked his car by mine. I exited his to walk to my Jeep, feeling unsure what would happen next. In the past, some dates would kiss my cheek. Some would stumble around. Some gave up the standard "I'll call you." Some had me in the backseat of their car with the windows steamed for a different conversation.

Not Will Christiansen.

His hands circled my upper arms, pulling me gently toward him. He had me waiting and waiting, his forehead brushing against mine as *this is it* passed through my brain.

"Hattie."

The seductive murmur of my name in my ear followed by a soft kiss at my temple was a huge turn-on. He sampled my jaw, leaving a path of tender lingering pecks which trailed along my throat. My body grew all shimmery. Maybe even levitated.

I smiled into the soft spot on his neck. After a sniff there, I found he had no scent. I wrapped my arms around his shoulders and shoved my body into his for more. "Mmm."

My eyes half-closed. His head moved toward mine. His lips parted. He drew me closer for the long-anticipated liplock. This man wanted something, and I liked the something he offered.

He kissed me. And again. His tongue deepened with mine. His hands captured my face. His thumb caressed my lower lip.

As my eyes batted open, I swallowed.

His smiled conveyed what he really wanted. "Let's go to your place."

Necking in a parking lot had disadvantages, and one possibility could be leftover happy hour co-workers spying on us. Drunk from the alcohol and the kissing, my mouth formed a languorous smile, "yes."

Considering my condition, I concentrated on my drive home. With my luck, one of Allan's cop buddies would ticket me, which would be unfun.

Will followed and periodically, I glanced in my rearview mirror to locate him. His gaze locked with mine. He winked.

Someone more prudish than I wouldn't do what I was about to.

Will and I rushed to my apartment where I led him boldly to my bedroom, shoving the door shut behind us. Off dropped his charcoal suit coat, blood red and silver tie, and his once-crisp white shirt. I ran my hands up and down his arms, feeling the smooth skin and arm hair.

His hands bundled my locks to my neck, tilting my head, as his lips sealed over mine.

Upon gathering folds of my dress—the chocolate linen sheath trimmed in pink, the one I'd carefully selected for our date—I pulled my dress over my head in one big swoosh and dropped it to the ground. I toed off the coordinating heels.

Lastly, his arms snaked around my back. He unlatched the hooks of my bra, and then peeled away the sheer coffee-colored undergarment. His hand trickled across my breasts, pausing to lightly massage and tweak each nipple. Delight and lust glistened in his gaze. "Gorgeous."

Feeling the quivering sensation low in my abdomen from each pinch, I tipped back my head and closed my eyes, letting my body succumb to the urges thrumming down low. Instinctively, my pelvis rubbed against his.

Our lips met and our tongues twined. We broke apart and then stared at each other, panting and heaving with anticipation.

I needed him in me. Pretty simple.

I unbuckled his belt and then unzipped the suit pants. When I unveiled the blue silk boxers tented in front, I grinned. Since I knew what was what, I slipped my hand under the elastic band, past his lower abdomen to finger the fluff. I cradled his thickness which summoned forth pleasurable moans and groans. My desire heightened. My neck bowed back as he tasted the tips of my breasts, sucking, pulling each into his mouth. The tension between my legs pulsed even more.

Will's hands dipped inside my undies and clutched my buttocks. "Firm not pushy."

Cute. And hopefully, very true.

Quickly, he kicked off his pants and followed with his boxers as I slipped off my panties. We grabbed each other and stumbled and bumbled our way to my bed, toppling onto the covers.

He rolled on the condom he'd found in his pants' pocket and slid into me with a slick action.

The immediate sensual contact sent my body zooming skyward. We went for mind-numbing, bouncing-the-creaky-old-iron-bed-around-the-room sex. I was pretty sure I screamed.

Round One felt very good.

Round Two felt very awesome.

****

The next morning, I woke and rushed to the bathroom where I saw in the mirror wild bed head, making my 'do resemble a ratted beehive from the sixties. I peeled my tongue from the roof of my mouth, and an odor like stagnant pond scum filtered out. Quickly, I ran a comb through the hairy bush and then scrubbed my teeth and flossed, topping with a mouthwash rinse. I popped a couple of Ibuprophen for the hangover. Luckily, my pink polka-dotted pajamas hung on a door hook. I slipped them on.

I slithered as silently as a snake into the bed.

Will murmured, "Morning," and tugged my head to his shoulder with his arm wrapped comfortably around my hip. He buzzed my forehead.

I arranged my head just-so to avoid his nasty breath.

He squeezed my waist. "Would you like to picnic

at Sommerville Park?"

"Sure." I had no other plans. "What would you like to eat?"

"How about chicken?"

The all-American picnic food. We split food duty and agreed to meet at noon. After he left, I took another pain reliever and sipped a soda while perusing the paper at the kitchen table. Again, the lead article was about the murder at NLB. The autopsy results were supposed to be released.

Not so good for potential customers.

A glance at my phone said *time to go*, and I set landspeed records in showering and changing.

I purchased a bottle of Chenin Blanc from the new-fangled gourmet market at Super Saver Grocery store, pecan-crusted chicken, vine-ripened tomatoes, and accessories for the meal. I saw Mrs. Wellborn and crouched behind the potato bin in major avoidance mode as she squeezed and sniffed mangoes.

Once done, she bellied up to the cart and turned the corner, heading toward the paper goods aisle.

I paid, but all the while, I glanced over my shoulder to make a clean getaway. She could read my story the same way my mother could, and today's would tell of my rendezvous which didn't include her son.

Will picked me up at our prearranged time. "Hey." He gave me a sear-me-to-the-soul kiss—one which almost caused us to modify our plans.

But I managed to stay strong and resist the power of Hunky Greek God. As I settled in his car, my lips continued to vibrate.

Sommerville Park was an incomparable secret and

one stingily shared by the surrounding community. A modest lake where occasional rowboats, canoes, and small sailboats could be seen drifting lazily in the middle of this extraordinary place. A delightful Discovery Garden bordered the east side with lush plantings and inspiring vistas.

Miles of hiking and biking trails looped the lake's perimeter. Branches from large old elm, oak, magnolia, and redbud trees dripped over the paths, banks, and much-coveted picnic areas. In the spring, daffodil blossoms peeked out of the warming ground, bringing their cheerful yellow. In the fall, the leaves transformed into their breathtaking autumnal colors of vivid crimson, burnished gold, and flaming yellow.

After spreading a green-and-black picnic blanket on the grass, I distributed paper plates, plastic silverware, napkins, and wine glasses. A cool breeze skimmed over my skin, and sensing the change, I drew a tweed jacket in blue over my short-sleeved black T-shirt. Strains of a golden oldies tune from a passing convertible drifted our way.

"Here's my share. You're lucky I don't cook." Will handed me a grocery bag which held a container of Caesar salad loaded with croutons and shaved parmesan chips. For dessert, he had chosen brownies.

How sweet. He'd remembered my chocolate craving, which added more points to his desirability factor. I placed the chicken, cubed into bite-sized pieces, and the tomatoes, sliced into wedges, on the salad.

After food and a couple of glasses of the tasty vintage white, my tongue loosened. "You know, you have a reputation with the ladies."

His eyes rounded with a fake look of amazement as his finger pounced against his breastbone. "No way."

"Yes, way. They say you play the field and have left a trail of broken hearts." I placed my hands against the center of my chest and heaved a phony sigh.

He stabbed his last piece of lettuce with his fork. "My assistant says so as well."

"Cathy Bartholomew—right?" I stuffed the dirty plates and forks into the empty grocery bags. I laid down on the picnic blanket and stared at the sky and the clouds. The food and the warmth of the sun made me sleepy. "I met her in the break room."

He nodded. "She takes good care of me. Anticipates my every need."

I just bet she does. But does she do the same for Allan? "How admirable. Then why were you fixing your own cup of coffee?"

He shrugged. "Sometimes, what she gives me is too bitter. But she's excels in other ways. She'd probably do anything for me and my staff."

Interesting.

He said, "Hattie?"

But I didn't really hear him as I drifted off.

"Hattie." A slight pull tugged my lips.

"Mmm."

"Wake up, sweetheart."

Sweetheart? Allan called me that. I blinked to life and sat upright. "I fell asleep." I tucked a strand of hair behind my right ear. "How embarrassing. I hope I didn't snore."

"No big deal, and you didn't."

Then, I recollected he had. I rubbed the back of my hand along my hairline, wiping away the thought.

Will kissed the sexy beast to life. His intimate touches delighted me.

I placed my hands on his shoulders and drew him closer.

His nose nuzzled my hair. "Let's go to my place."

A late afternoon of mind-numbing sex didn't come along every day. Since I'd already pet-sat my friend Lucky, I let Will drive me there.

Round Three was very good.

Round Four was very awesome.

****

On Sunday, Will took me to the indie theater for an early showing to watch a charming French comedy. By unsaid agreement, we skipped the sex since the next day was Monday, a work day—difficult call considering how good and awesome the other times were.

I was embarrassed to admit to myself I might be getting sore. Anyway, I needed to return to Allan's to check on my kitty friend.

When Monday morning rolled around, the phone rang, and someone from the office informed me to get to work as soon as possible.

Chapter Thirteen

"I don't understand, Mr. Northside. I've been calling Will all morning, and he's not answering."

The instant I overheard Cathy Bartholomew's drawl through Mr. Northside's speaker phone, my body went into ice pop mode. She sounded confused and anxious. I dumped my handbag on my desk. Sitting, I eavesdropped intentionally as I ever-so-gently opened a drawer and set my bag inside.

"He wasn't scheduled for an out-of-town audit," she said. "Doesn't have an appointment away from the office. He's never sick. I've tried his cell phone repeatedly and have had no luck in reachin' him."

I theorized this:

A) William Christiansen didn't show for work today.

B) No one knew his whereabouts.

C) Not calling was decidedly not the norm for him.

Something was wrong. My hands began to shake of their own volition. *Should I phone him?*

Mr. Northside summoned the other NLB managing partners to his office for a consultation. Their consensus was to contact the police, which Mr. Northside did. The police told him they would connect with Will's apartment manager and advise him of a potential problem.

Another phone call later, and the SPD told Mr.

Northside the manager opened Will's door and didn't like what he sensed, followed by what he smelled. Two officers entered and discovered Will Christiansen very dead in bed. Several hours later, the coroner called Mr. Northside, saying Will's body had been transported to the morgue and asked him to drive over to identify him.

Mr. Northside returned from the confab quite disturbed. Again, the partners filed into his office.

I heard him tell them, "The police want to investigate further. They will be searching his office and interviewing the staff..."

His door closed behind the group.

I didn't hear anything else. I held in check my insides on the verge of exploding. I couldn't stop jiggling my foot around.

The partners left Mr. Northside's office in a solemn single file. From their contorted faces, they looked like they had gone two rounds with a prize fighter. Punched, pinched, and puzzled.

Mr. Northside called Will's father and informed him of his son's passing. A few minutes later, he motioned me into his office and shut the door. "Please have a seat, Hattie."

I sat; however, confusion passed through my head as I waited.

"I don't know how to say this"—he brushed his hand over his close-cropped hair as he paced in front of me—"I've heard you and Will had a date."

Wow, no one is discreet at NLB. I glanced down at my hands folded in my lap. "Yes."

He cupped his hand on my shoulder. "You'll have to tell the police."

I nodded.

"Be…prepared."

Prepared? I squeezed together my laced fingers. *For what?*

His ringing desk phone interrupted us.

He crashed down the handset and turned. "The Sommerville police are here. We're to gather in the conference room. Because they are still investigating Phil's death and because of Will's demise, they've decided a more thorough examination is warranted."

My stomach began to roll and pitch. I literally felt green all over. Flinging open Mr. Northside's office door, I rushed to the ladies' restroom, locked myself in a stall, and vomited. When finished, I sat on the toilet, absentmindedly peeling paper from the roll in the stainless holder. Peculiar ruminations raced through my head. Feelings of shock and disbelief coursed through my body. My tears stained my blouse.

Will and I'd had so much fun. How could someone I had experienced a romantic weekend with now be dead?

Was I the last to see him? Maybe. But I didn't kill him.

Was he seeing someone else besides me? He had the *player* reputation. After the movie on Sunday, he'd had plenty of time to hook up with someone else.

After a while, my waterworks subsided. I closed my eyes and could even then feel the warmth from his vibrant body when he'd covered mine. I leaned to my right, resting my shoulder against the granite dividing wall. As my crossed arms cradled my torso, any remnant tears dripped on the restroom's black-and-white tile floor. I stared at the lock, unable to shift, unable to feel, transported to another time zone, totally numb. After a long while, I tore a section of toilet paper to dry my eyes.

When the stall door next to mine bashed against the wall, I jumped, then heard, "That bitch. That bitch. *That bitch.*"

I didn't recognize the voice dripping with hatred. I didn't know who the person was talking about either. Obviously, the person speaking was a woman since we were in the women's restroom, but *why would she be saying such ugly things?* The partition dividing the stalls nearly touched the floor, so I couldn't have seen her anyway unless I bent way over and identified the shoes but doing so might give me away. No, I'd play the incognito card.

And who was she talking about?

The water ran at the sink and the sound of a paper towel auto-rolling from the dispenser grabbed my ear. The door opened and closed.

I listened for more, but heard nothing, so I left the stall. After washing my hands at the sink and tidying the mascara runs with a dampened towel, I then wiped the paper along the back of my neck. The wet coolness provided relief. I glanced at my watch and an awareness of how long I'd been away from my desk moved me to go to the conference room to hear what the police wanted to do and how NLB would respond.

Shutting my eyes, I inhaled and exhaled several times just like I'd learned in yoga. I dug six feet deep for strength to get me through whatever would arise. Based on these past few weeks, something surely would. After all, didn't bad things usually come in threes?

First, Phil.

Second, Will.

And third?

I enlarged my eyes and scrunched them. Repeated and relaxed. I stared at my reflection for a moment longer. Before exiting, I mouthed to my mirror image, "Hattie, you can do this."

As quickly as I could, before anything could change my mind, I departed from the restroom.

****

The detective had corralled everyone in the conference and asked questions, grouping people, narrowing the groups to individuals for further grilling, which ended up being Cathy Bartholomew, Bookie Dave, and me. The end result was this:

A) Cathy Bartholomew because she was Will's assistant and Phil was under him.

B) Bookie Dave because he worked for Will and supervised Phil.

C) Me because I ate lunch with Phil and had one date with Will.

Looked like the three of us had the most contact with the deceased.

Cathy Bartholomew looked scared and chomped her chewing gum like it was the last piece she'd ever have.

Resembling a shifty-eyed rat, Bookie Dave's gaze swung from left to right like a clock pendulum.

The embarrassment I experienced flooded my body with heat.

We were questioned more, statements taken, and then dismissed. Right before five o'clock, I learned through Mr. Northside, Detective Allan Wellborn had left a message, arranging for a second interview with me, which also meant he'd returned unexpectedly from his business trip. Since my cat-sitting services wouldn't be required, I drove home, utterly spent.

After my apartment door banged shut behind me, I walked to the kitchen where I stuck my head in the open fridge. Jenny followed, not saying a word. I contemplated the cool depths and the near-empty shelves. Nothing inspiring. But there never really was anyway. And I wasn't that hungry, thanks to today's events. I could fall back on my go-to chocolate which, due to the abundant birthday supply, would be an easy one. I straightened and shut the fridge portal.

Jenny rubbed my shoulders. "Hey. Got your text about Will. Not good news."

"The ultimate in sucky news. I ran to the restroom and cried and cried." Remembering had caused tears to form, and I squeezed the corners of my eyes to stave them. "Thanks, I need the kinks massaged away."

"What's going on at Northside, Lancaster, and Brookside? Two dead guys from work doesn't happen every day." Jenny propped her derriere against the counter, her arms overlapped. "Need a new job?"

"I don't know anything. I just do my work and go home. I do know I have an interview with Detective Wellborn for tomorrow, which I'm not looking forward to." I contemplated. "Yes, I probably need another job."

She snagged an apple from the fruit bowl and bit off a chunk. After munching for a while, she asked, "What's the problem with Allan?"

"I'll have to be honest about my relationship with Will Christiansen." I pointed at her. "Pizza?"

"Pizza. My treat. I have a coupon." She finished her piece of fruit and lobbed the core in the trash can.

Jenny ordered my favorite pie, Canadian bacon and crispy bacon with lots of cholesterol.

While we waited for the delivery, we discussed possible interrogation scenarios.

"You'll have an interesting talk, but you've done nothin' to be ashamed of. You aren't dating Allan anymore. And your ex isn't in charge of your sex life. You are." Jenny laid napkins on the table. "Besides, why would Allan have to know?"

I added plates and a spice jar of pizza seasoning. "He'll want to trace Will's whereabouts for the whole weekend—the whole weekend he spent in bed with me."

"So, what this boils down to is you're trying to avoid telling Allan the truth?"

"No…yes." Frustrated, I let my hands fly to the ceiling. "I can't lie, especially in an interview with a police detective. I have to cooperate."

"Tell him. He could realize he'd made a mistake with Blonde Bimbo. You did everything you could, and you have every right to get on with your life."

As usual, Jenny gave wise advice.

I pinched the bridge of my nose.

She passed me an envelope. "Hey, that guy wrote another letter."

Jenny had picked up the mail. In her remark, I'd heard her unspoken question.

Peter Redmond, the Mitchell-wear guy, had written me formally about the job with his company, and I was betting there was a contract tucked inside. *Darnit.*

"Great." I slipped the missive under my arm. I would review it without her presence. "Thanks."

"Why would you say great? Who mails letters

nowadays? Who's Peter Redmond?"

"I told you he's a guy I know from my days at Tuckers."

"His name sounds sexy."

Sexy as in a dark Heathcliff way. Dark hair. Ice blue eyes. "I'll tell him you said so."

She twisted her mouth. Her examination made me uncomfortable. She knew me too well.

"You know, Hattie," she said, "you don't lie well."

"Me? I'm not lying. You know I'm a crap liar."

"That's not what I'm seeing in your eyes and posture."

"One body language class and you are some expert."

She resumed her spot against the counter. "Me think-eth you defend-eth too much."

"What are you talking about?"

"Like your mom, I can tell when you're keeping something from me."

I shook my head. "Aren't I entitled to a personal life?"

"Personal? Since when did personal mean keeping secrets from a best friend?"

"There's nothing to say. Peter's coming to town. I have a luncheon date with him. That's all." *Liar, liar, pants on fire.*

"I. Don't. Think. So. You're hiding something." Jenny's glare bore the look of anger and disappointment. At the delivery man's ringing of the doorbell, she broke the link and stalked over to the door to answer.

After paying, she tossed the box on the table, grabbed two slices, and went to her room. Closing her door nearly deafened my ears.

Crap, crap, crap.

****

Like my prior interview when Phil Meadows had died, I met Detective Allan Wellborn in the small conference room.

Will's death had hit me hard. Generally in my relationships, I didn't have two days of hot sex and then discover my lover murdered the next. Maybe that happened to other people. Maybe that happened in books and movies.

But not to little ol' me.

I stopped by my desk to freshen my lipstick. Clutching my handbag to my tummy as a form of body protection, I went across the hall to the conference room.

"Hattie." Detective Wellborn stood as I entered the room. He moved to my side, escorting shaky, nervous me to sit in the chair opposite his.

As I sat, I wrenched my trembling arm from his light touch.

"It's okay. You don't have to worry. It's me. You know me."

I had a hard time responding. Relationships were so…personal. I rested my hands in my lap, clenching and unclenching them. Little half-moon nail marks showed on my palm. Noticing, I set my hand to my forehead and crimped the skin. "Hmm."

He squatted next to my chair.

Out the corner of my eye, I stole a sideways glance at his face and saw concern there.

"Thanks for taking care of Lucky."

His lame attempt to help me relax. "Hmm."

"Hey, I don't trust just anyone with my furry friend. He likes you best."

True. The right side of my mouth crooked up at his light banter, but I didn't say anything.

"Are you ready?"

I gave him a brief glance, but I couldn't hold the look. "No."

He patted my arm again.

This time I didn't pull away.

"Hattie, we have to do this. We have to follow police procedure. I have to find out who killed William Christiansen and Phil Meadows."

"I know." Reluctantly, I looked him in his eyes, the beautiful dark ones the color of chocolate syrup. My heart swelled with remembering the love I'd found there. As a result, my angst intensified. "You're sure they were murdered?"

"Yes." He moved to his chair. "Preliminary autopsy report is in."

I stared at my hands clasped in my lap and lowered my chin. "Oh. I'm surprised the paper didn't report anything."

"The paper doesn't know."

Of course, it didn't.

Being interviewed was a problem. I minded being interviewed by Detective Wellborn. Requesting another detective seemed like a good alternative, and considering our past circumstances, shouldn't I be interviewed by someone else? Eventually, the information would be shared with him anyway.

I gave it a shot. "Shouldn't I be talking with a different police person other than you?"

He straightened his six-one frame. "Sommerville's

force isn't that big. We've called in everyone on this case." He gestured to me then himself. "You and I are not…together. So if I do my job correctly, all will be fine."

I saw that all of his papers were tidily stacked, bringing to mind the way he'd organized his apartment. My brain flashbacked to Will's untidy place.

"Ready?" he asked.

I let my head dip in a bare nod.

He started the recorder, stating the date, time, my whole name, Harriette Lee Cooks, and his. Pausing briefly, he checked my condition once again, and then proceeded. "Ms. Cooks. We've obtained statements from some of the NLB staff who said you attended a happy hour with Mr. William Christiansen, a Senior Audit Manager with Northside, Lancaster, and Brookside, last Friday at six-thirty at Jack's Bar."

An awful seizing took hold of my stomach. *So he knew.*

During this interview, Detective Wellborn directed his questions with a strong edge, one with authority.

Despite so not wanting to go there, I raised my head and looked him right in the eyes. Now, I'd confirmed he knew, and he knew *I knew* he knew.

He returned my look with one of steely-eyed professionalism.

"That is correct," I said. "I met William Christiansen at Jack's Bar for happy hour last Friday at six-thirty." Not exactly a lie. "We arrived at approximately the same time."

"Other NLB employees stated the two of you were seen leaving together, and later in the evening were behaving"—he swallowed, and his lips tightened—

"you were seen behaving intimately in the parking lot."

Turning aside my head, I focused on a blank spot where a horse painting used to hang next to a conference room window. I re-crossed my legs. The last thing I wanted to do was admit to a former boyfriend what I'd done with newly dead boyfriend. In my mind things—meaning these two male friendships—were separate and shouldn't come together.

"Ms. Cooks, would you answer, please?" Detective Wellborn asked.

A smidge of ire settled in my shoulders. I didn't like him pushing me for a response. I felt bullied.

"Ms. Cooks?"

I blurted, "Yes."

"Yes, what?" he asked.

"Will Christiansen and I kissed in the parking lot." *So there.* When he took too long to ask another question, I glanced at him through my lashes.

Finally, he cleared his throat. "I realize this is a personal question. But in order to determine the exact chain of events, we need you to clarify your answers. Are…were you dating, uh, William Christiansen?"

I sighed and frowned at the prospect of sharing more details. Truth be told, miserable with the murder and the interview, I wanted to cry like I'd never cried before. Focusing again on the blank spot where the painting once hung, I told Detective Wellborn what he wanted to hear and what I didn't want to say.

"Yes, we were together. Will heard through the employee grapevine about my birthday and invited me to dinner after happy hour to celebrate. He asked me to pick the restaurant, and I chose Mamma and Pappa's Italian Bistro on Boston Avenue—"

I caught the rigid stare the detective put on me, and then looked quickly away. Could it be he had thoughts about the restaurant, too?

I refocused on him. He moved his finger in a *continue on* twirl.

"We ate lasagna, salad, garlic bread, and drank glasses of Chianti, followed by cherry chocolate cake," I told him.

"Garlic bread? Not so good for the breath."

So not funny. I shifted my eyes into narrow bands. "Afterward, he returned me to my Jeep still parked at Jack's Bar."

"Who told him about your birthday?"

"I don't know for certain. I didn't. Stuart Steems and Cathy Bartholomew were at my party. One of them could have said something, but like I said, I didn't ask him."

"He took you back to your vehicle. Did you leave him there?"

I pursed my lips. *No way would he run roughshod over this gal.* "Afterward is none of your business."

"Ms. Cooks, please answer my question. What happened after Will Christiansen dropped you off at your vehicle?"

A solid gold below-the-belt hit. *Okay, fine. He'd asked.* I had to say. "Afterwards, he followed me to my apartment, and we went inside—" I stopped, I couldn't go on. I couldn't tell him everything.

Detective Wellborn maintained his police composure.

I could see with the flick of a glance and a slow, deliberate gulp from a bottle of water, he knew what had transpired. Did that bother him?

"He spent the night at your place?" he asked.

"He did," I barely croaked out.

"What time did he, uh, leave?"

Might as well go all the way. I wiped a small tear from the corner of my eye before a chance trickle could run down my nose. "He left at nine Saturday morning." Anger fizzed up, an all-consuming rage. I wanted to leave NLB and the police and every part of my life. Run to where there were no complications. "What else do you want to know? Did we use protection? Is he a great kisser? Did I orgasm?"

He stared at me like he'd never seen me before. Heartbreak and confusion darkened his pupils. Yet, he didn't utter a word.

He spooled his pen on the table top. "Did you see him later on?"

"He picked me up at noon, and we picnicked at Sommerville Park."

"And afterwards?"

"Afterwards, we went to his place and"—I wiped away another tear. My soul hurt for Will. And Allan— "had sex."

"What time did you leave?"

"He took me home around ten Sunday morning."

"Did you see Mr. Christiansen on Sunday?"

"Yes, at about one, we saw a movie. Would you like the stub?" I set my handbag in my lap and jammed my hand inside. I fished for the paper and upon locating the receipt, I shoved the torn strip over the table top.

He didn't even pick up the slip.

"The last time I was with him was when he left me at my door. I had several personal errands to run."

"Okay. Let's review. He took you home at ten,

came for you at one to go to the movies, and after the movie, you ran several personal errands. What were they?"

I felt as if I was in some sort of hangover fugue. Messy. Muddy. Mottled. My thought waves had to breast stroke through the depths. After extreme concentration, my focal point returned to Detective Wellborn. Slowly, I said, "My roommate and I shopped in the lingerie department at Tuckers to replace underwear which had been stolen from my gym locker. Second, I did a pet-sitting service for a friend. The rest of the time I was at home, reading a book for book club which my roommate can confirm."

His head tilted right. "Replace your underwear? What happened? Did he rip it off?"

This question had crossed the personal line. "Seriously? You're asking me that?"

He didn't say anything.

I'd been grinding through this grilling long enough. Time to put on some moxie. "He didn't quote, rip, end quote anything off. The last few times I've showered at the gym, I found someone had stolen my friend's and my underwear from our locker."

"Interesting." As he mulled over the unusual tidbit, he rubbed his forefinger over his chin. "Why would someone—presumably a woman since this took place in the women's locker room—steal your underwear?"

"That is the sixty-four-thousand-dollar question. Maybe there's a pervert. Who knows? I wouldn't wear someone else's undies. That's icky." I shrugged. This line of questioning was a huge relief. Thankfully, it had taken the attention from my sex life. "I just hate being forced to spend money when someone was so crude.

Maybe the police should do a stake-out."

"That would be a fun assignment." Now, he tapped the retractable part of his pen on the tabletop. "You were in Mr. Christiansen's apartment?"

I banged my fist on the counter. "What the hell do you think I've been saying all this time?" Did he want me to feel guiltier or more miserable? I glared. "Yes. We spent an entire weekend together. I was all over his bedroom. Fingerprints, hair, and unmentionable DNA. You name it."

"Do you drink coffee?"

A very *surprising from left field* question—yet, one which bothered my head. In a jiffy, I remembered why. "You asked me the very same question when you interviewed me about Phil Meadows."

"Please, refresh my memory. Do you drink coffee?"

"Not at all. I *never* drink coffee." Mom didn't drink coffee, so we didn't develop a coffee habit in our home. Not coffee, instead we consumed lots of chocolate.

My gaze swung to the exit. *Please hurry five o'clock because I desperately need more peanut candies, like the largest bag I owned, and most likely, would be the one he'd gifted me.*

He rattled off the date, his name, my name, and terminated the recording device. "We'll be in touch. Thank you."

Greatly relieved, I stood, tugging my jacket into place and bumping the chair aside with my legs. With all the composure instilled in me by Mom's lessons on deportment, I walked to the conference room doorway where I couldn't help but to open the door and step outside. I looked in the sidelight and observed

Detective Wellborn sitting at the table.

The pen, the one he'd been dallying with throughout our conversation, tapped against the tabletop. It tapped so hard, the surface would be pockmarked. Then he flung it away. With a violent sweep of his arm, he shoved the files and notepad to the floor. "Goddammit to hell."

I covered my lips with my right hand. Evidently, Allan did have a fuse, and something I'd said or done had kindled his anger.

He stabbed his fingers through his short hair. His chest heaved with fury. Before the door completely shut, I heard him say, "I'd hoped she'd understood."

Understood—*who, me?*

Understood what?

Chapter Fourteen

What I'd wished would be another mind-cleansing workout, wasn't. More tired than I really knew, I steered my car homewards. Inside, I walked to Jenny's bedroom door on which I rapped and cracked open approximately three inches. "Decent?"

"What's up?"

I took that as the go ahead to enter.

Jenny swiveled to show the back of the spectacular cherry silk dress she wore. "Can you give me a zip?"

"Wow, you look great," I said, distracted for the moment by her stupendous appearance. "Would you like to use my clutch embroidered with flowers? It's the perfect accessory."

"Too late. I already borrowed it."

I pulled up the zipper. "There. Same guy?"

She faced me and shimmied the sides of the dress into place. "You ask me the *same* question every time."

"Guess I'm becoming monotonous."

"You? Never." She picked up the borrowed clutch. "Same guy."

I grinned. "Sounds…serious."

"We like each other. A lot." Her mouth fashioned a smug smile. "So what has you so hot-and-bothered and not in a good way?"

"Someone messed with my locker at the gym."

She laughed. "Going commando?"

"Hell no. I learned my lesson and stashed a set under my bra strap while I worked out. Only, I didn't shower once I'd found the mess exposing how someone had plowed through my belongings while I'd been on the treadmill. I couldn't wait to get out. I'm seriously considering moving my membership elsewhere."

Her frown turned studious. "In my opinion, someone is deliberately stealing your underwear to make a point. But that's the million-dollar query—who is it? What's the point?"

I fixed my hands on my waist. "I don't buy exciting stuff. The only really pretty set I have is the lacey pink one you gave me for my birthday last year. You know, I wore them one time and lost the undies. I haven't worn the set until lately," my voice tapered to a bare nothingness, "when...I, uh, found the, uh, panties..."

"What?"

Her scream almost burst my eardrums.

"You found the pink bikinis? Where?"

Me and my big mouth. A blunderous admission. I should have foreseen her question.

"Didn't you lose them at Allan's?" A mischievous tone traced Jenny's probe.

Miss Smarty Pants had all the answers. However, telling anyone about my undercover operation was not a good idea. I fast-tracked to the living room.

She shadowed me. "Hattie? Is there more?"

I did a hem-haw thing while staring at the ceiling, followed by a dramatic sigh, one perfected by four-year olds, knowing I should tell the truth because sooner or later she would wiggle it out of me. "In Allan's dresser drawer."

"You were in his drawers?" Jenny shook her head. "What a Freudian slip. I can't believe I said that."

She regrouped from her faux pas, tried to ask something a couple of times, but nothing came out. Finally, she said, "No." Her head shook a second time. "I don't want to know. That would be too much information."

Oh, what the hell. She would find out and best heard from the original source-me. "You know the other day when I was pet-setting Lucky?"

"Dare I ask?"

"I searched Allan's townhouse."

Gasping, Jenny's chin nearly touched the floor. "You-you d-did what?"

"I searched his apartment."

"You did not!"

"I did. The whole turkey from top to bottom." I measured from above my head to below my knees.

"Ordinarily, I'd say I'm speechless. Today, the words won't come." Jenny thumped her palm against her forehead. She plunked into the khaki club chair. "Hattie, I can't believe you did that. You have to be out of your freakin' mind. Have you sunk to an all-time new low? Have you lost the few brain cells you have left? What if he finds out? He's a policeman, for God's sake...and he's supposed to be—*he's a detective*. He's trained to be observant."

My head drooped. "I know, I know. If you were in my shoes, you'd do it, too. I wanted to figure out what he and Cathy Bartholomew were up to."

"OhmyGod, Hattie. You invaded his privacy. I don't believe this. I don't believe I'm hearing this." Jenny gave me an intense stare.

Yikes. Similar to one my mom affected. The pin-the-tail-on-the-donkey-and-not-miss one.

"How would you feel if he'd done the same to you?" Then, she clapped her hand on her mouth. Through her splayed fingers came, "Oh no."

"What?"

"What would your mother say?"

"You think I'd tell Mom—my mom? Not me. Nooo way. She'd trot out the Respect lecture." I shrugged. "Besides, I have a very good reason."

"When I get over how outlandish this is, I'll want to hear your explanation. I cannot believe you did that."

Jenny walked to the mirror strategically located next to the front door for primping. She straightened the dress' spaghetti straps. "How did the second interview with Detective Wellborn go?"

I welcomed her changing the subject. I flopped on the couch and clutched a pillow to my chest. "I was upset. Not every day I'm interviewed by a former boyfriend about a new dead boyfriend and have to discuss my sex life with new dead boyfriend to old boyfriend. Doesn't crap like this happen only on a TV sitcom?" I rubbed the spot right above my right eyebrow. "I'm not sure, but I have a funny feeling—"

She poked my arm. "Tell me."

"Ow!" I kneaded the owie, hoping a bruise wouldn't materialize. "It's just a feeling, but the police may be thinking I'm the bad guy—slash—girl—slash—person."

"You? Twice in one day, you've managed to stun me, Hattie Cooks. Why, you're afraid to kill spiders."

"I know, I know." And big roaches. I placed drinking glasses over the bugs and let them suffocate.

The crunchy squashing sound which accompanied stomping on large insects sounded gross. And live roaches were juiced with bug guts. That was when Killer Kella came in handy. She stomped on them without hesitation.

"Why you?" Jenny asked for the second time.

"The police believe I was the last person to see Phil and Will, and my guess is they look at that person very carefully, making me numero uno suspect in their books."

"According to the cop shows, being a friend with the dead guys is not enough to lock you up."

"I know it. You know it. But do they know it? Twice, Allan has asked me if I drink coffee. He knows I don't drink coffee. That's why I think it's possible Will's and Phil's deaths have something to do with coffee."

"Interesting." Jenny considered this. "Was Phil Meadows' coffee messed with?"

"Could be. At least, that's what the NLB rumors are saying. Bookie Dave said the police techs took away the cup which sat on his table. I think—I don't know for sure—but I think it's standard operating procedure to check food stuff."

"So, someone gave Phil coffee—who?"

"Beats the hell out of me." I shrugged. "The one and only time I ate lunch with Phil, he didn't drink coffee. He ate kiddie yogurt and drank a soda. And then, I came upon him eating in the break room a few days later and spoke with him. He dies. Bookie Dave found him, and that's The End."

"You need to go over in your mind the exact chain of events."

Jenny gave good advice. So I told her exactly what happened, mentally pointing a finger here, here, and here, trying to plot my movements. Then, I guess, my subconscious said aloud, "As I was leaving the break room, I passed Cathy Bartholomew going in. She said 'hi' which…was the…laaasstt…thing—"

Jenny jerked upright. "Your face is all twisted funny-like. Did you remember something?"

Gazing into outer space, I attempted to summon the great almighty remembering thing. "I might have."

"What? You were talking about Cathy Bartholomew and the 'laasstt thing…'" Her drawl imitated my inflection. "Hattie? Hattie. Snap out of it."

I broke from my memory ozone and faced her. I elongated my spine, my eyes stretched broad. "Now, I remember what I couldn't remember to tell Allan when he interviewed me the first time. Is it coincidental that after I spoke with Phil, I passed Cathy Bartholomew walking in the break room? Do you think…maybe I should…no, I can't…do you think I need to tell Allan I saw her?"

I slapped my cheeks like the "Home Alone" kid before she could utter a word. I stared at her in hopes she could provide the outstanding answer I craved—a huge no. "OhmyGod, Jenny, I can't tell him." The pen-throwing episode materialized in my thoughts. "He's-he's not happy with me."

"Doesn't matter how he feels about you. He has to know." She directed her finger at me. "You call him on the phone and clear this up. Right now, missy."

Jenny was a practical and mostly wise girl. "Not me. No way. I had difficulty talking with him about Will. He made me cry. He was angry, too. After pitching his pen against a wall, he knocked his papers on the floor and cursed. I just can't."

"Hattie." Jenny put her hands on my shoulders and gently shook my body. "You could be a suspect in the murders of these guys. You have to tell him. I don't care if it's about the Blonde Bimbo he's dating. You've got to tell Allan. This is what's important. She could be the last person seen with Phil Meadows—not you."

Jenny left me to pace in front of the couch while wringing her hands. "God, this whole thing is so incestuous. First, you date Allan. Then you don't. Then Cathy dates Allan. You work with Cathy. Her boss is Will. You date Will. To top it off, two guys at your job are murdered."

She picked up my cell phone off the kitchen counter and thrust it into my hand. "If you don't call him, I will."

I called Allan, but I was nervous and my foot tap-tap-tapped, betraying my angst. Luck might be on my side, and I'd get his voice mail.

"Yes, Hattie." *How does he know?* I wondered if he possessed highly bizarre telepathy powers, but probably my name coupled with my number appeared on his caller ID. I'd made it to *contact* status on his device. "Hey," I said. "I've thought of something."

"I'm listening."

Wasn't there a TV psychiatrist who said that phrase? "I didn't mean to bother you. I'd planned on leaving a message."

"This better be important. I was almost out the door."

"Sorry. Jenny thinks I should tell you."

"If this is about the investigation and your

interview this morning, I need to get some stuff." I could visualize him as he walked over to the computer desk. "Okay, I'm back. Shoot."

My words spilled out fast. "It's not exactly about this morning's interview. It's about Phil Meadows and the last person I saw with him."

"That is important." Allan took on his detective voice. "I think I want to hear what you have to say in person. I'll be right over." And he hung up.

Damn! I shook my phone. I didn't want him over here.

Jenny ejected from the club chair where she'd been keeping an eye on the action. "What did he say?"

"Thanks to you, girlfriend, he's on his way to our place. I look like warmed-over shit." I took a sniff of my stinky, sweaty, and smelly body. Even I wouldn't look at me like this.

Her laugh followed me as I raced to the shower where I turned the water on full blast. In one quick swoop, I yanked off my shirt and exercise bra. I started to drop my shorts when I heard the doorbell ring. *If that is Allan, he drove way too fast.* Maybe he'd used his lights and siren.

"Jenny, can you get the door?" I didn't hear her answer. She'd probably already left. I yelled, "Coming."

I turned off the shower, applied fresh deodorant, and rapidly wiped my arms and neck with a wet washcloth. I tidied my ponytail and removed any smudgy makeup. Then, I slipped on an unsoiled bra and yoga shirt, pulling it into place as I ran to the door.

I checked the peephole and *yep*, I was right. Mr. Perfect. I flung open the door, breathing harder from the racing around the house stuff. "You might get a ticket driving so fast. I know I would have. I'm guessing you have special privileges."

He chuckled. "I have fun looking for people like you."

"Sounds warped. Seems you did look for me on one occasion."

"So I did. Luckily, you don't live too far." The corners of his mouth quirked up.

I loved his smile and half-smile.

He stood firm and tall. Biceps bulged, strong thighs flexed. A five o'clock shadow roughed his jaw. Even slightly sweaty, Allan looked migh-tee fine in his running shorts and his ratty *Accountant's Rule* T-shirt not tucked in the waistband.

Weren't memories attached to clothing funny? He had worn his much-loved shirt when I asked him to choose me. More recently, I found it in his drawer with my underwear which caused me to remember the…well, maybe not fateful, maybe more like fatal day.

I'd give anything to smash myself against him. But I didn't. "I see you have on your favorite shirt."

He grinned and rubbed a circle on his belly. "Don't leave home without it. I'd changed for a run and was headed out when you called."

"Why did you come over? I could have told you what I knew when I phoned."

"You said the magic word, Phil Meadows. Worth hearing in person. May I come in?"

There was an alluring twinkle in his eyes when he asked. "You don't look very official. Where's your badge? Your almighty pen?"

"Official enough."

When focused on his job, he always looked official. Frankly, not wearing his coat and tie and carrying his little recording device to hear my tidbit surprised me. Maybe he'd immortalize what I'd had to say on his phone.

I ushered him into my apartment and closed the door. The unsettled feelings burst in my stomach because of this morning's bad interview. However, Mom would expect me to be the polite hostess. "Do you want a drink?"

"Water." He flapped his hand. "Whatever."

Fine by me. I slid around him, stepped into the kitchen, and removed two bottles of water from the fridge. I placed a package of popcorn—in my case, aka dinner—in the microwave. I handed the water squashed in a coozie to Allan who checked out my iPod player propped against some books in the bookcase while the corn popped.

His brow lifted in question, "You like Diana Krall?"

"A lot. You would, too. She's jazzy and a lot of her music is the old standards our grandparents listened to."

"Sounds good."

The microwave dinged. I ripped the bag and poured the fluffy, popped corn in a bowl, snagging a few kernels as I carried the container to the kitchen table. Allan and I dropped in the chairs, not talking for a while, just drinking and munching like the best of friends who knew each other's actions and words.

He picked up the paper napkin I'd deposited with the drink and pressed his fingers to the fold.

The silence between us almost killed me. I needed

to tell him what I remembered about Cathy Bartholomew. Finally, my hand inched across the table, my fingers curling over his arm. After another moment when nothing was uttered, I slid my hand into his, friend-to-friend like.

His clasp tightened around my fingers.

"Allan, what are you thinking?"

He didn't raise his head. His thumb caressed the top of my hand. Back and forth. Back and forth. "About how you could go to jail."

"I'm not going to jail. I'm not capable of murder." I hauled my arm to my side of the table and slapped the tabletop. I pointed my finger. "You won't let me. You know I didn't kill Phil or Will. I didn't kill anyone."

With a sigh, the kind which comes from the depths of one's hub, he planted his hands on the table. "I know and you know, but I can only do so much. I might as well tell you…today after you'd left, the police took your office computer."

Really big news. I bit into my lower lip. "My computer? Why?"

Reclining back, he sipped his drink. "I can't say."

I could add and *two dead NLB auditors* linked to *one office assistant* equaled *evidence.*

He rotated his bottle. "I don't blame you if-if you don't trust me."

"Allan, this isn't like last time. I trust you." What a big turnaround for me. After I'd discovered he'd withheld information regarding June Short's death, I hadn't felt him trustworthy. If he'd divulged more than he had, he might have prevented the slashing and stabbing showdown with Opal. Lesson learned.

But not one he'd repeat.

Nor me.

He gave me a direct look. "I can't say at this time. You are a tie-in to the very dead guys. So far, the department believes you're the last person to be with them."

"I wasn't the last person to see Phil."

He tossed back a handful of popcorn. "Tell me about it."

I took a drink. The cold momentarily froze my throat. "Here's what I'd forgotten during my first interview. After my lunch with Phil, I passed Cathy Bartholomew entering the break room."

He sat straighter. "You saw Cathy outside the break room?"

"Yes. I saw her go *into* the break room, and I said 'hi, Cathy.' Like she would respond—which she didn't."

"No one else saw or heard you?"

"I don't know. All I know is only Phil was in the room when I left. He hadn't finished his sandwich. I didn't see anyone else lingering in the hallway after I passed her."

Abruptly, Allan pushed himself away from the table and stood. He smushed his palm across his forehead while he paced around the living area. As he reviewed what I'd said, confusion alternated with irritation passed over his face.

Standing, I stepped closer and twitched his T-shirt's hem. With a soft gentleness in my voice, I asked, "You'll have to talk to Cathy Bartholomew?"

He nodded.

"I'm sorry. You're in an awkward predicament."

He nodded again.

"Are you angry with me?" Ducking my chin, I said even quieter, "Please don't be. I'm just the messenger."

I didn't mean to sound funny and kinda hoped he realized I had to tell him. I didn't want to, but I had to. And now, he was in a tight spot. Did he feel like I had when we'd talk about my former co-workers—all squirmy, flushed, and embarrassed?

Allan centered all his concentration on me.

My gaze locked with his.

A golden ring of fire burnished his chocolate irises. His finger stroked a loosened strand of hair from my temple to somewhere around my neck line, then skimmed along the divot where the collar bone and neck intersected, something he'd done in previous intimate times.

His light touch caused my whole being to flip to high-alert. A burn flamed through my blood. My eyes closed and my body propelled me to step nearer. So close, I absorbed everything—his essence, his warmth, his pine scent.

His head dipped low. His exhale wisped across my cheek.

I opened my eyes and looked into his, to stare as overwhelming emotions roiled through me, ready to blow up like a volcano.

"I'm sorry about this morning," he said.

Somehow, I managed to pat his upper arm and rest my hand there. To hide the awareness I felt playing over my face, I dropped my gaze and studied the silly slogan silkscreened on his shirt. "Me, too."

"I had to do my job and hurting you was a consequence. I wish I hadn't screwed up."

And then...I realized...*I'd* messed up. Slowly, I

lifted my chin.

Allan yanked me to his chest. His mouth found mine with a firm, forceful, fast kiss.

I locked my lips with his. He felt too good.

Rising to my toes, I almost scaled his body to get even closer. My arms looped around his head as he broke the kiss, regrouped, and slanted across my mouth in the other direction.

Cathy Bartholomew and Will Christiansen were flung out the window. But I didn't let them go, not really. Breaking away, I buried my face in his collarbone, my words almost muffled. "I'm sorry. I shouldn't have kissed you."

"Why?"

His hands cradled the back of my head, holding it so I had to stare into his face.

"I grabbed you."

Shutting my eyes, I shook my head. Being with him made my muscles ache for more. "I could have stopped you. But I didn't. It's not right. It isn't fair."

"Sweetheart, what's wrong?"

I sighed, let my forehead dip to the comfy spot, and let my fingers pluck his T-shirt. "I'm not the kind of girl who flits from one guy to the next, and I don't want you to think so little of me. You matter. What you believe about me matters."

"It's okay," Allan whispered into my hair right above my ear. "This is about you and me. And I decide what's best for me. I know you. You are the one. You always have been. You always will be."

The truth flooded through me. No denying now, I knew how I really felt. What I'd had with Will Christiansen was just about sex!

Oh, Lordy. I blinked away a tear. Now may not be the best time to say how I really felt. But I had to before my courage evaporated. "The other guy isn't...wasn't...ever in the picture. I love you." I fisted my hands in his hair as I kissed Allan with heart, depth, and longing.

His hands crept down my back, down my arms, and over my bottom. His chest brushed accidentally against my nipples.

They constricted into tight knots, wanting his touch, his mouth. Desire bloomed low below my belly and began pulsing, throbbing with an urge for more. I broke away when his stubble sandpapered my face. "Ow."

"I'm sorry. I-I..."

Resting my hands on his shoulders, I murmured against his mouth, "There's nothing to be sorry for. You're such a man."

And his arms embraced me with a longing I'd wanted for many months.

His hands slipped under the hem of my athletic top. The shirt flipped over my head, dropping to the floor. His palm covered my breast, molding and manipulating the flesh.

"OhmyGod." My head crooked to one side while his lips buzzed light kisses to my ear. My hands skated past his waistband and his underwear, grasping his bare firm bottom.

Abruptly, we stopped groping, grabbing, and kissing. We took a long solid look at each other.

I wanted him no matter what and read the same intent firing in his eyes. Seizing his hand, I yanked him into my bedroom and slammed the door shut.

We enveloped each other.

His forehead met mine. "God, Hattie, I can't stop. I've wanted you for so long, ever since I can remember."

My lips found the soft spot below his ear. I inhaled the light trace of scent which spelled all man. "I know. Me, too."

We began moving frantically, taking more of the other.

I tugged off my exercise bra. I loved the feel of his hands on my body as they sketched here. There. Everywhere. *How does a man know exactly where to stroke a woman?*

We shuffled to the bed and fell awkwardly on top.

His mouth fastened on my nipple.

As his lips pulled and teased, a throbbing sensation intensified in my tummy, followed by hot burning and insatiable urges. I needed him in me. I needed satisfaction. "OhmyGod. OhmyGod."

My spine arched. I almost orgasmed. After I stripped off his favorite T-shirt, I ran my fingertips up and down his spine, playing with the muscles in his back.

His mouth began working his way down my neck, across my shoulders, to the elastic in my undies, and back to my chest.

My body screamed in delight as his male part nudged my female part. My mouth pulsed. Removing his shorts became my goal.

Buzz-buzz, like the sound of a tiny mosquito taunted my ear.

He lifted his head from my chest.

Buzz-buzz.

Feeling a slight interruption, I barely moved, reluctant to leave my out-of-body experience.

Buzz-buzz.

We stopped, really aware of the sound coming from his smart phone.

Frustrated, I rolled to my right then left. "Not again."

"Shit." Allan shoved me aside as he sat up, fishing the phone from his short's pocket. He looked at the number as he stood.

For a millisecond, I'd hoped he had second thoughts about answering.

He depressed a button and walked away, settling his shorts into place. "Hi, Cathy."

Not her. Stunned, I collapsed on top of the bed. I set the back of my hand to my forehead. We were about to make mad, passionate love, and the idiot—anger, like none I'd ever known before, ignited inside me—was talking to the Blonde Bimbo.

Last I heard, only his mother, sister, office, and me had his cell phone number. Now, add Bimbo to the list.

Why? Why? Why couldn't we finish what we started? An undercurrent connected us, a powerful one which clearly meant something extraordinary. We felt a need to solidify our…whatever. And in all these months, nothing had happened. Granted, I was partially to blame. But I'd made noteworthy efforts to fix things.

Damn! I hated being yanked from one extreme to another. I had to be going crazy. My clenched hand hammered my thigh which would probably leave a blue-ish purple-ish yellow-ish bruise. *Cathy Bartholomew. I hated her. Hated her.*

Crossing my arm over my bare breasts, I said very

loudly and on purpose, "Goddammit."

His sideways glance took me in.

I noticed and snagged my shirt from the floor. I marched to the living area, stuffing my head and arms in the openings. The manufacturer's tag rubbed high on my neck. I plucked it away and discovered the garment was inside out and backward. *What the hell* and overlapped my arms. I stood by the front door, my foot tap-tap-tapping while Allan finished his call.

When done, he pocketed the phone and walked slowly toward me. His other hand held his shirt. He halted by my side and thrust his head and arms into the openings, then reached for me. "Hattie."

I sidestepped his maneuver and quickly finished his sentence. "You've gotta go." I rubbed my eyes to wipe away the spilling tears.

"Look, sweetheart. Nothing is what you think."

"What I think? You have no idea what I'm thinking. No. I'll tell you. I'm your little lay on the side. All I was and ever will be. Well, buster, no more. I've learned my lesson."

He drew away like I'd slapped him. "You're wrong."

His response sounded harsh. "That's what you say, but not what you do." I had to know. "Did you get what you want?"

"No."

"What, Allan?" I hurled up my arms, and then let them fall by my side. I stood and waited.

But he said nothing. He did nothing. And nothing was going to take place.

I opened the front door. "You know what I think? You don't know what you want."

"I want you, sweetheart."

"If you do, you have a funny way of showing me. You can't decide if you want me or Cathy Bartholomew, and I feel...jammed...in limbo. I'm confused and not coping where you're concerned. And every single time we've tried"—I grounded out through clenched teeth—"to be intimate, the damn phone rings. I don't feel like I'm first with you. The bald truth is"—I swallowed deep—"I'll never be first with you.

"For the life of me, I don't understand why you're with Cathy Bartholomew. She's not your type. I used to think *I* was your type. The whole universe did. Boy, were we all wrong about you."

I went for the entire corn chip casserole. I pounded my fist against my sternum six times. "Thanks to you, my heart is hurting. I don't like it, nor want to anymore." A sob caught my voice. "I can't believe I-I asked you to choose me. Do you know difficult that was?"

"Yes—"

"At least, I know Will Christiansen was a fling. And I didn't flaunt him in your face like you just did." I motioned toward the door. "Get out. Go to Cathy Bartholomew. She's who you really want. You certainly do jump at her beck and call."

Allan's finger almost stroked my hair.

I knocked it away, and my hand met his cheek. The whack hurt my ears and stung my hand.

His jaw dropped. His eyes went wide. Staring at me like he didn't know me, he very slowly massaged his cheek up and down, up and down. "Hattie."

Somewhere in my name, I heard amazement and a slight plea. With my arms locked to my side, my fingers curled in my palms. The urge to smack him again pulsed in every nerve. Pushing through the odd sensation, I said, "Don't. Come. Back. Don't. Ever."

His pupils tightened to pinpoints. "You don't understand."

"How can I when *you* don't? We've played this game before. Don't come back."

"This isn't what I want."

"Too bad."

He raised one brow in a very serious lift. "We need to talk, sweetheart."

"No. This is what I want." And boy, did I show him. Mustering strength from God knew where, I shoved Allan out the door. Then crashed it closed behind him. I shrieked, "And Don't. Call. Me. Sweetheart."

With my back pushed against the portal, I slid to the floor and planted my head in my hands, grinding the heels of my palms into my eyes. The tears I'd held back burst forth. After a long mournful moan, one where I had nothing left but exhaustion and dullness, I raised my head and smoothed my fingers over my face, catching a couple of droplets.

He and I would never come together.

If he'd really wanted to, he could have done a better job of dumping Cathy Bartholomew.

****

Stupid. Stupid. Stupid. I berated myself all the way to the bathroom. I'd sunk to an all-time low, something resembling a walk of shame. After snatching off my clothes, I studied myself in the mirror. I saw horrible. Not horrible from sticky, sweaty, and smelly, but horrible with remorse and idiocy.

The roller coaster my life now traveled was unfamiliar. Spent, I propped my hands on the bathroom counter for the support because exhaustion had taken over, and I could hardly keep myself upright. College Boy and I'd had an uncomplicated relationship. All seemed so easy. Never any arguing. Just lots of loving togetherness and pretty good sex. Maybe if we'd stayed together, our relationship would have evolved into something different. But I'd recognized I needed more.

Allan and I exchanged strong words and almost-wild, almost-sex—not exactly conducive to building a good relationship. He hadn't acted like this when we were younger. He was Sarah Ann's quiet older brother. Today, I saw a whole new side to him. Chin hanging to my breastbone, I held open the shower curtain and turned on the water.

I lathered myself from neck to toe with the grapefruit shower gel squirted on a squishy sponge. I paused when my thoughts reverted back to us as a couple. Foolish feelings about being involved so quickly with Will Christiansen crowded my brain. Self-conscious and stupid. I didn't love Will. Maybe I—

No, I knew. Misery slumped on my body. Deep inside, I knew I'd always been in love with Allan.

Which is why love could hurt.

The refreshing water cascaded over me, baptizing me in my newly acquired revelation.

Fling best described my relationship with Will. And in all probability, our affair would have died eventually. I could accept responsibility for my behavior and move on. The truth energized me, and I vigorously washed away the stink of exercise and exorcised men.

While rinsing, I questioned whether I'd attacked Allan with remnants of the lust-filled weekend Will and I'd spent together? Or had I attacked him with remnants of the lust and love I'd felt for him?

I sent my head from side to side. *Didn't matter.* What did matter was making sure I did a three-sixty with my life—romantic and career-wise. I turned off the valve and wrapped a towel sarong-like around my body, tucking the end under my armpit.

One thing I knew for certain, I cared a great deal for Allan. And as long as he ebbed and flowed in and out of my life like the tide, I would have difficulty separating from him. Considering our close family ties, we would meet sooner or later—which would be mortifying. But for the sake of sanity and with a stiff British 'tude, I could do it…*if.*

If I stuck to my plan. Allan had made his choice, and I'd made mine.

Nundom, I resolved. I hauled on the pink flowered pajama bottoms.

Nundom. Because I didn't get in trouble in nundom.

Chapter Fifteen

The next morning at work, I found on my desk a plain white envelope, inscribed with my name in a familiar handwriting—Allan Wellborn's.

What now? I stared at the card and noted this would affect my stay-away-from-Allan plan. Unfolding it, I discovered the contents confirmed my beliefs— asking me to baby sit Lucky while he traveled out-of-town.

He'd signed off with "sorry."

Yea, right. He was sorry. I was sorry. The whole freakin' world was sorry.

I refolded and dropped the note into my handbag, thinking once again, Allan had been at NLB doing his deal, and now, he'd disappeared on a business trip. And good ol' dependable Hattie had been called upon to play mama to his baby.

I didn't mind taking care of Lucky, and he knew I would do so. I liked furry friends. Still curiosity abounded as I wondered why he asked me to cat sit when he could ask his mother or Blonde Bimbo. And how especially puzzling was he'd asked me after our disappointing close encounter of body-to-body kind the previous night.

I sighed with the knowledge Allan wouldn't turn over a new leaf any time soon and share with me.

Yep, he is sorry. I am sorry. The whole world is

sorry.

"Hattie," Mr. Northside said from the doorway.

My musings interrupted, in a flash, I swiveled my chair in his direction, my hand spread against my chest. "Oh, Mr. Northside. You startled me. Is there something you need?"

"Everything's fine. I wanted to talk to you about your computer."

I turned to my left where the monitor normally sat on my desk. Small dust wads of hair and unmentionable fibers and crumbs, two dimes, and one paperclip decorated the spot. I'd forgotten. "I didn't even notice."

"The police have it."

Allan had disclosed the police had taken the computer. Had I left anything incriminating? I didn't think so, but you never knew nowadays. The rumor was nothing really disappeared on the internet. My brain sorted through the emails I'd received. *Clueless.*

I tilted my head. "Why take mine?"

His shoulders did the raise-and-drop thing. "They have some theory going. The techs picked up several others. I'm not sure what exactly they're looking for, but I didn't want you to think confiscating the one you used was a bad thing."

The police had to do what they had to do. Still, I felt as if a spotlight had been aimed at my head, making me look and feel guilty. "I didn't kill Phil or Will, Mr. Northside."

"I know." He patted my shoulder. "We have to let the police do their job. They are suspicious of everyone and everything…" He turned away and then paused. The corner of his mouth lifted into a sideways-up grin. "I suppose if you have work to do, we could hook up my extra laptop, 'though it's kinda old."

Poor man. Having one's business under siege had Mr. Northside coping in unusual ways. "This isn't easy for you, sir."

"Somehow, we'll manage. Accountants are a resourceful lot." He stuck a hand in each coat pocket, as if searching for something specific. "If only I could find... Never mind. Having a can-do attitude is important. I have enormous faith and trust in the NLB employees."

He wouldn't say that if he knew the truth about Blonde Bimbo.

"If you don't mind, I'll use your computer," I said. "I didn't finish reading the revised employee orientation doc and should check your calendar. Having the police here threw everyone off."

"I'll be right back." Mr. Northside went to his storage files and returned with his laptop.

We hooked up some cables and plugged in the power cord. When all had been deemed operational, he returned to his office and shut the door firmly.

As I waited for the laptop to go live, I drummed my fingers on my desktop, and then glanced at the empty place where the computer I'd used had sat. The dust outlining the spot called me to take a tissue and wipe everything while restraining the urge to sneeze.

Just great.

****

As I made my way through the convoluted hallways of NLB, I became aware of the hum of keyboards clicking, soft ringing of phones, and the sweeping swish of the copier making duplicates. The familiar office noises meant the accounting profession at NLB continued to operate. Even if the phrase did sound hard core at times, indeed, *life goes on.*

The other employees I'd passed mumbled an uninspired and unenthusiastic "hi" or merely nodded which I understood, seeing how I shared the same reaction, especially since the computer I'd used had been appropriated.

In the kitchenette on the nineteenth floor, I retrieved coffee for Mr. Northside and bought a soda for me from the vending machine. In addition, I bought three bars of gourmet chocolate-coated toffee and slipped two in my jacket pocket. The gloomy atmosphere from the murders hung in the air, and candy would be my cure.

I ripped a bar open and took a large bite. I snagged a napkin in case chocolate goo smeared my fingers. A paper taped on the refrigerator next to the envelope for this week's football pot seized my gaze. Stepping closer, I saw a new poem. This intriguing missive had replaced the old one and also caught the attention of the guys gathered around the coffeemaker for their morning sports break.

Two down, one to go.
That's what you get
When you play with a 'ho.

A tax auditor I'd met a few days prior lifted his cup toward the stainless appliance and said to his buddies, "Hey, did anybody read this?"

"Yup, a new poem."

"It's a new, bad poem."

"Where's the old one?"

"Dunno. Sounds similar."

"Yea, but what does it mean?"

"Who knows? I think maybe the Dragons won two games."

"Duh. Old news. What I really want to know is who won the football pot?"

"Ask Bookie Dave."

Even a rocket scientist would say this note had been penned by the person who'd scribed the first one. The wording and cadence were similar. And there were other comparable characteristics—Times New Roman, size fourteen font.

I took a minute to study the rhyme and determined from the discussion going on around me, the note referred to Miller, the new quarterback for the Dragons, the one the guys had discussed in depth last week. The whole '*ho thing* left me clueless. Perhaps, like the guys had said, the Dragons won two games and the part referring to *the 'ho* could be Miller, the overpriced acquisition. Maybe *acquisition* was the correct word since I continued to be football ignorant.

"Hey, Hattie." Bookie Dave sidled up on my right. "Thinking of playing? Last week, Mr. Northside cleaned up."

"He won big and asked me to order flowers for his wife with the winnings." I scrunched my brows. "I don't know about participating. Usually, I'm a loser with a capital L."

My parents hadn't endowed me with the *winning* gene. I picked the wrong bank drive-thru lane or checkout line at the grocery store which meant waiting for extended periods of time. In reality, we all did this, and in my thinking, probably more than we knew. According to my mom, these every day inconveniences were really a lesson in patience in disguise.

"It all happens for a reason," Mom had preached. "Perhaps, a small reminder for us to slow down our hectic lives."

I could live with this Mom-ism. Now, if only my life would slow down. "I'm not very good at sports stuff," I explained. "I love baseball. When I was a kid, I liked to watch the Texas Rangers with my dad. He always said the best catcher ever was Pudge Rodriguez. My dad once attended a perfect game."

"Baseball?" Bookie Dave stroked his chin in a professorial manner. "The World Series is coming up. Maybe…"

Snagging Bookie Dave's coat sleeve, I drew him to my side. "We need to have a tête-à-tête."

"What's a tête?"

"It's French for head."

"I don't speak French."

Refraining from rolling my eyes, I sighed. "A talk. A chat. A discussion."

We shifted to a spot farther from the other auditors. "What's up?"

I looked at the group of suits and lowered my voice, "The police took my computer."

He arched a brow. "I heard."

"Have you heard who else's?"

"Yours, mine, Phil's, Will's and, oh yea, Cathy Bartholomew's." He counted off his fingers, one stained with ink.

Wow. What can the police be looking for? "Really? Know why?"

"Nope. They didn't say, and I didn't ask." He pointed toward the game paper. "Go with any ol' square. The more who play, the more fun. Which box is your favorite?"

I pushed my way through the guys to the fridge. I sensed all gazes locked on me, increasing the tension and forcing me into an unwanted spotlight. I studied the grid. Since most of—what I perceived to be—the good squares were taken, I wasn't sure what to do.

When I heard someone cough behind me, I worried about holding up the others and hurriedly scribbled my initials in the two/five square. As I slipped a five-dollar bill inside the envelope, I heard the choked laughter from the staff surrounding me.

Facing them, I shrugged in questioning naiveté. "What? What did I do now?"

The guys sobered. A second-level auditor said, "We hate to say, but those numbers aren't the best for winning."

"Doesn't matter."

"You won't win with those numbers," Bookie Dave said.

I glared. "Then why did you insist I play? Geez Louise." I stomped off with the annoyance one gets when dealing with the male species. *Men—they always think they know everything.*

Stranger things had happened.

****

The same evening, I drove to Allan's apartment and parked my car in his lot. I stared at his front door, hoping to find something to propel me to go inside and do what I'd said I'd do. However, when I spotted his cute critter sitting in the front window, I decided I'd better get moving. I couldn't put off any longer taking care of Lucky.

I opened the door and the frisky feline attacked my

ankles. I stooped to pick him up, and he skittered playfully away. He acted like he craved company—which he probably did with his dad gone.

The inspiration to search once more didn't resonate. Anyway, last time had been enough. The energy or desire which once had possessed me had vanished. After a quick reconnaissance around Allan's apartment, I established everything appeared normal. Mr. Perfect wouldn't be labeled messy.

Spending little time in his place seemed like a superb idea. If possible, I would take Lucky home, but my complex only allowed small aquatic ones who lived in one gallon-sized containers. An elaborate fib about a four-legged pet might cover my ass for a while, but I didn't tell whoppers well.

I returned the borrowed video to the DVD shelf by the television, paying particular attention to the alphabetical order. As I picked up my handbag I'd deposited carelessly on his desk, a lime stripe snagged my curiosity. When I realized my handbag rested on a manila file folder, and the stripe was the header of a label, I tilted my head and looked at it harder. I returned my bag to the desk top and picked up the folder. Someone had typed *Cold Case-Louisiana* in the white area.

A funny hunch flitted through my brain. Perhaps Allan Wellborn had gone to Louisiana for this particular case, and in a hurry, he'd forgotten to take the file. I fanned the file wondering if I should take a peek inside or not.

No, Hattie, my subconscious said.
Yes.
No. This is police business. If Allan Wellborn

wanted you to know, he would tell you.

Just an itsy bitsy look. He never tells me anything.

No.

But I didn't listen.

Tag me way too snoopy for my own good. I glanced around the room to see if anyone watched. For all I knew, he had security cameras recording my every move—

OhmyGod, they could have been operational when I'd searched his place. My brows scrunched together. *But wouldn't I been busted if true?*

My gaze swept the room one more time. Instead, I found Lucky who sat patiently by my feet. He pawed my leg to get attention.

"Hey, buddy." Carefully, I pinched back the file's edges, and since nothing calamitous happened, I opened it. A piece of white paper floated in a feathery drift to the floor. Picking it up, I discovered a phone number scribbled in blue ink. When I looked at the backside, I found nothing else.

I studied the number and recognized the area code was one used in Louisiana. Mr. Northside worked with a big client from Baton Rouge and phoned the number often.

I suppose I could call.

No, Hattie. More from my subconscious. *Do not call the number.*

I could retrieve my cell phone from my car and try.

Tsk-tsk. It's still wrong.

I gave up. My subconscious was right, and besides, I carried guilt easily. Sure, calling the number seemed like a good idea, but truthfully? I was a big fat scaredy cat. Besides, this was Allan's big-ass police business.

But the most important reason of all was because Mom didn't raise me to be nosy. However, she would have completely understood the apartment searching I'd done previously, because it fell under the category of *retrieving forgotten items.*

I opened the file one last time and found articles on Alprazolam and Oxycontin clipped to the cover. The information had been obtained from a pharmaceutical database, telling of the benefits of each and the dangerous side effects of a combination.

I replaced the folder, tapping it—*crossing fingers*—at the right angle in the right spot. If Allan asked, I could say I'd dumped my bag on his desk, the folder accidentally fell, and then apologize. What was the saying a lot of men used—*it's better to ask for forgiveness than permission?*

I could play the game, and he would never know.

I filled Lucky's food bowl and patted him *bye.* With the lamps switched on in the living area, I secured the door behind me.

****

On Saturday, the NLB mishaps were quickly forgotten with the arrival of the Funsisters' Fall Field Trip—an outing to the largest Trade Days market in the whole United States exactly one hour due East. The venue was so colossal, the whole thing couldn't be covered in one day. The market began on a Monday when county court was in session. Vendors took spots on the sidewalk surrounding the government building. Eventually, the city had to purchase land for the vendors, and thus, Trade Days was born.

Desperately, I needed a change in scenery. I held high hopes our getaway would enable me to focus on myself, my needs, and set aside the murders and the oh-woe-is-me Allan feelings I stuffed in my gut.

Maggie had borrowed a large SUV to accommodate all of the Funsisters. We also agreed Kellar could find a piece of furniture, and we would have to determine how to pack the car, even if we had to sit on each other's laps to make room for her acquisition. No way would we leave her bargain behind.

These kinds of trips enabled us to utilize our finely honed pro-shopper skills:

1) *Yes* is not a four letter word.

2) Be supportive and repeat the pro-shopper's mantra, "I think you should."

3) Carry bargain crap around for a minimum of six hours.

4) All calories consumed were to aid our energy level for shopping and therefore, didn't count.

5) Shop clearance racks first.

New rules were added on occasion.

Because we were pro-shoppers, we'd prepared in advance with snacks, water, large shopping bags, and a rolling cart. Without a doubt, we would fill them with special items. Because we were pro-shoppers, we refused to rent a battery-powered scooter. Anyway, most of the scooter users needed to walk.

We liked this flea market for the large variety of bargains. Schlepping around barns and along dusty paths, we found antiques and treasures to add to our collections of vintage postcards, Christmas ornaments, pottery, and other unique pieces which caught our whimsy for a few pennies.

We rejoiced over old jewelry and decorator items,

fun clothing, crafts, and furniture. We oohed and aahed and heavily deliberated, occasionally consulting with each other for pro-shopper advice. And in the end, Kellar purchased a small patio table and chairs.

"It's not too big." She used this phrase every time we shopped here. We lugged everything acquired so far to the SUV and maneuvered our purchases around the ample storage area and her booty.

Halfway through our shopping bonanza, we paused for lunch. We had a variety of food to choose from which included turkey legs, red beans and rice, hamburgers, hot dogs, soup or baked potatoes—all good choices. However, we delved into the dark side. A restaurant in the middle of the whole shopping extravaganza served one of my favorite sacred foods, lemon meringue pie.

We had a whole sacred foods theory: Delectable items which caused an orgasmic experience when eating them. Whatever we felt extra-special food-wise made the list. For example, fabulous lasagna eaten at an Italian joint in New York, a handmade apple tart inhaled at a restaurant in Colorado, or Mom's chocolate lava cake could qualify.

My list was fairly simple: my favorite soda, chocolate-covered peanut candies, pizza, and a few other tasty items. I also liked chocolate meringue, but not coconut meringue or banana cream pie. A perfect steak and a well-made Caesar salad.

Jenny added pecan pancakes to hers which I also agreed with, but only if covered with real maple syrup and a side of crispy peppered bacon.

Maggie, on the other hand, liked green beans. What was her deal? Why veggies when pie was available?

Absorbed in paying reverence to a huge slice, I heard Jenny say, "I bet you haven't heard the latest."

My hearing fine-tuned.

"Tell us," Keller said. "Does this involve Hattie?"

"Absolutely. Who else could I tell tales on?"

I looked at my BFF and wondered if aliens inhabited her body.

She flicked her hand at me. "Hattie could be implicated in two murders."

Oh that. Not even murder could stop me from this eating adventure. I sighed and continued to eat my sacred food. *Not new news to me.*

"Really?" Tracey asked. "This sounds interesting. I knew about the murders from the paper, but I had no idea Hattie was involved. Do tell."

I wished the Funsisters would pick on someone else in our Book Club. I forked a delectable bite, closed my eyes, and savored a taste of perfect meringue—light and sweet, layered over delicious satiny lemon filling. *Mmm.*

I scooped another bite. Really, I wasn't interesting. Each of my friends had just as many opportunities to have idiotic things happen to them. I knew of a few memorable incidents. Unfortunately, since I was so involved with my pie, the events escaped me.

A few months back, at Maggie and Kellar's birthday party, Jenny and Kellar had deliberated my love life with Allan. Their discussion turned, and the Funsisters debated the merits of tiny lacey panties versus crotch-less ones.

Now, they deliberated me as a murderess.

"You know she was the last to see Phil Meadows and Will Christiansen a-live," Jenny said.

I squirmed in discomfort, wiggling my bottom in my chair. Who could ever be accustomed to having their private affairs being bandied about in the minutest detail in front of them? I particularly didn't want everyone knowing about sex with Will. A one-on-one confessional with a Funsister wasn't so embarrassing. Funsisters were sister psychologists. Yet, when confronted in a large group? Mortification gushed through me.

Of course, if this situation continued on a regular basis, a possibility existed I would never be embarrassed. *Would that be something to look forward to?*

Finished with my treat, I glanced over my shoulder at the slices of pie arranged prettily in the refrigerated case and ran my tongue over my top lip while contemplating another piece. The seductive chocolate meringue beckoned with a siren's song of "over here, no calories today."

The plateful of tornado twisters topped with spicy seasoning and ketchup which I had eaten earlier didn't dissuade me. I'd shared a portion with my friends and hadn't met my daily calorie allotment.

While I mulled over a second piece, I considered whether or not the Funsisters could be diverted into discussing condoms, an old, but informative subject. They had extensive experience with this topic, and I had acquired new knowledge about the flavored varieties like bubble gum and grape. The raincoats could be purchased in fun colors like glow-in-the-dark yellow and cherry red. Some were studded for *her pleasure*.

"So what's the latest in condoms?" I asked.

Jenny ignored me. "Not Hattie. She wouldn't hurt a fly."

Mostly true. I scrunched my nose. Wasn't looking good for the condom stuff.

"Shall we hire a hit man?" Trixie ruffled her short hair into interesting spikes. She originally hailed from the Windy City where the mobster era had ruled. Undoubtedly, she meant to eliminate the real murderer, whoever he or she may be was moot at this point.

"I think I'll find Hattie another job as there's a curse on Northside, Lancaster, and Brookside Accounting," Trixie said.

They all nodded. Two murders at one accounting firm were not normal.

In my opinion, Trixie will have to locate a new job for me anyway as NLB wouldn't want a murderess in their employ.

On and on. And of course, the Funsisters wanted to know how Allan figured in the whole thing, meaning in my life, and if sparks were flying between us. If they only knew about the almost-wild, almost-sex, then I'd be in for some serious ribbing. Thank goodness Jenny had missed the excitement the other night when she left for a dinner date before Allan's arrival.

And I explicitly didn't tell because of her big mouth reasons. I succumbed to my weakness and purchased the coveted piece of chocolate pie. Meanwhile, the Funsisters discussion flowed over, around, and by me. Who could get a word in edgewise anyway?

They continued their chat. Yet, I could only ignore their discussion for so long. I slammed the table top to draw their attention. *Ow.* "Have you out-of-your-freaking-mind people forgotten his current girlfriend, Cathy Bartholomew?" I fingered my sore wrist resting in my lap.

Time turned to ice for a moment. The Funsisters looked at me like I had no marbles in my head.

Sometimes, I didn't have any, but everyone had those moments.

"Hattie," Maggie said. "We call her Blonde Bimbo for a reason. Face the facts, it's just a matter of time before you and Allan work out this whatever you have going on."

"Remember the stupid comment she made about our favorite sweet?" Tracey asked. "She's toast."

After my birthday party, Jenny had sent an email as soon as she could, informing the Funsisters about Cathy Bartholomew's dimwitted comment regarding chocolate being fattening. We would chase pie with candy.

"She is unbelievably stupid," Kellar said.

"And her hair?" Tracey held her hands away from her head, mimicking Cathy Bartholomew's voluminous hair style. "I've never seen the likes before. Looks like something revisited from the eighties."

"Yuck," they chorused.

"She isn't his type at all," Trixie said.

"So who is?" Kellar asked.

As if a symphony conductor waved his wand, the Funsisters simultaneously turned their gazes toward me.

I pressed my fork to my breastbone. "Who…me?"

"Yes, you."

Little ol' clueless moi. They'd chatted about my love life in great detail behind my back. And regardless of Allan's current situation, they determined the ending of his love affair with Blonde Bimbo wasn't near, and I would eventually be paired with him.

"I can't wait to hear about Hattie and Allan's next romantic encounter. Any bets?" Trixie opened her wallet. Several of the Funsisters raised their hands, and they exchanged dinero.

Maybe Trixie can hook up with Bookie Dave. He was short, but not bald, just balding, and liked to gamble, too.

I could share a huge bombshell told to me while we were shopping. *He-he-he.* I rubbed my palms as I savored a juicy tidbit. My lovely sister Tracey had a big secret.

Since my birthday party, Tracey had been dating Stuart Steems regularly. Their relationship had progressed muy rapido, and hot things were happening under the bedcovers. Almost too much information, but—*he-he-he*—information worth sharing. Using this opportunity to turn the tables and announce something of prime importance to the Funsisters would be ideal— for me.

I practiced patience and timed my announcement to perfection. "Tadaaaaa…Tracey is dating Stuart Steems." I had the satisfaction of watching my bon amis' heads rotate my sister's way. Pleased with my attention-grabbing results, I added, "And they're doing IT under the covers."

More head swiveling in Tracey's direction who nodded with enthusiasm. The girls gave her hugs and high fives.

Amazed, I raised my hands in disbelief. *Why aren't they razzing her?* "What?"

"Well, what did you expect?" Trixie asked. "They

danced the whole time at your birthday party, and Stuart took her home—with your blessing I might add. The infamous love at first sight stuff."

Poom! The expression of being shot down like a cartoon coyote. Why weren't the Funsisters discussing Tracey in a more probing manner? What about lots of discussion causing her embarrassment and humiliation? What about her racy underwear? What about her sexual positions? What about her condoms? And was Stuart really hairy all over?

My BFF's fawned over Tracey, and then the discussion returned to Allan and the murders.

Rats. I slumped in my chair. *Can't blame a girl for trying.* I stole some leftover chips from Maggie's plate and munched.

Later on, Tracey did ask me if I could give her some pointers to help improve Stuart's dress code.

I'd start with his ties. Then, remembering his unusually hairy legs, she might want to wax his back. And his unibrow...

He-he-he. Little did Tracey know Stuart had asked about implementing a makeover for her.

Chapter Sixteen

Today, I broke my all-time record by walking/running two miles on the treadmill. Afterwards, I hummed a happy congratulatory tune as I made my way to the women's locker room for a shower. I rounded the stairway next to the water dispenser and *bo-ing!* Purely by accident, I smacked into Cathy Bartholomew, knocking her handbag to the floor.

How odd we met serendipitously through bumping into each other. First, we did at work, and now, at the gym. This time, she rounded the other side of the central staircase, and because sweat was dripping in my eyes, I'd bodywhacked her.

As I bent to pick up her belongings, I couldn't help but notice Cathy Bartholomew looked amazing in her workout clothes. The baby blue-and-navy-striped top stretched skintight over her tatas and emphasized her tiny waist. Cropped yoga pants rode low on her hips, exposing her diamond-studded belly button and flat tummy. Her big blonde hair had been knotted with a colorful elastic band.

My body perspired profusely, sort of an involuntary by-product, when I exercised. Sweat turned my bangs to limp and they plastered on my forehead, my face flushed red, and mascara raccoon-like runs ringed my eyes. I wore the usual—not pretty, but utilitarian—black baggy knit shorts and a short sleeved *Run with the Big Dogs* T-shirt, a Christmas gift from my dad.

"I'm so sorry, Cathy. I didn't see you." With the back of my wrist, I cleared droplets from my eyebrows. "Are you hurt?"

"Not at all. I should have paid attention. Are you?"

"Peachy. I haven't seen you at this gym before. You come here often?"

"I joined a few weeks ago," she replied, smugness oozing from her smile as she turned her body. "I work hard to maintain my figure."

I watched her pose from side-to-side like a wannabe Miss America contestant. I eased my teeth into my lips, choking on what I really wanted to say. Cathy Bartholomew did have a great figure, probably thanks to bulimia or anorexia and the imported tatas. Did she even eat at all? I had only seen her drinking coffee. And everyone knew she didn't eat chocolate.

"Yea." I picked up a small tissue pack. "How often do you work out?"

"Usually, seven times a week."

"Wow. You take this exercise stuff seriously."

"And doesn't the effort pay off?" Cathy Bartholomew struck a new stance, hands on hips, to further display what she possessed.

And I didn't. And wouldn't ever have. Of course, her method of binging and purging wasn't healthy either.

She opened her bag.

I lobbed the rest of her belongings I'd gathered inside.

"I was on my way to get some coffee," she said.

I pointed to the stacked cups and pitchers. "I was thirsty, too." From under a nearby chair, I retrieved two orange prescription bottles and extended them toward her.

She snatched the containers in a not-so nice way from my hand and shoved them in her bag, snapping the clasp forcefully.

With our conversation paused awkwardly, I followed her to the drink station where we poured our beverages of choice. We stood around, probably thinking the other would say something first. Perhaps, we could talk murder, or the football pool, or gossip about the other employees.

But no, I had to ask something else. "So, how's Allan?"

Cathy Bartholomew's face darkened. Her forehead pleated and lips thinned into tense tight lines. Her hands curled into fists and waves of angry tension emanated from her body. Her posture stiffened into a threatening stance.

She might sock me. I stepped outside her boxing range.

"Listen, you bitch." Cathy Bartholomew pushed into my personal space.

So close, I caught a huff of coffee on her breath.

"You stay away from Allan Wellborn," she said in a voice no one else could hear.

Stupid. I should have never asked this question. I knew better. She was one crazy insane gal about him. *Stupid. Stupid. Stupid.*

Stabbing her index finger toward my face, she came within a half-inch of hitting me in the eye with a very pointy, but well-manicured, nail. "You hear me?

He's all mine." Poke. *"Mine. Mine. Mine."* Poke. Poke. Poke.

Whoa. Instinctively, my head jerked a couple of times to avoid the eye jabbing. I didn't want to argue. I would lose because of my lack of defense weapons. I'd filed my nails short, not into sharp spears.

Raising my hands, I backed away with quick looks to my left and right to see if anyone else had observed what had transpired. "Sure." I hoped my careless manner sounded calming. "I haven't seen him except at the office on police business."

"And keep it that way. I have my eye on you." Venom dripped from her words. "He. Is. Mine."

Cathy Bartholomew leaned closer, her index finger pawing my throat. "Will Christiansen got what he deserved when he screwed you." Her nail scraped me from notch to sternum. She straightened and crossed her arms, feet planted in the same place with an evil slant shaping her eyes and a grit setting her teeth.

OhmyGod. Her comment stunned me. My jaw dropped and my eyes rounded. How did she know about my rendezvous with Will? Without a doubt, the whole office saw us together at happy hour. But how would anyone know about our lust-filled weekend?

I skimmed my fingers over the barely bleeding line, knowing I'd have to use some kind of antiseptic 'cause bacteria had to be prolific under her long claws.

I broke away and headed toward the women's locker room, pausing for a brief look…or two…or three over my shoulder to see if she had followed me.

She hadn't physically; however, her gaze had.

Yep, "crazy" and "insane" best embodied Cathy Bartholomew. No way did I want her anger directed toward me. My body shuddered as chills crept up my spine. One lunatic woman had attacked me, and I didn't want to be attacked by another ever again.

What in the wide world caused her to hate me so? Who knew she could be so terrifying? I snatched a couple of white towels and made fast tracks toward the showers, knowing I could disappear there.

Upon my subsequent return to my locker, I found no Cathy Bartholomew anywhere and blew out a tension-filled heave as I picked out my clothing, only to find my underwear had disappeared. And this time, I didn't care. I didn't even bother searching as I slid on my skirt and buttoned my blouse. Tracking to the exit, an old school rhyme ran through my mind, "I saw London, I saw France. I had on no underpants."

I might want to re-evaluate using this gym or at the very least, re-evaluate showering here.

****

I found my way home quickly and easily. Once there, I tossed my stuff on the coffee table and plopped on the sofa, snagging a decorating magazine of Jenny's. My cell phone buzzed. I checked the ID and noted Allan phoning, probably to check on Lucky, and I'd like to think me, too.

We hadn't really talked since our meet at my apartment which most likely was a good thing, considering my altercation at the gym with Cathy Bartholomew. No way would I mention I saw her, nor would I mention to her he'd called me. I entitled this plan *Self-Preservation 101*.

Even with our brief conversation, jitters skittered along my extremities while speaking with him.

"When will you be home?" I asked, trying not to

think of nails ground into pointy barbs. Hopefully, his return would remove my anxiety.

"Miss me?"

He sounded way too cheerful. I wasn't going there.

Paperwork shuffled in the background and he said, "Hang on."

I waited while he retried whatever, raising my chin to stare at the ceiling, rotating my head from side-to-side to relieve the angst cramping the tendons. I tried, tried, tried to focus on nundom, my new goal. I even mouthed the word—*nundom.*

"I'll be back in two days," he said. "Can you continue to take care of my pal, Lucky?"

"S-sure," I whispered with a hitch. I checked over my shoulder to see if Blonde Bimbo was around, capable of overhearing us. I knew doing so would seem silly to some folks; however, lately, I felt her presence everywhere.

"Do you have a cold?"

"No." I coughed to one side to clear my throat. "No, I'm fine."

"You sound funny."

"Sorry. Must have swallowed a frog. Of course, I'd love to take care of Lucky. He should probably be my cat."

"Maybe. Maybe this is my way to keep you around."

My stomach coiled into knots the size of grapefruit. Allan's mission was to torment me.

Yes, I missed him. Feelings, emotions, love was hard to turn off. With our poor attempt the other evening, I felt in the end he had clearly indicated I wasn't in his life as he ran off to answer Cathy

Bartholomew's call. Yet, he continued to throw around hints, insinuating something else. "Allan, don't say things you don't mean," I said. "We had this discussion the other day."

"I mean it."

"No, you don't." *Please, please, don't let Cathy Bartholomew be listening.*

"Yes, I do. I know what I want."

From any other guy, the words would sound like a Michael Bublé song to my ears. But after the encounter with Blonde Bimbo, I had self-protection in place. Which would mean giving up on him.

"No, you don't," I said. "You're dating very scary Cathy Bartholomew. Remember you answered her phone call the other night? Remember your indecision? I'm not living in limbo any more. Please stop tormenting me."

"Scary?"

Oops. I'd dropped the wrong word. My grip tightened on the phone.

"How is Cathy scary?"

"Nothing."

"You said Cathy's scary."

"No, I didn't say scary."

"Yes, you said 'very scary Cathy Bartholomew.'"

"You must have misunderstood." *Lord,* I prayed, *and Mom, forgive me for lying. You know I don't often.* "I said she was"—my finger twisted a strand of hair which inspired me to substitute—"hairy."

"Hairy?"

"You know, like big Texas hair."

"O-kaayy. Are you searching my apartment again?"

Busted. I felt guilt crowd my shoulders over him finding out. "Who—me?"

"You, sweetheart."

"Why would I go through your place?"

"I'm wondering the same thing. Fingerprints don't lie. Next time wear gloves. Is this some kind of weird-ass girly thing?"

"Why do you ask?"

"'Cause Cathy did it, too."

How…strange. Why would she search his apartment? I suppose she could have had the same questions I'd had. And why would he fingerprint his apartment? He could be teasing, but most likely, he'd just tossed out a random guess to unnerve me.

"If you're finished," he said, "I have something to say about the other night."

Do I want to know this? I sat at attention. "I'm hanging hang up now."

"Give me a minute. This won't take long."

I waited.

"Hattie?"

"I'm here."

"I didn't move on with Cathy."

What?

"You picked the wrong theory. And someday, you and I will have to have to settle…whatever this is… going on between us. Man to woman."

Because of my recent emotional roller coaster, I depressed the *end call* button, screamed, and tossed the phone on the sofa—my way of putting distance between us. Remorse stole over me. I knew Mom wouldn't like me being rude, especially to Allan, the perfect prince among all men. I thumbed my lower lip.

I teethed my finger while thinking I didn't understand him. Not at all. We nearly had engaged in almost-wild, almost-sex, and he takes a freaking phone call from Cathy Bartholomew, then sprints from the room the other evening. *And now?* Was he possibly saying he wasn't with her?

The hell with being focused. Being focused was confusing. Another cry erupted from my whole being.

Jenny knocked before opening my bedroom door.

She sat on the bed by my side and patted my arm in consolation, the way BFFs and sisters do.

"I'm guessing Allan called."

I nodded.

"No wonder you screamed. It's the sound you make when irritated with him." She wrapped her arms around me and slanted her head against my shoulder. "Hattie, it'll be okay."

God. I didn't think I could feel any more awful. I gulped deep, cleansing breaths. "No, it's not. I'm so annoyed with him…with her…with everything."

Jenny let me rant and rave about everything bottled inside me.

"Maybe I can run away." I could, too. With a miniscule turn of my head, I glanced through my lashes toward my desk so Jenny couldn't see. A new opportunity was within a touch. Peter Redmond had followed up his letter and our chat with an email. All I had to do was pick up the phone and say a simple *yes*.

"You won't. You'd miss your friends too much. And ultimately, running away never solves anything. Besides, your mother won't let you."

Jenny knew my mom pretty well.

She squeezed another big Funsister hug and pushed

to her feet. Grabbing my hands, she pulled me to stand. "Come on, we need a soda."

"And chocolate," I said.

"And chocolate." She passed me a tissue from the box on my nightstand.

I brushed my nose with it. "And pie."

"Sounds like a food orgy to me."

****

I'd just finished eating all the bad-but-tasted-so-good stuff when my cell phone dinged—a call from Tracey.

She said, "Hattie."

Her wail had me snap to attention. Tracey wasn't a crybaby. "Trace?"

"St-stuart has been admitted to Sommerville Hospital."

"OhmyGod!" So amazed, I fumbled my phone. Pushing my hand through my hair, I stood and walked laps in front of the coffee table. "OhmyGod. What happened?"

"He has a b-broken right leg, bruised arm, ribs, and face. A messed up rotator in his right shoulder."

Stuart looked and acted geeky, but he wasn't clumsy. I asked, "How did he get hurt? I ran into him in the hallway by the stairwell. We talked. I'm at a loss."

Tracey didn't say anything, just sniffed.

"I saw him right before he took the stairwell," I said. "Tell me what happened. Tell me everything."

"I'm not sure if I have the whole story. Stuart hasn't been very coherent. He's on pain killers. He said almost everyone was gone for the day, and he had to run something down to the eighteenth floor—"

"I saw him then," I said.

"Someone pushed him as he started down the stairs. In the back. Really hard. 'Cause of the boxes he carried, he lost his balance and fell." She hiccupped and sniffed.

Off to the side, I heard her blow her nose. "Oh, sissie, how awful."

"Why would someone hurt Stuart?"

I was mystified. "I don't know. I can't imagine. He's just a nerdy accountant guy. Do you want me to come to the hospital?"

"No." Tracey gulped a cry. "He's sleeping now. Oxy is powerful stuff."

"So I've heard. The best. I can come, hold your hand, and bring something, anything. Food. Whatever. You name it."

"No, I just want to sit here quietly. I don't want him disturbed."

"How did you know he was pushed down the stairs?" I asked.

"He said so. Said he felt a hard shove in the middle of his back."

My hand cupped my forehead. "Any idea as to who might have done it?"

"Doesn't remember. He remembers laughing."

"Laughing? He laughed?" I asked.

"No, he heard laughing."

"Weird. Maybe he misunderstood what he thought he heard."

Tracey sniffed again. "M-maybe."

"Did you call his mother? She would want to know."

"I'll call her as soon as I get her number."

"Did someone from the firm call the police?"

"Whoever found him called 9-1-1. The detectives talked with him earlier. But he can't answer questions now."

Un-be-lieve-able. "So we don't know if he had an accident or the incident was deliberate," I said.

"No."

"Will you call me tomorrow? Call me when the police come?"

"Yes. I had to talk to someone, Hattie. I'm so worried."

"I know. Believe me, I understand," I said. "Thanks for telling me, Tracey. I'm glad you're there for Stuart. Love you."

"You, too." Tracey hung up.

"Jenny!" I ran down the hall to tell her what had happened to Stuart. I found her reclined on her bed, reading a book by her favorite mystery author.

She jerked upright.

"You won't believe what Tracey just told me."

Walking back and forth the length of her bed, I told her the whole sordid story about Stuart and the stairs. I, however, didn't bouncey-bounce on her mattress to annoy her. When I finished, I passed my hand over my jaw.

"I don't like the picture you're painting," Jenny said.

"Me, neither."

"You think he fell or was pushed?"

"I say pushed. He's not inept. With all the ballroom dancing lessons, he moves lightly on his feet." I scrunched my nose. "Yet, freak accidents do occur."

"Do you think this is related in some obscure way to the poisonings?" she asked.

"Poisonings?" I pushed one finger up and down between my brows. "What poisonings?"

"How soon you forget. The ones at the office? Remember Will, Phil?"

"Could be, although I didn't say anything to Tracey. Right now, her hands are full." We sat quietly for a while, thinking, and then I added, "I bet the police pay a visit to NLB."

"With two probable poisonings," Jenny said, "and a possible attempted murder, they'll be there."

I crossed my arms over my chest and wondered. *What is the deal with NLB anyway?*

****

I was not a detective. However, the events taking place at Northside, Lancaster, and Brookside were not normal. From my experience with Buy Rite Automobile Insurance Company, I'd learned when something seemed dangerous, it was.

Without a doubt, I should have heeded Allan's advice when he'd told me to pay attention to my intuition. I didn't. Being Mr. Policeman, he'd said his comment in such an off-handed manner that I didn't pay his counsel any credence. And it didn't help when he omitted much-needed details. Since I didn't like learning any lessons the hard way, I would do better this time.

Trixie wouldn't like my decision. I punched Jobs Inc. phone number to speak with her. "Trixie? Thank God you're there."

"Where else would I be?"

I heard a squeak from her desk chair. I could envision her rotating from one side to the other. "I need a new job."

"Oh, Hattie." The squeaking stopped. "Tell me."

****

Allan didn't come home from his trip, and he didn't phone me either, which seemed unusual. He was pretty spot-on about checking in daily. And I wouldn't be the person to contact him because the Cathy Bartholomew threat still hung over my head. So I continued to care for Lucky with the plan to avoid him.

After work on Thursday and a less-than-worthwhile trip to the gym, I showered at home. I'd stuffed my outfit in a duffle and carried it with me to the elliptical, believing I could outwit the thief. No way would any more of my underwear be stolen.

I opened the apartment door and threw my handbag and bag of clothing on the coffee table. I dropped my bod in the khaki club chair and checked my cell phone for messages. Finally, one from Allan.

"Hi, sweetheart."

Sweetheart? I stiffened. Why did he continue to call me some pet name when I'd asked him not to? He had to have scrambled eggs for brains.

"I wanted to let you know I'm staying in Louisiana and will be back on Friday. I hope to see you then. Call me. Bye."

Did I hear him right—he's in Louisiana? The great Detective Allan Wellborn revealed something? Wasn't he breaking some kind of regulation policeman code?

Mystified, I fingered circles on my temple, letting and even feeling the *two and two* come together. His comment confirmed what I'd found in the file folder on his desk, the one marked "Cold Case-Louisiana." Then, a niggly something about someone from the office hailed from Louisiana snuck in my head. Who was it?

What would he be investigating in Louisiana?

Allan had asked me to call him back.

Again, self-preservation took over. *Better not to.*

****

After a quick shower, I checked in with Tracey, who was at the hospital.

She said she would be standing steadfastly by Stuart's bedside until he recovered. "The painkiller does the trick. He seems comfortable."

"Good news." I asked, "Does Stuart remember anything about anything?"

"Not yet."

"Have the police been by?"

"Yes, and he told them what I told you. He felt a hard shove in his back and laughter behind him. Afterwards, he tumbled forward and hit his head on the concrete and steel stairs."

I winced. Just the thought of him hitting his head got to me. "He could have been gravely injured on those steps. Cracked his skull, his spine, or something."

"I know. He's very blessed. Everyone says so." Tracey blew a whoosh of air. "I have some really, really good news."

"Tell me."

"Stuart asked me to marry him."

OhmyGod. I juggled my cell phone.

"And yes, I accepted his proposal."

She said yes?

"I want to marry him."

Stuart and Tracey had known each other—*for what? A few weeks? And she said yes?* More importantly, what would Mom think? Surely, Tracey wasn't right in the head. I bet a box of donuts she'd accepted because she was distraught with him being in the hospital.

She said yes?

"Yes, Hattie, I'm marrying Stuart. You'll have to get used to him being a part of our family."

Me? I hated to tell her I wasn't the one who had a problem with him being a part of the family. She should be more concerned about Mom.

A wham of ghastly proportions smacked me upright. Would we be required to wear nametags at the wedding?

Chapter Seventeen

For the umpteenth time, the detectives returned to the office of Northside, Lancaster, and Brookside. They stepped up their inquiries to pursue Stuart's contention he'd been pushed down the stairs.

NLB employees were on a razor's edge. Fewer groups congregated in the alternate break room. Less activity and chatter occurred.

Returning from the mailroom, I observed a detective who stood outside the small conference room where he had been conducting staff interviews. From his stance of spread legs and a watchful stare, I could tell he searched for a particular someone, and I prayed to the One Above he didn't want me.

Then our gazes intersected, and he hustled in my direction. "Ms. Cooks?"

Rats. Looks like he found his victim. I arched a brow in a nonchalant inquisitive manner. "Yes?"

His hand waved toward the conference room. "Would you come with me, please?"

Not what I wanted to do. I shifted my mouth sideways and squinted. "Is something wrong? I really need to get back to work. Mr. Northside is expecting these documents."

"I won't take long. I'd like to cover a few new items."

I compressed my lips and wondered if I needed to

find an attorney.

Again he signaled toward the door.

I shrugged. "Sure." I followed the detective to the conference room and took a seat in the now very familiar chair he'd indicated, the same one I'd sat in while Detective Wellborn interrogated me. Did a Guinness World Record exist for participation in police interviews? I crossed my legs in a sophisticated-girl manner. My name should be stenciled across the chair's leather back.

The detective switched on the recorder and said the date, time, and interviewee name thing. "Ms. Cooks. The police are asking questions about an incident involving Mr. Stuart Steems, employed by Northside, Lancaster, and Brookside, Accountants. Do you know him?"

Shit, Jenny and I were right. Once again, I stared at the empty space by the window, remembering what Tracey had told me about the incident.

"Ms. Cooks? Ms. Cooks?"

"Sorry," I said, "I heard you. I was thinking about what you said."

"Could you answer the question? Do you know Stuart Steems?"

"Of course. I know Stuart. He's a Senior Audit Manager for NLB and interviewed me the day I was hired to fill the temporary position as Mr. Northside's administrative assistant. Subsequently, Stuart and I attended a party together, and he's recently engaged to my sister, Tracey."

His left eyebrow arched. "Two days ago, the day of Mr. Steems' accident, you were seen speaking with him in the hallway next to the stairwell."

Sooo...someone else saw me with him. I nodded. "That's correct. Before the end of the day, I walked by Stuart who stood in the hallway next to the stairwell. We talked briefly."

"Tell me about it."

Aha. The detective line, the one the cops learned in cop school, and the same one Detective Wellborn had mastered. At least *he* wasn't conducting this grilling. I would be glad to cooperate and do anything to help Stuart. "I've been helping my sister, Tracey, with a makeover on Stuart. I complimented him on the new suit he wore."

Confusion crossed the officer's face. "Makeover?"

Clearly, *makeover* terminology wasn't included in detective vocabulary. "Stuart is clothing challenged," I explained.

"Clothing challenged?"

Golly, if he repeats everything I say, this will be one long chat. "Stuart wore a new dark blue suit, blue-and-silver striped tie, an expensive white shirt with a navy checked hankie jauntily stuffed in his coat pocket. I told him I liked the outfit, and he shifted about to show it off. He even wore his father's cufflinks which were inscribed with an 'S'. When I commented on his stunning appearance, he blushed." I leaned a little closer. "His uni-brow was gone."

"Uni-brow?"

Here we go again. "Yes, uni-brow. You know, one large eyebrow instead of two."

The detective's eyes rolled upwards. "I see."

What a phony. He'd agreed because he hadn't understood what *clothing challenged* and *makeover* meant and didn't want to look ignorant. And he knew I knew. A dose of reality TV like an episode of Successful Man wouldn't hurt him.

His gaze dropped to his own outfit—a frumpy black-and-gold tweed jacket over too-long black slacks, a burgundy shirt, and a gold tie with matching slashes.

The detective needed my fashion expertise as well.

"Why would Mr. Steems ask you about clothes?" he asked while patting his tie.

"He didn't. My sister had on his behalf. I used to be an assistant buyer for men's sportswear at Tucker's Department Store. My family and friends consult me as a style expert."

"Oh." He blinked. "Is it common to use the stairwell to travel between floors?"

"Absolutely. Like most buildings, the elevator is slow, or seems slow; so we use the stairwell. We run up and down the stairs several times a day. I think of it as a Stairmaster-like exercise and good for my hips." I smoothed my palms over the dark skirt covering my legs.

The detective gave me the once-over from head to tabletop. "And nothing else?"

"Hmmm, let me think." I pressed my finger to my chin. "Yes, there's something, but it's—"

"Anything you have to say would be helpful."

"It's silly, really." I fluttered my hand. "I congratulated Stuart on winning the football pool. He's a big fan and plays the game every week—"

"What game?"

"The betting game. Maybe you've seen the one posted on the fridge in the downstairs kitchenette?" I pointed over my shoulder in the direction of the break room.

"I have." He nodded. "And some kind of weird poem, too."

"That's the one."

"Stuart Steems won the football game?"

"He did. He said he didn't know and thanked me for informing him."

"Did he win a lot of money?"

Oops. Will someone get in trouble over illegal gambling? "Here's the deal. I'm a newbie at this betting stuff."

The detective's mouth crooked in a one-sided grin.

"My understanding is the bet is five dollars a game and if all the squares are taken, someone wins something like five hundred dollars. Ask Bookie Dave for the exact amount."

"Bookie Dave?"

Lordy, this guy. "He's a manager under Stuart and runs the football game."

"So, it's okay to bet at NLB?"

I shrugged. "Why not? It's only for fun. Nothing big-time."

"Five hundred dollars sounds like a lot of money. Has Stuart won before?"

"I don't know for certain, but he loves football and participates regularly."

"Could someone be angry over his winnings? Angry enough to hurt him?"

His questioned shocked me, making my eyes widen and my spine extend. *What a horrible, terrible question.* "I have no idea. All I know is last week's game was posted on the fridge in the break room. Like I just mentioned, I told Stuart to check. He said he didn't know he'd won and thanked me."

"Anything else?"

"Not really. After our conversation, Stuart passed through the door and presumably down the stairwell to the lower floor," I said. "I returned to my desk."

"Did you see anyone else in the vicinity?"

I propped my elbow on the tabletop and rested my chin in my palm. I deliberated hard for a moment and then brightened as I remembered what I'd told Detective Wellborn. "Right after I left Stuart, I passed by Cathy Bartholomew as she entered the same hallway. Excited for Stuart, I said in passing, "Cathy, isn't it great? Stuart won the football pool!"

The detective terminated our interview and pitched a hurried "thanks" over his shoulder as he rushed off with this new information.

****

Jenny beat me home from work. I joined her in the kitchen where she prepared a salad for dinner. While slicing cherry tomatoes in half, she asked, "How's Stuart?"

I fingered a parmesan crisp she'd purchased at Super Saver grocery store. "Tracey says he's recovering and by the end of the week, he should go home."

"Good news."

"It is." I picked up a knife and chopped romaine lettuce. She sniffed while cutting onions and her shoulder caught the weep.

"He has to rest a while with the broken leg," I said, setting the knife aside. "Tracey's insisting he stay with her. She said she has plenty of vacation time to use, and she would rather spend the time taking care of him now instead of honeymooning later on."

"True love. How sweet. What about staying with

266

his mother?"

I gave her an "I am clueless" look. "I didn't ask. Tracey said something about her being on a cruise and would rush home if he wanted her. I think he said no."

"How was the rest of your day?"

"Funny you should ask." I snagged another crisp and leaned a hip against the counter.

"Why so?"

"Because we called it. Another detective interviewed me. They're conducting an investigation into Stuart's accident. Do you suppose the police think this could be a possible attempted murder? And I'm beginning to feel picked on."

Jenny's knife clattered to the floor.

Shocked and amazed didn't even begin to describe the look covering her face.

"OhmyGod."

"Yea. Me, too."

"What did you tell them?"

"Anything and everything I knew. The detective seemed curious about Stuart's winning the football pool and asked pointed questions about it. I did remember seeing Cathy Bartholomew in the hallway near the stairwell. Then I saw Mr. Northside a few seconds later." Setting the cutting board next to the bowl, I brushed the lettuce inside.

"Did you mention him?"

"No. Didn't think to. Just her."

A thoughtful crease shaped Jenny's brow. "Cathy Bartholomew." She wandered over to the oven where she slid in a tray of buttered bread for warming. Not long later, the scent of garlic drifted into the room.

"I want to think about her."

****

Rats. After I'd eaten half of Jenny's salad at dinner, I remembered I'd forgotten to feed Lucky. As far as I knew, Allan could still be out-of-town. Not hearing anything different from him, I'd better take care of his furry pal. I hopped in my Jeep and headed to his place.

As I approached, I saw through the picture window different lights burned inside—the one on his desk and the pot light at the top of the stairs. Usually, I switched on the sofa table lamps and adjusted the drapes before I left. Like most people, I didn't fancy being alone in a gloomy atmosphere in strange places. Just the small glow would cast a homey ambiance.

Besides, Lucky shouldn't be in the dark.

Possibly, Allan had returned early. Since I hadn't called like he'd asked, for all I knew, he could be home. I knocked once-twice-thrice, but no one replied. *Okay, maybe he's taking a shower and didn't hear me.* Using my key, I unbolted the door. "Allan? Allan? Are you home?"

No answer. What surprised me was Lucky popping out of the shrubberies next to the apartment door and wrapping his pliable body around my legs. I picked him up and nosed his forehead. Kitty was soft. I draped him over my shoulder. "Hey, Big Guy. What are you doing outside? Looking for love in strange places?"

I guess Allan might, on occasion, let his feline friend enjoy the great outdoors—*wait a minute.* My free palm thumped against my forehead, causing Lucky to wiggle and nearly plop to the ground. I regrouped and hugged kitty to my chest. *How stupid.* Allan was out-of-town. He couldn't let Lucky outside.

So how did he escape?

268

I whispered calming sweet nothings in the kitty-cat's ear and carried him inside to investigate. After shutting the door behind me, I dumped him on the couch and wandered through the apartment. As I walked about, I turned on the lamps I favored and darkened others while I checked out the premises.

Clink, clink.

My heart stopped. A fear-ridden, deep gulp clogged my throat. Sliding my hand in smooth small increments up my neck, I made a slow turn, looked, and released a deep breath. Lucky followed me, his tags clink-clinking with each step. I blew out another relieving breath and massaged my scalp to release the tension.

The kitchen and living areas looked the same. The mail rested on the computer desk where I'd laid it. Upstairs in the loft, I found the bath and bedroom to be undisturbed. Other than the odd lamps, something seemed different, but I couldn't put my finger on what had changed.

I made my way downstairs, my forefinger tapping my lips, trying to call forth what I struggled with recalling. I filled Eating Machine's bowls, and then locked the door after I exited, giving a shove against the portal to be sure I'd secured in properly and there would be no more cat escapes.

****

Alarming news greeted me at NLB the next morning: Cathy Bartholomew hadn't reported for work. Several of us phoned her apartment. No one answered, not even a voice mail pick-up. And for those who had her cell number, no one got a response either.

Based on office talk, Cathy Bartholomew had low

absenteeism. Maybe she had a family emergency out-of-town—wherever that was—and forgot to notify someone at NLB. Maybe she had car trouble. Maybe she had to go to the hospital. Nevertheless, one constant imprinted our minds. Many of my co-workers mumbled their speculations. We were concerned and rightfully so, considering what had happened with Phil, Will, and Stuart.

I reported the unusual absence to Mr. Northside.

He sighed. "Another problem. She could be sick and doesn't want to answer her phone. Keep checking."

With a casual examination, I could tell Mr. Northside looked as if sleep eluded him. New wrinkles furrowed under his eyes, and he responded a tad slower than usual, his body morphing into a little crooked man with a mass burdening his shoulders.

The more we colleagues chatted about Cathy Bartholomew, the more information surfaced. Everything about her could be described as mysterious. She didn't divulge where she had been born and raised, but one co-worker tossed out the thought she might hale from Louisiana based on the Southern drawl lacing her words. She never told anyone what she did over the weekend, but instead, asked others about themselves, turning the conversations on the instigator. No one knew her hobbies.

I knew from our encounter at the club she exercised a lot…or pretended to.

And interestingly, no one knew she dated Allan Wellborn, except for me, which I didn't divulge.

How interesting.

****

On the following morning, I walked to the

kitchenette on the nineteenth floor for the surprise birthday party for Mr. Northside. Finally, someone had told me what the "did you know" question meant.

I set a birthday card next to the sheet cake which had been placed in the center of a round table. His name was written in orange frosting underneath *Happy Birthday!!!* Clusters of blue flowers and emerald tendrils decorated each corner. Numbered candles of "4" and "8" sat off to one side of the dessert. I loved everything about cake and this one looked stupendous.

A couple of auditors escorted a blindfolded Mr. Northside into the room, and then whipped off the bandanna covering his eyes. Mr. Northside was very surprised. His grin was the size of a sideways banana and his eyes danced with laughter.

I hadn't seen him look so happy in days.

We all sang the traditional song. Bookie Dave made a speech and told us how much he appreciated the secret being kept.

After Mr. Northside blew out the candles, he took a knife and cut neat slices.

I said "hey" to Bookie Dave and the other guys hanging around the fridge. After I filled a cup with water, I, too, paused to read the new poem posted on the fridge.

Two down, one to come.
Bet the 'ho
Doesn't think this is fun.

Several beginning auditors crowded around me. One said, "Another joke poem."

"I see," I said. To my experienced eye, the poem had been printed on the same kind of printer paper as the other two, written in the same Times New Roman, size fourteen font. And presumably, the same person who wrote these poems continued to mock football players, in particular singling out Mr. Miller, the quarterback, and the outrageous salaries football players commanded nowadays, comparing him to a 'ho.

"Whatever," another auditor said. "It doesn't mean anything."

"I agree. It could be more original and the poetry's terrible."

"I'm more interested in my winnings."

"Me, too. Did you hear Stuart Steems won last week?"

"No way. That's fantastic. I know he's a big football fan. Did you see his new suit?"

"Yea, he looked good, too. Was it ruined in the fall?"

"That would be a shame. Sure hope he's feeling better."

"He is," I added, glancing around the group. "Before we know it, he'll be stumbling around here on crutches."

Their light nods accepted and welcomed my statement.

"Hey, Hattie." Bookie Dave pushed through the auditors now crowding my body. "Guess the two/five square you picked last time didn't work out, huh?" He laughed at my frown.

The other guys snickered.

"Are you playing this week?"

I pursed my mouth before replying, "I think I should read up on football before I give this another go."

The guys tittered like a birdies lined up on the top

of a fence. I bestowed on them a playful dirty look. Like most suckers, everyone saw me coming. Never won raffles. Never won contests. But was loved by animals.

"Sure wouldn't hurt," Bookie Dave said.

A good choice was *not* to play anymore. I could save up and treat myself to my favorite accessory: a new handbag.

Now, that is money well spent.

****

A grocery store pit stop after work would provide much needed necessities—bananas, low-fat milk, and whole wheat bread. Chocolate wasn't required after the big cake bonanza I'd amassed at Mr. Northside's birthday.

My luck flip-flopped when I spied Mrs. Wellborn in the produce section, selecting apples. I tried the evasive squat-like-a-duck and turn-the-corner move.

Mrs. Wellborn's eagle eyes spotted me at the same time. "Harr-riii-ette."

Darn her radar.

Everyone in the produce section stopped what they were doing and stared.

I couldn't be more embarrassed.

Like a dog with a favorite chew toy, she wouldn't let me wiggle away.

With caution 'cause you never know what a mom would do, I lengthened my stride and gravitated back to the fruit bins. I always believed Mrs. Wellborn was scary, and there was a possibility she might want to yell at me about her son.

With a warm smile tilting her mouth, she embraced me like a hardly-ever-seen grandmother. "Harriette, I have to say again what a nice time I—we all—had at your birthday party. Elaine is a master at organizing such an exceptional event."

"Thanks, Mrs. Wellborn. I enjoyed it, too."

"You be sure and tell her I said so. The unique M&M theme caught my fancy." She leaned closer and cupped her hand beside her mouth. "I'm a closet chocoholic also. Can't get enough gourmet malt balls."

What amazing news! Never in a bazillion years would I have guessed Mrs. Wellborn and I would bond over chocolate. And who knew about gourmet malt balls? I'd have to try those.

"Have you seen Allan lately?" she asked.

I guess Mom hadn't confided her son and I weren't dating any more. "No. He's traveling so much. I was stunned when he asked me to take care of Lucky. I thought he'd ask you."

"I would have been glad to. I'm concerned about his frequent trips to—of all places—Louisiana." Tsking, she frowned. "I wish he would tell me more. He's always been rather close-mouthed."

I could sympathize. Most moms felt the same way. My mom prayed daily I would confide in her.

She sighed. "I guess he has to be careful, considering his job. I couldn't believe he wanted to change careers and become a policeman. It's such dangerous work. And he took a pay cut, too."

"Isn't he doing some accounting on the side?"

"He is. Wants to keep in his hand in."

"He seems to like police work," I told her. *He had mastered Interrogation 101.*

"Yes, he does which is what is important—him doing what he wants." Mrs. Wellborn whipped to another topic. "Oh, Harriette! You won't believe why I'm shopping. Sarah Ann dashed into town for a visit yesterday. I was so surprised."

"Fantastic, Mrs. Wellborn! How's she doing?"

"She's fine. And the baby is beautiful."

I'd had no opportunity to visit with Sarah Ann in a couple of months. "I would love to see her. Would you mind if I stopped by?"

"Sure, Harriette. Why don't you come now?"

And so I did.

****

Fifteen minutes later, Sarah Ann opened the door and her earsplitting scream almost burst my eardrums. "Hattie!"

Her arms embraced me in a big hug. I clasped her close. I felt an empty spot in my heart. Boy, I'd missed my friend.

"I planned on calling you later today." Taking my hand, she led me into the house. "I'm so happy to see you. You look great." She scooched the black denim tote trimmed with ribbon flowers and beads off my arm and turned it from side-to-side. "I love this handbag. Tres chic. It's perfect with your black dress." She set it on the entry console table. "Did you run into Mom at the grocery store?"

I nodded. "Over apples in the produce section. I tried hiding, but her radar zeroed in and found me. Tell me your news. How's your baby girl?"

We walked over to the living room couch and cozied together like the best of companions do. "She's fine. She's such a good baby, able to nap everywhere," Sarah Ann said. "Hattie—"

"Life in Denver?"

"Fine. Hattie—"

"And how about handsome husband Tom?"

"Tom's fine. Everyone's fine. Everything's fine."

"Tell—"

Sarah Ann grabbed my sleeve. "Hattie, stop. We need to talk."

Unsure over what she wanted, I squinted. A great deal of time had passed since Sarah Ann and I'd held our last girly-girl talk fest. "What about?" I asked. Because of the nature of her statement, something felt odd and worried my head. My fingers hovered over my lips. "Are you okay?" But before she could open her mouth to reply, I blurted, "Oh-oh-oh! I know! I know! You're having another baby!"

Sarah Ann shook her head in a slow, careful way. "No, Hattie. No baby. That's not what I wanted to discuss."

Frowning, I looked at her. "Should I be worried? Do you have some scary scarring disease?"

"No," she said. "I'm worried about you."

Why would Sarah Ann be worried about me? With a head tilt, I studied my bestie. "Why me? Everything's hunky-dory."

"I'm worried about you and my brother."

"Not that," I whined and overlapped my arms. Being bombarded with the "Allan Wellborn" stuff was irritating. "Everyone wants to talk about him. Your mom. My mom. Jenny. Now, you. Don't you have any other hobbies? Crochet, needlepoint, world peace? There's nothing to say."

"From what Mom and Allan told me, you two were an item."

I crossed my eyes. "We set a short record in the

item department."

Sarah Ann gave a little laugh at my face and bounced her finger on the spot where the forehead and nose come together. "Your eyes are going to stick. You'd better undo them."

I did and massaged the bridge.

"I know about the unfortunate incident when he shot your co-worker. Allan said a little, and Mom told me a lot. The Mothers Always Know Network still holds court over produce at the grocery store."

"Yep, like I said, she found me there."

Sarah Ann giggled. "Mothers always know. I guess I'll learn the tricks soon enough." She looked me over. "Seriously, Hattie. For a while, Allan sounded lost."

"Hmm." I stopped rubbing my eyes to understand everything about what she'd said. "Me, too."

Of course, he hadn't acted too lost if he could go on a date with Cathy Bartholomew a few weeks later. But I didn't tell her anything about what had happened.

"He didn't mean for you to be hurt."

Sure he did wafted through my thoughts, but I didn't verbalize the sentiment in the sarcastic manner I wanted to. And I knew differently. Allan had given me a small apology and attempted to explain everything. I acted too embarrassed to listen. This knowledge unnerved me, and I hugged one of Mrs. Wellborn's needlepoint pillows to my stomach. "I know. I treated him badly, but I was sorta confused. I felt betrayed for a while. I had to sort out the detective relationship from our personal relationship."

Remembering caused emotions to wash over me. I divulged the second most important declaration of my whole, entire life, the first being when I'd gone to Allan and had asked him to choose me. "I miss him, Sarah Ann. I haven't told anyone my feelings. I miss being with him a lot. We had so much—oh, I don't know—fun together. I have never felt like that with anyone before or since. Not even with College Boy." My tears threatened to do a Niagara Falls spillover. Again, I shoved my fingers to the corners of my eyes. "I love him. I really do."

After a long pause which involved Sarah Ann staring, she said, "Well, stop being a crybaby and do something."

How many times would I have to explain what I'd done? I'd asked Allan to choose me and he didn't. My heart accelerated to ninety miles per hour. Heat washed my entire body. My foot began tapping involuntarily. "I tried. I more than tried. But he preferred another and you should see her." I let the expression on my face do the talking.

Sarah Ann shook her head. "You're wrong."

"Believe it. You know how nervous I get with any kind of confrontation, much less, an intimate one. When I realized how much I do care for him, I overcame those uncomfortable emotions and pulled my act together. I drove to his apartment and asked him to choose me. After letting me stumble and bumble through a laborious explanation, he said, and I quote, *no*, end quote."

"I still don't believe it. I know my brother. He's not mean. You"—she pointed at me—"misunderstood him. You've got to try harder."

"Tell me," I said in a not-so nice tone, "what is there to misunderstand about N period, O period?"

"Not much." She twisted her mouth to one side.

"And he began dating what's-her-name about this time?"

"Well, maybe a little before that. I'm not sure."

She guided my head to rest on her shoulder and circled her arms around me. "Hattie, you're the only girl he has ever cared for. Even when we were younger, he liked you best."

This was interesting news. I drew away from Sarah Ann's embrace to study her. "When we were younger? Really? I didn't know. I mean, I knew he stared occasionally, but I thought he stared at every girl. Why didn't you tell me?"

"I wanted to. I had a hard time not saying a word to my best friend. Frankly, he swore me to secrecy. And he was right. His business wasn't my business."

"It's not true." I shook my head in fast shakes. "You're making this up. Allan never said anything. I was such...a nobody. You know how I suffered from the uglies. No one paid any attention to me."

"We're talking about Mr. Shy," Sarah Ann said. "And you weren't any better. The two of you were so bashful and hid behind your glasses. You were meant to be together."

With each bit of new information, my heart ticked to a faster beat.

"Time for you to find one another," she said.

I sat straighter and stared at her hard while wrapping my thoughts around this. We'd found each other, but had problems getting things moving in the right direction for a real relationship. And then Cathy Bartholomew stepped in. I had to know. "Why hasn't Allan married?"

"Who knows?" She shrugged. "I suspect he wanted

you two to settle into a good relationship first."

"Oh." I dropped my chin, focusing on my toes.

"Lately, I'd kinda tease him, saying things like 'now it's your turn.'"

"What did he say?"

"Something like"—her voice lowered to a he-man depth—"I'm getting around to it."

I could hear Allan in his quiet, conservative way brushing off Sarah Ann's intrusions. We were nearing our thirties, him closer than me, and had never married. I owed my single lifestyle to wanting more experience and even rejected College Boy's proposal because of a maturity I felt I lacked for a commitment to marriage.

Allan on the other hand... He possessed lots of hands-on experience, admirable virtues, and qualities women searched for. He was a good catch.

Sarah Ann turned me by my shoulders so I'd face her. "I need to tell you something. It's kinda of a long story, so bear with me."

"Okay."

"And don't be mad."

Where is this going? "O-kaaayy."

"Remember when we were thirteen, and we had the boy-girl Halloween party here? We had planned to the nth detail. And do you remember the kissing game, the one with secret partners?"

The Night of My Very First Kiss. I nodded. Who could forget such a momentous life event?

"I made two sets of numbers. One set went in one bowl and the identical second in another. Girls drew from the left and boys drew from the right. On a poster board, I wrote the number and a specific time the pair met in the hall closet."

I remembered this was how our fun little game had been played. As my thoughts leapfrogged ahead to determine the exact direction she was headed, my brainwaves muddled a bit.

"We agreed you would draw first to start the game, to break the ice. You picked number four and at nine-fifteen on the dot, you met your matching number four in the closet."

Okay, what I remembered, too. Why was she making such a big deal?

"I was sworn to secrecy," she said, "I never told you this."

I gave Sarah Ann a more perplexed than ever look.

"Your number four was Allan."

"Get out." I slapped my hand over my mouth. My eyes widened. I remembered the kiss, My Very First Kiss. It was very good. In fact, it was splendid.

For a long time, I'd recalled every teeny tiny detail. I would lay on my bed, memorizing the heaviness on my lips, the light touch of his tongue swiping across my aperture, and a slight slip of moisture left there. Our pounding hearts. His body against mine. A clean fresh scent of lemon on his skin.

Then I reached back to remember the first time he'd kissed me a few months ago.

Oh my God, it was the very same!

"Hattie." Sarah Ann cuddled my hand in a way only best friends could.

I twined my hand with hers.

"Allan was desperate to make this happen. He begged me to rig the game so he could kiss you. He paid, too. For a whole month, he did my chores. He never complained."

My pulse thumped out of control. He'd paid dearly. Mrs. Wellborn was the guru of doling out chores.

"Being the young romantic I was, I helped him." She lifted one shoulder. "You would come over, and he would just look and look and stare and stare like you were Cleopatra, Queen of the Nile, and he was the lowly slave worshipping you from afar. I was mortified with how much he watched you.

"Please understand, Hattie," she said. "I love you and my brother so much, and I thought what he asked me to do was sweet. So I tricked you. When you drew your number four, all the numbers were a four. I switched to another bowl for the rest of the drawing. In college, Allan dated other girls, but they weren't right."

Sarah Ann grabbed me by my shoulders and gave me a shake. "Now, do you understand what I meant when I said you have always been The One?"

I had to think about all of this. I drew back from her embrace and then drooped into the couch, tilting back my head to lean into the cushions. While staring at the ceiling, I put this new information together. This wasn't about teenagers kissing. This was about wanting someone for a long, long time. Longing for a lifetime.

Once a silly, naïve young girl, I didn't know a thing outside of my world, explicitly about boys. A family of girls didn't have a brother to learn from; so I didn't know what boys really thought or felt. Evidently, Allan always knew what he wanted. Me!

Thank God, Sarah Ann had finally made the truth known.

Reality had a funny, unexpected way of creeping in. I glanced at my hands resting in my lap. "But Sarah Ann, he's dating Cathy Bartholomew. She's everything

I'm not. She's the petite, pretty cheerleader with great big hair and imported tatas. You know the kind."

"So what?" she said matter-of-factly. "I think you know at our age big boobs aren't important. You must remember you're everything she isn't. You're fun-loving, sincere, honest, efficient, warm, and very beautiful. The best friend a girl could ask for."

Thinking of her caring made me smile. I didn't know what to add.

"I don't think Allan likes her," Sarah Ann said and her head moved lightly.

I heard disbelief in her words.

"Something's weird. I don't understand. She doesn't sound like his type. As far as I know, Allan has cared for you for most of his life." She bounced her index finger against her chin as a thoughtful wonder grew in her eyes. "What's really going on?"

My friend grasped both of my hands and made her pitch. "Regardless, Hattie, you have to chase him down. You know you love him. Don't let Allan go. And maybe, someday, we could be what we always wanted to be—real sisters."

Somewhere, deep in my gut, I knew she was right.

"You know what you could lose?"

I knew. Hopes and dreams. I could lose the man of my hopes and dreams.

Chapter Eighteen

Flopping across my bed, I considered what Sarah Ann had confided. Perhaps, on some level, I knew Allan Wellborn and I could be together. He had always known what he wanted—me! I was slower to recognize what I wanted—him.

Thank God, people changed.

Since I now knew Allan had been the young man waiting inside the closet to play the kissing game, I remembered everything with a very different perspective. To prepare for the party, Sarah Ann and I had removed the coats and other stuff people collected for who knows what reason from the closet.

"What are you doing with these things?" Mrs. Wellborn asked.

Sarah Ann managed to placate her.

The closet had plenty of room for two people. At precisely nine-fifteen, she'd crossed off number three and called out number four.

I tucked my glasses in my shorts' pocket. Without them, I couldn't see anything beyond a few inches from my face. But leaving on the glasses would have been a dead giveaway as to who I was.

I took a deep breath while butterflies flicked in my stomach. This is it, I thought, as I licked my lips, tasting my lemonade-flavored lip balm. If Sarah Ann could do this, I could, too, and made my way into the closet.

Once situated inside, I had closed my eyes and recalled hearing "hi" murmured softly by the unknown male. Hands fumbled around my upper arms, pulling me closer. Our tummies touched, and I shivered at the intimate contact. With timidity, I circled my arms around his neck. My cheek slid against his. Then his head turned and his mouth found mine. My First Kiss felt soft, warm, and slippery—thanks to the lip balm.

When we had broken apart, I gasped for air. Then, without warning, he snatched me back to his chest and kissed me more thoroughly.

A heat licked from my head to my toes. Time suspended. Somewhere out there, I heard the soft *ding!* from Mrs. Wellborn's kitchen timer, signaling our fifteen minutes were over.

I remembered an unknown force tore us apart and feeling reluctant about ending. With my chest heaving, I peered into the darkness to see who was in the closet with me, but without the glasses, I couldn't tell except tall, thin, and soapy.

Before exiting the closet, he said a deep and quiet, "Thank you."

Thank you? I wasn't up to par on kissing etiquette; however, saying "thank you" seemed odd to inexperienced me. I didn't utter anything. Flushing due to my ever-present awkwardness, I left in a daze. My First Kiss and looking back, I was glad Allan Wellborn had been the kisser to this kiss-ee.

A small grin curled the corners of my mouth as I recalled he hadn't worn his glasses either. Nowadays, his kisses had improved, being deeper, even more intensified, and his hands gripped into an all deepening and satisfying body exploration.

Boy, did I like that.

For all time, for me—Allan Wellborn.

I considered somewhere on our respective roads through life, we'd selected paths which caused us to be shaped into who we were. Both of us had gone to college. Both had had past relationships. Both had taken detours with jobs. And ultimately, both had circled our ways back to each other, only to diverge again.

Where will life take us next?

I couldn't begin to imagine what would happen. On all man-to-woman levels, I knew I wanted to be with him. One small obstacle remained, but she could be taken care of. Yep, I determined, time to shove Cathy Bartholomew out of the way. The girl would be in the smallest of pieces when I was through with her. I would not lose the man.

****

Once again, Cathy Bartholomew didn't make a guest appearance at work.

When notified, Mr. Northside informed the police she had been missing for several days and had not answered her phone, texts, or emails. They called the complex manager, and together, entered her apartment. Not only did they discover she wasn't at her place, they found not one iota of her belongings. The manager said her place looked rather…sterile.

According to her apartment neighbors, she had moved several days prior, and no one had seen her since.

We found this item interesting as she hadn't told any NLB co-workers she was moving. Or quitting. No nothing.

The police returned to NLB to trace Cathy

Bartholomew's movements.

Mr. Northside wanted to let her family know what had transpired. "Hattie, would you get Cathy Bartholomew's contact number from Human Resources?"

I studied Mr. Northside. His face was an odd color of grayish-white and his hand shook. "Can I get you something, sir? Perhaps, a cup of coffee or a pain reliever?"

"My prescription has disappeared." He shook his head and walked off.

Mr. Northside had had a difficult few weeks.

I wrote the number I'd procured from Human Resources on a note card. I looked at the sequence a second time while an irksome awareness crept up my spine. Previously, this number had been put before me. *But where?* I thumped my pen against the desktop and traced my past days, looking for a prompt.

I tipped my head with light side-to-side rolls while thinking *there I did this. And there I did that.* And so on. When I tracked the second time I'd fed Lucky, an epiphany broke through. I'd placed my handbag on top of a file which lay on Allan's desk. The file—*yea.*

I remembered tugging with my subconscious, deliberating whether or not to take a peek inside. When I had opened it, I found a phone number written on a sheet of paper. Looking at the card for Mr. Northside, I realized the phone number was the same one as Cathy Bartholomew's parents', the one with a Louisiana area code.

Wow. What a huge coincidence.

But why would Allan possess a file with Cathy Bartholomew's parents' phone number? A puzzled thought narrowed my brow into piercing lines, which according to my mother were highly undesirable. I considered. *Wouldn't he have hers in his cell?* Maybe she gave him the number for a silly reason, and he stuck it in the file accidentally.

Is it possible she had been involved in something dreadful in Louisiana? And isn't Louisiana where Allan had spent a lot of time on business trips?

Once again, I heard small strains of office gossip circulating. Whispers made the rounds about men regularly dumping her after getting past her seductiveness and her incredible Miss America-styled body. Some said she was way too possessive, and after knowing someone a short time, she became marriage-minded. Other co-workers said underneath her politeness, she was mean and spiteful—something I'd experienced firsthand on the ride home and at the gym.

Another rumor linked her with Will Christiansen. Maybe they had felt like exploring a relationship. I wondered if NLB had an ethical stance on employees fraternizing, especially a supervisor and his assistant.

So why did he ask me out? Was I just a conquest for him? A momentary thing?

Speculation ran she had been forced to leave her former employer, though no one knew the particulars. The general consensus was she didn't talk about her family, friends, or past life. She did work hard and her skills were well respected, but no one truly liked her enough to be her friend, since she alienated everyone by pontificating on every subject known to mankind.

Fed up, I called Trixie again.

"Hattie, I've been wondering about you." Exasperation laced her tone. "What's happening at

NLB?"

"Trix, I'm really truly ready to find another position. Everyone situated with this company is dying, or hurt, or disappearing."

"I agree those aren't normal working conditions."

"The police have taken my computer and questioned me three times, too."

"Just a few more days, Hattie," Trixie pleaded. "Please? I'm swamped right now. Do it for the paycheck. Please."

I sighed. She was a dear friend and I was easy. Plus an income stream was exceedingly desirable.

I stayed.

****

After work, I drove to the gym for a run and finally achieved two miles on the treadmill. And icky me felt ecstatic with the results. I headed to the women's dressing room for a refreshing shower. And after opening locker number 108…wouldn't you know it?

My underwear had been poached yet again.

Unbelievable.

How on earth did someone get into my locker? Yes, I knew better not to shower at the gym. I'd thought keeping the key with me at all times, even tucking it under the towel which lay on the floor outside of the shower, would cover my ass.

What I get for underestimation. I could have showered at home or changed to a different locker, but…but…but… If…if…if…

Being experienced with going commando was not an attribute.

****

Before going to Allan's to feed Lucky, I made an

unscheduled pit stop at home to put on replacement underwear.

Jenny sat at the kitchen table, eating a Waldorf salad she'd picked up at the Super Saver's Grocery Store's gourmet take-out on her way home from work.

Since my game plan never included going without food, I hoped I could pilfer some of hers. Laying on thick compliments would help, too. "Mmm, that looks delicious. That deli makes the best salads. My mouth is watering just staring at your dinner."

She nodded. "It's pretty good." She stabbed lettuce and crunched.

Maybe I'd been too subtle. "Are you eating the whole salad by your lonesome?"

"Ha. I was until you showed." She gave me a knowing look and set aside her copy of *About Moi* magazine.

Jenny knew I would talk her into sharing. I retrieved a fork and a glass of water. She slid her plate to the middle of the table, and I helped myself. "Thanks."

"I think we should talk about the bad things at the firm." She speared a chunk of cubed apple.

"Okay, but pass the pepper." With a liberal hand, I sprinkled cracked black pepper over my portion. "Shoot."

Her right hand index finger shot up, counting count one. "First, Phil Meadows is found dead, possibly poisoned."

"Correct."

Two fingers up. "Second, Will Christiansen is found dead in bed, possibly poisoned by the cup of coffee on his bedside table."

I flicked my fork in a "continue on" expression. "Again, correct."

Three fingers stuck up. "Third, Stuart Steems is pushed down the stairwell at work."

"Okay," I said, "now we know exactly what happened to these guys, but what we don't know is the why."

"Wait a minute. I'm not finished." Four fingers popped up. "Four, Cathy Bartholomew is missing."

I raised my hand to cut short her analysis. "Wait a minute. Why would you think it's important to note Cathy Bartholomew is missing? Is her absence connected to the guys?"

Jenny frowned. Her fork plopped on her plate. She rested her chin in her left hand and stared. "I'm not sure. Let's just leave her in the equation for now. There's a connection between these people."

"I haven't a clue what. When you figure it out, let me know."

Her index finger pounced on the table next to her plate. "Think for a minute, Hattie. You're working at NLB. You know these people. Who is intimate with Phil, Will, and Stuart?"

"And Cathy Bartholomew."

"Her, too."

"Well, lots, especially the people at NLB."

"Do you know if they have any other connection besides work?"

I pondered her question. "I don't know since I haven't been employed with NLB long enough. Besides, Phil was brand new to the firm. I don't think he even knew all of our co-workers."

I stabbed my fork into the salad. Around my

mouthful, I said, "Let's see. Cathy worked for Will, and Phil worked for Stuart. And Stuart and Will are Senior Audit Managers."

Jenny picked up her fork again and idly twirled it in the salad. "Who could be associated with them in order to kill them?"

I began recounting events with Phil Meadows. Phil and I ate lunch. We talked. I visited with him another time at lunch. Left. Yadayadayada. Afterwards, he was found dead, possibly from a tainted cup of coffee. I remembered Cathy Bartholomew had entered the lunchroom as I left.

Then, my recollections turned to Will Christiansen with whom I had an awesome weekend-long affair. He was highly respected by our boss, Mr. Northside. Then he didn't show for work, and his assistant, Cathy Bartholomew, made several attempts to contact him. He died, possibly by a tainted cup of coffee. And an unusual rumor circulated Will and Cathy had been more than friends.

Stuart and I had met outside the connecting stairwell and talked about his new suit and football winnings. As I left, I said "hi" to Cathy Bartholomew as I passed her in the hallway outside the stairwell. I made a small remark about lucky Stuart winning the football betting game. Cathy Bartholomew used the stairwell also.

Cathy Bartholomew was missing. She hailed from Louisiana. And Allan dated her. He'd left a file on his desk with her parent's phone number on a piece of paper. And the number I gave Mr. Northside was the same one within the file.

Click.

A great fear froze my whole being. *This isn't good.* My heart nose-dived to my stomach. My breath sucked from my chest. The bad guy was right in front of me the whole time.

Jenny stopped eating. "Hattie, you look funny like you're scared. Something's wrong. What is it?"

I turned my head slowly toward her. She'd fixed a very concerned look on me. "I know who connects the three."

Wide-eyed, Jenny swallowed deeply. "Who?"

Chapter Nineteen

With a quick, hasty motion, I jerked to my feet. My chair hit the floor with a clatter. I raced around the room in a reckless fashion, banging my arm, then my leg, and my foot against furniture while I searched for my handbag. I swept books, magazines, any and everything to the floor.

Desperately, I needed my keys.

Desperately, I needed to get to Allan Wellborn.

Jenny twisted in her chair from left to right, watching my wild search. "Hattie, what are you doing? Where are you going? Why are you tearing up the apartment? Who will clean up this mess?" And in a louder pitch, she said, "Who connects all three?"

"Oh, Jenny, I think I know. It's the notes." I threw the answer over my shoulder as I raced around the apartment. "I think Cathy Bartholomew's killing people. I think she's the one who poisoned Phil and Will and pushed Stuart down the stairs. In fact, I'm positive she's the bad girl."

God, I couldn't be any more stupid. *Stupid, stupid, stupid.* Cathy Bartholomew had been right in front of me the whole time. I saw her after visiting with Phil and Stuart. She was Will's assistant, and I believe she went to his apartment the Sunday afternoon he and I had spent together. Most importantly of all, she was Allan Wellborn's girlfriend.

The ideas raging in my head about where this was headed weren't good.

"Cathy Bartholomew didn't come to work today. And Allan's late calling me. Like clockwork, he checks on Lucky. I'm so scared."

"Lord!" Jenny said. "Are you thinking—"

"I think Cathy Bartholomew was the one who wrote the tacky poems about the '*ho* and the '*ho* is me." I pointed to my chest. "I think she has killed two men, and I'm afraid the next one is Allan." I paused and stared. "Oh my God, Jenny, what if she has done something to Allan?"

The keys were on the counter right where I had left them. With a greedy snatch and with speed I've never shown on the treadmill, I dashed to the door.

Jenny said, "I'm calling the police."

****

I dashed to my car. The cool breeze rushed in through my open window as I stomped on the Jeep's pedal and sped my way to Allan's apartment, ignoring yellow lights, hoping the police wouldn't pull me over.

My brain was possessed. All I could think of was getting to him. All I could think of was Cathy Bartholomew fixing him a coffee cocktail. All I could think of was him dead.

How unbearable. I swallowed a slug of fear. I didn't want to lose what I'd just found. The worrisome tears which fell from my eyes and littered my cheeks were brushed aside. Remembering Sarah Anne's words about "stop being a crybaby," I concentrated on my driving. A blithering idiot would be useless help.

Finally, I turned into his apartment's lot and slammed my car's transmission into park. My gaze grazed over the cars and locked on his granite-colored 4-Runner not far from his front door. I studied Allan's window to see if possibly anything—something— anything could be taking place inside.

Did I see a shadow flit in the shrubberies? I tensed and looked again.

Maybe I was mistaken after all. Maybe I was overreacting. Maybe he was home, and everything would be okay. "Is the air conditioning causing the curtains to ripple?"

Feeling a little relieved, I exited the Jeep. I rapped on the door and waited for an answer. But he didn't answer. *Okay, he could be showering or on the phone and didn't hear me.*

Using the same key he'd lent me for cat-sitting, I let myself inside. A peculiar, almost uncertain feeling, like an intuition one gets when on edge, had me being very careful as I quietly shut the door behind me.

I took three steps from the apartment doorway into the living area and what I saw terrified me. On the floor next to the computer desk laid Allan. I dashed to his side and squatted, touching his upper arm. He appeared to be unconscious. His head dipped to his right and his eyes were shut. His wrists and ankles were bound with duct tape. My fingers slipped to the groove along his trachea and I checked his pulse. Still beating.

Not sure what to do, I smoothed my other hand over his forehead with an instinctive, caring gesture. Softly, I said, "Allan."

He didn't respond.

I looked closer at his right shoulder and discovered he had been shot.

Blood stained his clothing and the wound had

pretty much ceased bleeding. His facial coloring didn't have the usual healthy glow. His breathing appeared normal, or sketchy—I couldn't tell. I was no expert on gunshot wounds, but he appeared to be mostly okay. *If only he'd open his eyes.* I explored his shoulder with a tentative touch.

"Allan," I said again, hoping my voice would call him back to me. He still didn't answer. I continued to pat his arm and think. Then a creepy feeling inched up my back, causing me to stiffen.

"Hello, Hattie."

Something slammed into my back, causing my body to sway. My head narrowly missed hitting the desk chair as I crumpled to the floor right next to Allan's shoulder.

After an unknown bit, I came to. I blinked several times, bringing my surroundings into a hazy focus. The pounding in my head hurt like hell. I touched the lump on the left side of my head, thankfully, not near my temple.

Cathy Bartholomew stood with Allan's gun aimed right at me. I curled my legs and shifted myself to a hip sit. My tongue tasted like cotton balls, and I managed to control the urge to vomit by shutting my eyes and swallowing. I cradled the side of my head upright. "Cathy. What…did you…do?"

No reply. She watched and waited.

"Did you…shoot…Allan?"

Still no answer.

"Why?"

Surveying the room, I was astonished to find underwear strewn around. Most I recognized as mine. Then two plus two added up to Cathy Bartholomew was who had swiped Jenny's and my underwear from the gym. "Why are my under things here?"

"I stole them," she said.

Calculated. Cool. Calm.

"I charmed the master key from the towel guy."

God, my head hurt. I had sorrowful feelings for the towel boy who unquestionably would lose his job. Cathy had used her womanly wiles on him and hit pay dirt. "Why?"

"Please, don't act so stupid. I know better, Harriette Lee Cooks."

I shook my head and a sharp pain shot through it, sending a white light to my eyes. I wasn't a wussy, yet this really stung. I lightly probed my hairline.

"You know what's going on here. I've been waiting for you. I knew you would come. You can't stay away from him." After a moment passed, she said, "I had no idea how much fun I'd have watching you squirm."

In an instant, I understood why Cathy Bartholomew did all of this. She was very twisted with jealousy. In an incomprehensible way, she extracted a strange revenge by targeting the men with whom I'd had a connection.

"And don't forget this…" She kicked my knee.

"Ow!"

"And this…" Using her teeth, she ripped open a two-pound M&M package, presumably one Allan had stored in the top of his closet.

I watched in revulsion as she danced around, shaking the perfect chocolate treats over the carpet. When finished with the bag, she tore open a second one and spread it around as well.

What a waste of good candy.

The sweet tang of chocolate penetrated my head and sent my tummy roiling. Again, I batted my eyes and gulped, wishing all of this would disappear.

She re-gripped his gun. "It's supposed to be me."

I gave her a one-eyed squint. "You're supposed to be what?"

"I'm supposed to be his girlfriend." Her thumb stabbed her chest. "Me. Me. Me. Allan should love me."

Her voice lowered with a note of despondency. My body slanted away.

"But he doesn't. At your birthday party, he couldn't keep his eyes off you." Her mouth pouted. "Not even when we danced. You. Not me."

She refocused on me. "Other men react in a similar fashion. Why is that? Why would they like you? Why would someone want *you* when they could have"— Cathy Bartholomew's free hand swooped in a downward stroke—"me?"

With calculated steps, she circled the area where Allan lay and I waited. "Look at you. You aren't beautiful. You aren't talented. You can't even keep a job. God knows why you're here. You take up warped space until someone like me can get rid of you."

Her pointing the gun at my head boosted my fear. "What are you talking about?" I asked.

"Don't play games with me, missy. This began at the Italian restaurant. The dinner with your 'Funsisters.' I noticed when you spied us and knew at the precise moment you were an old flame. His whole attention diverted to you. You sparkled. Meanwhile, there I sat with him growing terribly unhappy as he watched you and your friends having a good time."

I watched her every move, and a peach-pit hardness tightened in my belly. Seeing them together had hurt me more than anything I'd known.

"I wanted Allan from the moment I laid eyes on him. He's perfect. And I knew I couldn't let you"—she gestured with the gun—"get in the way of what I wanted. I warned you to stay away from him. Remember? At the gym? Remember what I told you? He. Is. Mine."

If he was hers, then why had she shot him? You don't hurt someone you love by shooting them.

Slowly, Cathy Bartholomew walked closer.

She was crazy insane with resentment and jealousy. I could be next on her to-do list. I took a deep swallow of dread, searching the room for something to stop her.

Maybe I could grab...

Nothing there.

Maybe I could knock his gun from her hand...

No way. I was too scared to even think of doing this.

Oh God, please, help me think of something. Allan moaned and I turned to check on him, returning my hand to his forearm. After a moment, he settled. I set my gaze on her again.

Intimidated with a gun pointing at me, I lied to save my hide, "Cathy, you're so wrong. Allan and I were never a couple. Not really. We ate pizza and partied once. Nothing more."

Her eyes narrowed. Her grip tightened on the gun. She shifted her feet. "I-don't-think-so. You turned up like a putrid penny everywhere I went. Everyone I met.

Everyone knew you."

Cathy Bartholomew standing over me wasn't ideal. I had to think of something fast.

"You want to know how I knew?"

I nodded.

"I found your pink underwear."

Oh, shit. I bit my lower lip to stall the screams threatening to explode.

She nodded. "Yes, ma'am, the pink lacey panties which lay in his drawer next to his underwear. Only they aren't there right now—are they, Hattie? I checked. They aren't. I found them when I snooped the night Allan fixed me dinner. We ate spaghetti, watched a movie, and smooched on his sofa. We came this close to making love. I was so ready, juicy, hot. I rubbed his crotch"—her mouth twisted to one side—"only he stopped me and stood, saying he had to take me home, because he had to be at work early."

I'd been right about the date when I searched his kitchen and found the dirty dishes. But the chunk about them nearly having sex had me wanting to spew my guts. I so didn't need to know about her libido.

"Did you take the undies, Hattie?" She leveled her shoulders and took on an "I know everything" face. "Here's what I think. You"—she lifted the gun barrel—"had sex with Allan and at some point, the panties were left behind."

"Why do you think they're mine?"

"I'm not stupid, girlfriend. Anyone can see how he feels about you. The panties are yours. You found them in the drawer next to his underwear. You took them back when you cat-sat."

Not much else I could say. She had figured out

everything.

She cocked her head. "I didn't get why he wouldn't have sex with me. Allan is supposed to love me. *My* panties should have been in his drawer. Not yours. I did the only thing I could. I had to stop his fascination with you."

"But, Cathy, men never obsess over me. They like girls like you. You're perfect."

She stomped on my leg. "Shut up. You don't know what the hell you're talking about."

Gasping, I grabbed my calf and scuttled next to the chair.

"I found the underwear. After we ate, Allan drove to the convenience store to rent a movie. Of course, I rummaged through his belongings, his clothing, and his drawers. Doesn't everyone? Imagine my surprise when I found what you'd left behind."

Her brows creased. "Why would a guy keep a woman's bikinis if he didn't care about her? That's when I knew you had to be punished."

Punished? I had no words. My mind went blank. I wished for help. But the only help coming would be whomever Jenny had called. *Please hurry.*

Cathy hadn't confessed a word about what I suspected she had done. I had to know. "Cathy, did you kill Phil and Will and push Stuart down the stairs?"

"Ha, brain-child. I've killed more than those two idiots."

I held the breath I'd sucked in and froze. Did Cathy Bartholomew just admit she killed other men? *Oh God,* I prayed with desperation, *wherever You are, You're needed now.*

The apartment door opened and in walked Mr.

Northside.

What is he doing here? I was afraid to say anything because he could have hooked up with her.

He took in the gun, the injured cop, and me. Then his astonished gaze settled on Cathy Bartholomew. "Cathy, what have you done?"

She flew to his side. "I took care of them, just like you asked Hiram."

His eyes rounded. "I—what?"

"Didn't you want me to—" She took two steps away from him, cocked her head. Confusion rooted in her eyes.

"God, Cathy, you misunderstood. I wanted to be with you, but not like this."

Mr. Northside and Cathy? But what about Allan? Is she really mental?

"But you said they knew about us and needed to be taken care of—"

"Cathy, I could have reassigned Will and Phil. Not have you murder them."

Her mouth dropped open. "I thought you wanted them to die. I thought you loved me."

"You think every man who talks to you loves you." He took a few steps toward her, palm up. "Give me the gun."

With a mixed-up cloud in her crinkled eyes, she shook her head and stepped back. "I don't know—"

"Cathy, hand over the gun. We'll get you some help—"

"Help? I don't understand. I don't need any help." Her forehead crunched, and she wiped her free hand up her nose and over her eye. "I'm f-fine. Really I am."

"Please, Mr. Northside," I said very softly. "Can't

you do something?"

His head went from side-to-side.

Cathy was in la-la land, and Mr. Northside wouldn't or couldn't help. I found no comfort in that. Instead, my stomach boiled and churned.

Guess I'd have to think of something to stop her.

Allan rolled with a restless stirring. If only I had some means to comfort him. Slowly, I tucked my legs under me and squatted as I pretended to minister to him. Stroke here. Stroke there. Meanwhile, I kept an eye on Cathy Bartholomew and Mr. Northside. Maybe I could distract her with a confession of my own. "Okay, you got me, Cathy."

My saying her name caused something to register. She faced me and waited.

"I did go through Allan's stuff. I took my underwear because I was cutting all ties with him. I'm not proud I searched through his things. I violated his privacy."

Liar, liar, pants on fire.

Cathy Bartholomew zeroed in like a kamikaze pilot on her target. I watched her very carefully, steadying myself. Time to be a big girl. The gun quivered slightly in her hand.

Now! Thrusting my hands at her knees, I shoved her with all my might, knocking her backward toward the sofa. Her arm flung upward. The gun discharged into a down pillow on the couch. White feathers floated playfully.

I kept pushing.

Mr. Northside scrambled over to the couch's arm, but before he could twist the firearm out of her hand, a second shot discharged, hitting him. He said, "Eh," and dropped.

I didn't stop. The urge to kill claimed my mind. I thrusted harder. The gun fell from her grasp as her body dove between the couch and the coffee table. The sound of her head cracking against the corner caused me to flinch. But I didn't stop. I rammed her into the hardwood floor. And finally, Cathy Bartholomew stilled.

As if waking from a bad dream, the clouds of chaos parted. I found my hands on her knees, and my body poised over hers. I picked up the gun which lay by her side and slid it into the kitchen. I blinked several times when somewhere, out there, the scream of sirens assailed my ears.

Standing, my foot fumbled on something—a roll of duct tape. Good old duct tape with about a billion uses. While thanking God for Trixie's valuable handbook, I tore strips of tape with unsteady hands and bound Cathy Bartholomew's limbs, mimicking her job on Allan.

After I'd finished, I released the spool and stepped away, only stopping when my back bumped the bookcases. My body started shaking like a tower of strawberry-and-lime gelatin confection, and I coasted down the bookshelves to my bottom. My head hurt unbearably. The urge to vomit clawed at my throat. I looked around at what Cathy Bartholomew had done and sniffed back a tear, a nervous one from someone who wasn't used to doing what was needed in unusual circumstances.

Stop being a crybaby.

I glanced at Allan. I crawled to his side. I smoothed my hand over his forehead. Using my fingernail, I scraped a corner of tape away from his skin. "Please,

Allan, be all right. Please wake up. God, I need you. Please, Allan."

The door behind me flung open. "Police."

Thank God. I looked over my shoulder.

"Freeze."

Gladly. Rotating, I raised my arms above my head like a bad guy from a cop drama.

The two policemen surveyed the scene.

The first one said, "Wow. Did it snow?"

This reference was to the white feathery pillow down floating around like a playful snowstorm.

"Looks like a kinky party and I wasn't invited. There's candy and underwear everywhere. I didn't know Allan was that kind of guy."

As the second one walked toward me, he holstered his gun. His shoes squashed into the treats, making a crunchy noise. All the chocolate turned to rubbish. And now, the carpet would have to be cleaned.

He hunkered down next to Allan's side, felt his forehead, and then checked the shoulder wound. He noticed my arms lifted above my head. "You can lower your arms."

The stocky cop glanced at me. "Ma'am? Are you all right?"

Finally, something registered in my head, and I let my arms fall to my side. "Huh?"

"I asked if you're all right." He motioned to the mess on the floor. "What happened?"

"She hit me with his gun." Desperately, I needed a drink of water. I swallowed. "Allan and Mr. Northside need to go to the hospital."

"EMS is right behind us." Then he took a pad and pen from his pocket. "And who are you?"

"Hattie Cooks."

"Allan's mentioned you. Aren't you his girlfriend?"

"Cat-sitter—" *Where is Lucky?* He must have gone upstairs to hide.

"And who's this girl?" He pointed his pen at Cathy.

"Cathy Bartholomew. They've been dating. She"— I pointed a shaky finger at her turkey-trussed body— "was angry. Threw stuff. Shot Allan."

He scribbled down what I'd said then lifted his gaze a fraction. "And the other man my associate is tending to?"

"She shot him, too. Hiram Northside, managing partner Northside, Lancaster, and Brookside, Accountants. Our boss." I didn't care to talk about him. "Is Allan okay?"

"We'll know soon enough."

"Please, call his mom." Automatically, I rattled off the number I'd known for as long as I could remember.

"Can do."

While we waited, the cop cut away the tape from Allan's ankles. The sound of the ambulance's sirens grew louder with its approach. I couldn't stop looking at Allan. His lips parted, and his mouth moved ever so slightly. *Had he murmured my name?*

Two more cops entered and stood over Cathy Bartholomew. "What happened here? Who taped her up?"

I squared my shoulders. "I did."

"I like your style."

"Wellborn's down," the first guy said.

"Aw, shit." The second of this new duo pointed at

307

me. "Who's she?"

"Hattie Cooks. I think Wellborn has mentioned her."

"Something about dating her."

EMS barged in and took control.

I managed to stand and shift to the front window to wait. Surely, Jenny should be here by now.

After Allan's vitals had been checked, EMS loaded him on the gurney thing they used.

I took a slight step in their direction but spotted the detective's raised hand, making me wait.

Mr. Northside had been tended to and as he was about to roll by, he lifted his hand and the paramedics halted.

For a long while, we stared at each other. I didn't know where to begin. I saw on his face a grim expression. "Why?"

"I don't know. I'm just an accountant." His mouth fashioned a bare smile, just a tiny tilt to the corners.

At that moment, I detested Mr. Northside.

The EMS rolled him away. The metal doors slammed and with sirens and flashing lights, the vehicles sped away into the twilight.

Anxiety killed me. All I could do was wait.

A cop saw me touching my head. "You're hurt."

I felt the sore spot. "A little. She hit me. Blacked out some."

He shone a penlight in my eyes, and then examined my head. "No cuts, big bump. You don't appear to have a concussion. Do you want to go to the hospital and get checked?"

My head went no-no-no. "I'll be okay."

He opened the freezer compartment of Allan's

fridge and took something out. With a gentle move, he held a paper-wrapped ice pop to my goose egg. "You're sure?"

I set my hand over his and held the treat against my head. The cold relieved the ache. "Sure. I need to find Allan's cat and go home."

"Someone there to watch you?"

"My roommate."

He slanted his head. "Allan has a cat?"

I nodded. "Yes, a big fluffy gray one. He likes to hide under the bed upstairs."

"I'll check."

I set the ice pop on a bookshelf and watched the cop go up the stairs, saying "Here, kitty-kitty." He disappeared into the bedroom, and three minutes later, he came out, cradling Lucky in his arms. Great relief spilled over me when the cop pressed the cat in my arms.

Satisfied, he returned to the team working on Cathy Bartholomew. "She has a bump on the back of her head," the paramedic said. "But she'll be fine. We have to take her in, though, for a brain scan. Just routine."

The cop bobbed his head. "When she's okay, we'll transfer her to jail; then she'll be booked."

Moments later out rolled Cathy Bartholomew.

I murmured in Lucky's fur, "Good riddance. And please, lock up the filthy bitch."

The detectives from the Stuart, Phil, and Will cases arrived. They spoke with the cops who had arrived first on the scene. Then, they noticed me standing by the window.

One gestured my way with his pen and said to the other, "Isn't this girl the same one Wellborn stopped for a taillight out a few months ago?"

"She's Hattie Cooks." The detective flipped the pages of his notebook. "I interviewed her the other day at NLB."

"I think he's dating her."

Didn't the detectives mean Allan dated Cathy Bartholomew? I wanted to clarify their mistakes, but I wasn't capable of uttering anything.

Like bad guys in an old western movie chasing a wagon train, the group circled around me, discharging questions about what exactly had transpired.

"What happened?"

"Wasn't the other woman Cathy Bartholomew?"

"How do you know Allan Wellborn?"

My hands quaked. I squeezed Lucky hard. He meowed. I was only capable of vague answers.

Jenny peeked in the doorway. "Hattie. Hattie." Ducking under the crime scene tape, she picked her way across the threshold. "Hattie."

At the sound of my name, I focused on her, sensing welling tears. Lucky and I ran to my best friend. "Jenny."

She forced her way past the police and threw her arms around me and the cat. "Are you all right?"

My body trembled. "Not really."

Jenny looped her arms tighter around my waist, and I did what Sarah Ann had told me not to.

I cried like a crybaby.

Chapter Twenty

After routine questioning over the meaty bones of what had taken place, the detectives suggested Jenny take me home. They said they would contact me later to take a formal statement.

Fine by me.

Jenny, Lucky, and I shuffled our way through Allan's unsightly apartment. At the door, I took one last glance at the candy, feathers, and underwear. I may never again eat my favorite treat.

Jenny shifted closer to my side. In my ear, she asked in a soft voice, "What is it?"

I shook my head. "Nothing. Let's go."

With her arm supporting me, we walked toward her car.

I shrugged away. "I'm okay. I can drive myself home."

"Want me to take Lucky?"

"Thanks." I set him in her arms. "I can barely manage myself right now."

Jenny protested a little, but I convinced her I could.

"It's less than ten minutes away. I don't have a concussion, just an extra large owie. I'll follow you." I unlocked the Jeep's door and climbed inside, tugging it shut. I cranked the engine and followed Jenny for a few blocks.

I can't explain what happened next. I made a right

turn and drove without thinking….without good judgment…and ultimately, without consideration of any consequences, to the highway. I continued my journey and the next thing I knew, I was in Bayston, knocking on my cousin Corrinne's front door at one in the morning. A three-hour drive had passed, and I had no idea about how I'd done it. Only God knew how I even had enough gas to get there.

Corrinne opened her front door and squinted with the creases of interrupted sleep marring her face. "Oh." She threw her arms around me and held me tight. After another fierce assessment, she dragged me inside. "Harriette Lee Cooks, you scared the life out of me. Everyone is looking for you. I jerked aside the bedroom curtains when I heard a car stop and ran downstairs as fast as I could when I saw it was you. The whole family and friends are very worried. Everyone is texting everyone."

She examined me by running her hands down my shoulders and then the length of my arms. "Are you all right? Your body seems chilled."

She led me to the couch where we sat. Reaching behind her, she grabbed a crocheted lap blanket from the back of the couch and draped it over my shoulders.

Instantly, comfort swathed my body and only then did my whole being soften in increments.

She went to the kitchen and returned with a steaming mug. "Drink this. Chamomile tea. Always helps me."

I took a few sips. The warm liquid penetrated my insides. I sipped more and one-half a cup later, an awareness from fingertips to toes crossed over me. Tea was a good cure-all.

Corrinne fiddled with the lump on the side of my head.

The pain returned, and I curved away. "Ouch!"

"I'll be right back with something for the swelling," she said.

I heard the fridge door open and her rummaging around.

She returned with an ice pack.

Corrinne filled me in on what had emerged during my three-hour drive as she handed me a napkin and pressed the pack to my head. Half-listening, I sipped my drink. When finished, I gave her the cup and took the frozen thing shaped like an apple from her and wrapped it in the napkin.

She said she'd heard from Mom who'd heard from Jenny and Mrs. Wellborn. She said his mother was eternally grateful I'd rescued Allan.

Maybe Mrs. Wellborn won't look at me so weirdly any more.

The last anyone knew, I'd hopped in my Jeep to follow Jenny to our apartment and then, I'd vanished. A chill settled on me again.

"We've been so worried," Corrinne said. "Is it okay to call your Mom and tell her you're here? She'll probably want to talk to you."

I gave an affirming nod and braced myself for Mom's wrath.

While I listened to Corrine ask and answer, I rolled to my side and rested. Instinctively, I tucked my legs to my tummy like I do when sleeping. Exhaustion took over. The ice pack fell to the floor. Straight away, I dropped into a deep sleep, thus unconsciously thwarting Mom's lecture plans.

****

I awoke around ten in the morning, something I didn't normally do. I fluttered open my eyes to find my nurse-friend studying me.

When she noticed me stirring about, she handed me two over-the-counter pain relievers and a glass of water. "I called Maggie, and she said it was okay to take this stuff." She examined my head. "Fine, no stitches required."

I swallowed the pills and promptly fell asleep again. When I did rouse around lunch time, I spotted two sets of itty bitty eyes, examining me up close and personal. I brought into focus Corrinne's daughter, Lillie, and son, Joseph. They stood next to the sofa, holding hands, and staring.

"Hi." My voice cracked in a froggy croak.

Startled, Lillie and Joseph ran away, screaming, "Momm-mieee, Mommmiee," throughout the house.

The shrill little voices sent a dull throb to my temples. My fingers pushed circles on the spots to ease the ache. Maybe bad breath and Hattie looking witchy and scary was what frightened them.

Corrinne walked over to the sofa. While drying a saucepan, she studied me. "How's your head?"

Lightly, I touched the bump. "Almost gone. I'm just tired. Exhausted. Can I stay here for a while?"

"Sure. You need more rest."

"Hungry?"

"Famished. I want a burger."

She stared at me. "You want to eat...a hamburger?"

"Yes. I was wondering... Would it be okay if we stopped at the superstore and bought some stuff? I need clean underwear." I couldn't believe I'd mentioned undies. Yet, it was the truth. Cathy Bartholomew had depleted my supply and I hadn't any with me. "And get me food? My treat for you and the kids."

She grinned. "Not a problem."

Corrinne loaded Lillie and Joseph in their car seats secured in her Cherokee's back seat, and we drove to the store.

I stocked up a supply of malt balls, soda, some clothing, and toiletries. To make up for the witchy and scary part, I let the little 'uns pick out a cartoon DVD they didn't own. We hit the fast food joint in the parking lot. I wolfed down my share.

Back at Corrinne's, I carefully washed my hair, avoiding the tender spot on my head. I changed into the newly purchased black sweatpants and a long-sleeved, white T-shirt. I froze my favorite drink to a slushy, popped two more tablets, and parked my body on the couch.

Every time I closed my eyes, the last twenty-four hours played like a bad videotape jammed in a VCR. Over and over, the nightmare repeated. These kinds of dramatic situations don't really sink in at first. And the more I sat, the more I became…unsettled.

Lillie, Joseph, and I watched a children's show with puppets, another featuring a small girl who traveled, and other educational programs. Sometimes, the kids would climb over me in play. We would laugh and giggle. Perhaps, subconsciously, I wanted to substitute the bad memories with happier ones, utilizing the saying "it takes ten good things to replace one bad one." And all the while I ate candy, drank pop, and let my body find a way to repair.

What really happened was Corrinne's kids watched cousin Hattie take a mental vacation.

A professional might have classified me as clinically depressed or blue or paranoid. But I tended to think of my down time as regrouping, letting the magic of time heal. I craved blue sky. A warm breeze. Rustling trees. Serenity. And when done with that, I camped on the couch and, on occasion, visited the bathroom, or ate more gourmet malt balls.

After a few days of television, bad cure-all, and the freaky bag-lady act, Corrinne plopped beside me on the couch and took my hands in hers. "We need to talk."

I sorta knew what was coming.

"Hattie, it's time for you to go home."

Her words were edged with a firm tone.

"You're scaring Lillie and Joseph with the TV and chocolate and sodas, not to mention what a bad example you are. They won't even eat veggies any more. You don't do anything except barely go to the bathroom and the guest bedroom. You aren't eating right or sleeping well. This isn't normal behavior and certainly not normal for you. And my house smells like...well, worse than poopy diapers...sorta man-smelly. You need to go home and get on with your life."

She was right. I couldn't protest. I sniffed my armpit. She was right about the man-smell as well. I'd forgotten to buy deodorant. "I guess vacay is over."

Corrinne laughed and slipped an arm around my shoulders. "I know everything which has happened isn't what happens to average people. I can't begin to understand how deeply you're affected by the whole incident. I know you're upset. I wish I could take your hurt and pain away."

I was upset, but that wasn't why I didn't want to go home.

"You were incredibly brave to confront the Bimbo and save Allan. I don't know if I could have done what you did. You faced danger, and in doing so, you saved his life."

Hearing Sarah Ann's "don't be a crybaby" refrain in my head, I stifled a hurt surfacing in my chest.

She lightly cradled my cheeks in her palms. "You're the best—the best sister, the best friend, the best cousin. You're determined, despite your occasional shy episodes. I'm probably not the right person to counsel you about this, but I think you have to handle whatever is bothering you." She grasped my hands in comfort.

I scrunched my face, and then scratched my nose.

"Look at me," Corrinne said.

Her rough talk took me by surprise. She wasn't one to say ugly things.

"Are you afraid of something? I'm asking because I'm worried. I take great joy in being with you. You would do anything and everything for everyone, and we would do anything and everything for you. You have a very interesting life. And in my opinion, you have a man who loves you."

Startled, I lifted my head and stared. "No."

"Yes, he does. I truly believe Allan loves you and always has. Everyone else has been thinking the same thing. While you've sat here comatose, I've been fielding phone calls. Allan's flat on his back at his mom's and asking for you. Do you know what that means?"

He needs someone to ride to the rescue and save him from his mother? I shook my head and let a bare grin curl the corners of my mouth.

Corrinne gave my shoulders a little jiggle. "Yes, you do. Stop ignoring the obvious. Allan wants you. He wants to see you. You have to go home."

The dam in me burst wide open. I curled my lower lip under my upper teeth before replying, "He was almost killed because of me."

"No, Hattie. Allan was almost killed by an insane, jealous woman who craved attention from every man."

I stared at my cousin.

"Just because she fixated her crazy jealousy on you does not mean you're responsible for what she did."

I knew she was right. The ol' dilemma churned inside me. "If Allan hadn't been mixed up with me, she wouldn't have been j-jealous. He wouldn't have been shot."

"Wasn't Allan dating Cathy Bartholomew *after* you threw him out?"

"Yes." I gave this question more consideration then said a more affirmative, "Yes."

"I think it's possible, considering her background, she would have fixated on any woman he's friends with."

"Maybe." I crooked my mouth. "I guess."

"Hattie, just a few months ago, he almost got you killed."

Corrinne was right again.

"I give up." Her hands flew up. "I think you two are made for each other. I love you. You're always welcome here, but right now, I'm throwing you out. Vacation is over. Go home, and have great sex with your man."

I let a smile quirk my mouth. "Jenny said he must be a masochist."

Chapter Twenty-One

I returned from Corrinne's in Bayston. All the while, Allan had been recuperating for a fourth day at his parents'. Jenny had sent a gift bag filled with Oreos and a coupon for milk, something he would appreciate, and had taken Lucky to his mother's.

From the reports circulated by the Moms Always Know Network, I heard he felt a little weak but was mending nicely. The bullet had jammed in his shoulder, and fortunately, considering the caliber and the complicated shoulder area of tendons and bones, did minimal damage.

Mom told me Mrs. Wellborn said he had a hole-y looking, puckery scar. He would be out of work for six weeks, maybe more. After he'd rested, he would have physical therapy. The doctor had to evaluate him for clearance to return to work. He might have to see a psychiatrist to determine if he was mentally fit for police duty.

Allan survived the gunshot. The real question inquiring minds wanted to know was would he survive his mother?

Jenny kept me posted on the events which had followed the night I drove to Bayston. "Cathy Bartholomew remains in jail, and fully recovered from the crack on the head, but not in her right mind. While being transported by ambulance to the hospital, she regained consciousness and screamed like a loony tune, 'Al-lan, Al-lan, Al-lan,' over and over."

"Sounds scary," I said, taking another bite of vanilla ice cream with chocolate and caramel swirls.

She nodded. "I'm glad I wasn't there. The EMS guys restrained her as she thrashed with wild and unpredictable body twists."

I spooned another mouthful. "Strong from her workouts."

"Allan had taken the business trips to Cathy Bartholomew's hometown in Louisiana to get background information from the local police. They were investigating the murders of two other accounting professionals who could have been poisoned by none other than…Cathy Bartholomew."

What a crazy 'ho—to use her favorite word.

"The Louisiana police suspected her, but they had no real evidence. They had reason to believe she had headed for a large town to find employment in the accounting profession. They dispatched a bulletin, notifying all nearby law enforcement agencies in an attempt to locate her.

"Allan met her by accident at a local bar. He bought her a drink—at her insistence—and gave her his phone number—at her insistence. The Louisiana police expressed interest in her whereabouts, and the Sommerville police noticed, and everyone decided he should monitor her.

To him, she mentioned her Louisiana upbringing and past employment. No evidence had showed she possessed a predilection for prescription drugs and connected her to the coffee cups found on the victim's bedside tables. No fingerprints. No eyewitnesses. No

DNA. No nothing. Just suspicions."

Cathy Bartholomew was a first-rate mixologist. She concocted an Alprazolam and Oxcontin coffee cocktail. But she wasn't good at covering her tracks.

I went to the sink and rinsed my bowl, setting it in the dishwasher. I was aware Jenny watched me to gauge how much and how she should shovel out the rest of the story.

"Ahem," she said. "To continue. The Sommerville PD checked her laptop and determined she had purchased the Oxy from a Mexican internet pharmacy and had lifted Mr. Northside's Alprazolam prescription."

I returned to the island, bumped my back against the granite top and thought. "With her jealousy of me as a catalyst and Mr. Northside's off-handed remark about laying off employees, she began her plotting and planning. By coincidence, I'd connected her to Stuart, Will, and Phil.

"Phil had told her of eating lunch with me. She freaked and offered to fix him a cup of coffee. She slipped the blend in the coffee. He overdosed and was found a few hours later."

"Yes," Jenny said.

"Will let slip accidentally he and I'd had fun-filled sex weekend. In another of her wild rages, she confessed she had gone to his apartment. Poor Will became her next victim."

"Exactly." Jenny scratched her forearm. "Her fingerprint matched one found on his coffee cup, left on the nightstand by his bed. She'd gone through the police's routine questioning, but they were cautious and waited for forensic reports.

"She saw Stuart in the hallway after I'd informed her about his winnings and not surprising, she hated the fact he dated my sister. Stuart pinpointed her as the person who shoved him by recognizing her laughing voice—something like the cackle of a wicked witch—following him as he rolled down the stairs.

"The Sommerville PD computer tech team discovered the notes on the fridge originated from her work computer. By her using the device, questions would be thrown in several directions and possibly, away from her."

Jenny came to my side and set her hand on my shoulder. "The police psychiatrist believes jealousy consumed her."

Too bad, I thought and chewed on my thumb. *Lock her up for...forever.*

I didn't go back to Northside, Lancaster, and Brookside, Accountants. Too many bad memories clouded my brief tenure there. I didn't want to and felt they didn't want me.

Mr. Brookside, an NLB partner, emailed. "I'm sending you a paycheck and a bonus." He included a letter of recommendation too.

Lovely. And opportune as the moola he'd supplied would support me in my current lifestyle until the next job rolled my way. *Or if I decide to go in a different direction. Or get my hair done.*

"Not to worry," Trixie had said. "We'll find something suitable." She said more interesting jobs were available, but maybe I should have a less exciting one.

Hopefully, no employer would think I created problems. Meanwhile, I found great reprieve exercising at the gym.

First: The five pounds I'd gained on the chocolate-and-soda diet while on holiday in Bayston evaporated. I still believed chocolate was never fattening and instead, credited my weight gain to watching kid TV.

Second: No one stole clothing from my locker. With great relief, I didn't have to go commando.

Third: Exercise raised endorphins which caused me to feel better mentally and stronger physically.

So slowly, but surely, I, too, healed.

****

Several weeks later, the doorbell rang. I expected no one.

Jenny said she wasn't either but she answered the door anyway. "Hattie, you'd better come see this."

I joined her and discovered a brown paper bag with my name scribbled in pen flopped back against the open door, and a *Get Well* Mylar balloon shaped like a flower pot, tied to the bag.

Usually, Jenny and I cherished these kinds of surprises. But I couldn't. Not today. This surprise meant Allan was nearby, watching me. I slumped against the door. My heart drummed hard. Unpredictable and uncomfortable things resulted when I opened these presents. Scary feelings. Reconciling my feelings. "Not again."

Jenny smiled. "Well, you know who it's from. Open it." She said under her breath, "Wish someone would send me chocolate on a regular basis."

"Very funny. What makes you think I want it? A large supply left over from my birthday is still in the kitchen. Besides, someone's getting flowers frequently, and it isn't yours truly." *So there.*

Jenny glanced around. "What's the noise?"

"What's what noise?" I asked.

"I'm positive I heard a weird buzzing sound."

Buzz, buzz. "I hear buzzing, too. A bee?"

We searched the shrubberies and flowers outside the apartment door. Nothing there.

Buzz, buzz.

"Your cell phone?"

Jenny ran to the kitchen counter to check. "No."

Buzz, buzz.

"I can't find it."

"I'll keep looking," she called.

Oh well, might as well pick up the bag.

Buzz, buzz.

The bag vibrated? With a skeptical look, I held it at arm's length. Something was inside, and I was positive I didn't want to know. "Jenny, I am not opening this bag. Look! It's moving. Whatever's in it is strange."

Jenny gave me her favorite "you're so brainless" look. "Hattie, you know what he puts in the bag. It's just your favorite treat and a note. It does not buzz."

"Then please explain to me the vibrating?"

"Well, I can't. Bags don't normally pulsate by themselves."

"Maybe it's a bomb or a wasp."

"Ha, not likely, since it's from Allan."

"Alarm clock?" I got another "so dim-witted" look. "Maybe it's…" I closed my mouth, hesitating because I didn't say this word often.

"What?"

"Nothing."

"No, you were going to say something."

A flush covered me from head to toe. "No, really,

it's nothing."

"Hattie."

"Okay, fine." I shuffled from foot-to-foot. "Maybe the buzzing is from a…dildo." There, I said it.

Jenny laughed hysterically, doubling with so much laughter, tears crowded the corner of her eyes. "How do you know?" She grabbed her sides. "Dildo. Dillll-do."

I crooked my head and glanced toward the parking lot to see if anyone else could be listening. "I don't know for sure, but what else could it be?" I lifted the bag. "Not many vibrating objects fit in lunch-size bags."

Jenny wiped the tears from her eyes. "Since when did you become an expert on dildos?"

"Since last book club when we read the mystery about a sadistic villain with them, and Trixie furnished her own supply for us to see."

"OhmyGod. That's your total experience with— he-he-he—dildos?"

"Yea. So?"

"Girlfriend, you know shit about shit. You need to get out more."

She was right. I knew shit about dildos or B.O.B.s, what Trixie had named her Battery-Operated Boyfriend.

"I get to keep the M&Ms." Her shoulders shook with the leftovers of laughter. "Dildo." Taking the gift, she opened it and showed me…

A cell phone.

Surrrprrriiise. I tried to jerk the package from her hands. "Hey, where's the chocolate?"

Jenny danced out of harms' way with a little verse, "You're wrong. You're wrong." She extended the phone. "This is what's buzzing. Speak."

I grabbed the bag from her hand and looked inside, finding only a small, vendor-sized bag of my most cherished candy.

Jenny snatched it away. "I called the chocolate." She hid the package behind her back. "You"—she wiggled the black object in her other hand in front of my face—"get the phone."

"Nope. I already have one."

"This is yours, too."

She's lost her marbles. With the most defiant posture I owned—arms crossed, legs spread and firm, my feet planted square on the floor, lips taut and straight—I stared. "It's a throw away. Throw. It. Away."

"No." Wiggle, wiggle. "Hattie, answer this phone."

"No way."

With more determination, Jenny mirrored my pose. "Harriette Lee Cooks, answer this phone right now."

I set my hands on my hips. "You sounded just like my mom."

"Who wouldn't when you're so stubborn? I'll wring your neck if you don't answer this phone."

"I don't need to talk to…uh…whoever it is."

"You know very well who it is."

She waited for me to cave with my immovable act. I didn't.

"This is so rude. I'll talk to him."

"Fine by me," I said, calling her bluff. "See if I care."

Jenny shoved the package in her blue jeans' pocket and depressed the talk button. "Hello. Oh, hi-iii. Thanks, I'm great. You?" She weaved her finger in a strand of hair as she spoke with him.

A little bit of jealousy budded in my chest as Jenny looked more like she flirted over politely chatting.

"How nice," she said, giving me a brief sideways stare. "Are you working? That's good news, too." After a lengthy pause, she looked my way as she listened. "She won't. I don't know. Nervous? I think so, too. I think she misses you. Okay, I'll try. She's being stubborn. Here goes."

Jenny forced the phone in my right hand and then wrapped my fingers around the edges. She set the gadget to my ear. "Talk." She stepped back, tore open the candy bag, munching while waiting for me to make a move.

Truthfully, I didn't think I would ever be ready. However, I couldn't go through life avoiding my fears. I used to go through life avoiding embarrassment. Now, I needed to face a new obstacle, sorta like the quote in my favorite movie, "Strictly Ballroom." In it, the heroine, an ugly duckling turned beautiful swan, quoted a Spanish proverb to the handsome young hero about living in fear wasn't wholly living.

I wasn't wholly living.

Jenny gestured with a push-push of her hands.

As I stared at my feet, I held the phone against my ear, and listened for a moment. "Yes?"

"Hi, Hattie."

Of course, the caller was Allan. "Hmm."

"Talk to me."

He sounded so good, so strong and healthy. I shook my head. I had experienced what few people ever would. I had experienced a crazy insane, jealous woman hurting someone I cared deeply about. I chewed on my lower lip, and then I shifted the phone to my other shoulder. *Stop being a crybaby.*

"I'm fine, sweetheart. Please talk to me," he said. "Why are you twisting your mouth oddly?"

If I didn't talk to him, I couldn't get over my emotional turmoil—

Wait a minute. Wait. A. Minute. How did Allan know I'd teethed my bottom lip? I knew he could read my mind, but this? He had to be nearby. I raised my head and looked at the cars parked in the lot outside my apartment door. I blinked to focus and sure enough, I found him peeking around the corner of the building, holding a cell phone.

Our gazes intersected, he punched off, and then slipped the device in his pants' pocket as he walked toward me.

Relief tore through me. Wearing worn jeans and his ratty *Accountant's Rule* T-shirt, Allan looked so good. Better than good. After another glance, I determined he'd lost some weight. Jenny and her candy indulgence faded away like a puff of smoke.

When he stood toe-to-toe opposite me, he said a soft, "Hi." His arms enveloped my body to pull me closer.

I sighed and let my man hold me. *Heaven.*

"God, I've missed you."

He said the identical words passing through my head. The phone in my hand dropped to the ground as my arms surrounded his waist. After breathing in the soapy scent from the spot on his neck, the one I loved, I pressed a soft kiss.

In marriage, two people joined together to become one. Some said a couple came together as one when they made love. I think Allan and I came together as one right then. We absorbed each other's warmth, scent, and essence. His skin felt like a part of mine. His breath, my breath. I didn't ever want to leave this spot of ecstasy. We truly welded into one.

We stood together for a while rejoicing quietly in our feelings for one another.

Allan whispered into my hair, "I have something to ask you."

My head tilted as my gaze found his dark brown eyes to see if he really was as healthy as everyone had reported. My forehead scrunched.

"I'm fine. Could you listen for a minute?"

"Yes."

"Don't go," he said.

"What?" My brow creased.

"Don't go."

"Go where?"

"Jenny told me about the job offer in New York City."

"Oh." I frowned. "But how did she know?"

"I don't know. Maybe she's like the Powerful OZ. Sees all, knows all."

"She has a big mouth."

"I know it's a once-in-a-lifetime opportunity."

He was right. In New York, I could pursue a career as a buyer for a big department store, doing exactly what I wanted. And even better, I would be off the temporarily employed merry-go-round.

"I don't want you to go. I've thought and thought about this long and hard while recovering at Mom's."

Well, what else could he do at his mother's? I rested my hands against his chest. His pecs were well-developed which told me he hadn't lost strength there.

"I hope it isn't too late to ask."

Ask? My eyes popped wide. *Is he going to ask me to marry him?* Confusion slammed my brain. I was not ready. *No-no-nooo way.* Allan wouldn't ask me to marry him. I twisted around.

"Stop wiggling, Hattie, and listen for a minute." He fumbled about to hold me tighter.

But I was faster and quicker. I freed my arms from his grasp, stomped on his toes, and wrenched aside.

He danced on one foot.

In a quick motion, I stepped into the apartment and slammed the door.

"Hattie!" He hammered the door.

I cringed at the noise, just knowing the door would smash open.

"Open up right now. I mean it. Open this door. We need to talk, and I am not doing it out here where everyone can hear our personal conversation. Open-the-door-now before I hurt my shoulder."

Oh my. He sounded unrelenting, loud and demanding, and banging insistently with his fist. And using the "hurt my shoulder" line wasn't playing fair. I giggled into my palm.

Then suddenly, he stopped pounding. "Hattie, pl-ease."

I'd fallen for his pleading once before. A few tears rolled from my cheeks to polka-dot the floor.

"Okay. You don't want to face me right now. I understand. I feel stupid, talking to you through a door, but here goes. About the no, the one I said when you asked me to choose you. I want to explain. Awe, shit."

He slapped the door, emphasizing his frustration.

"Please, open the door. I believe our whole relationship is through a door. Try to be a nice guy…"

A few moments passed. "I need to explain nothing was ever between Cathy and me. Nothing at all. I saw her occasionally for work, for the case. That's it."

I rubbed the space between my brows then pressed my ear to the wooden surface.

"I didn't care about her. I care about you. The night I saw you at the restaurant was awful. It just about killed me. And when you drove over to my place and asked me—you know—to choose you, I had to say no. What you did was so brave. But the job was the only reason why I said no when you asked me to choose you. I made a huge mistake.

"You know how I feel. I love you." His voice lowered. "Don't be foolish enough to think I'd ever let you get away. You're the only woman for me."

My heart exploded into hopeful bits.

"I couldn't see you because of the case. I wanted to, but I couldn't. I wanted to explain a few times, but you were too embarrassed to listen. I don't blame you for feeling how you do. I was embarrassed, too. How could I tell someone I care for deeply, I couldn't be with her?

"Look at her. Cathy has awful hair. She chatters incessantly. She's loud. The night of your party, I wanted to phone a taxi to take her to some faraway country when she made those snide remarks. She wasn't my type, isn't my type. You are my type. You've always been."

I flattened my lips. I didn't want to feel too optimistic.

"I almost told you the day we were so close. But I

couldn't. I regretted giving Cathy my cell phone number. Things would be so different now if she hadn't interrupted."

Minutes of gut-wrenching silenced ticked by.

"And when Cathy found the...uh, you know, the pink underwear, she went berserk and focused her jealousy on you. I'm sorry. She was one crazy insane person. None, *none* of it's your fault.

"I've beat myself up thirty different ways over my so-called involvement with her. She killed four people and hurt another. Something to live with."

Me, too.

"I know you found the unopened box of protection in my nightstand drawer. I was just kidding about the fingerprints."

Oops. I'd forgotten.

"The bed was all messy from your bouncing. I know why you searched. Must be a girl thing. I bought the condoms with you in mind. Your searching tells me how much you care for me. More than you're saying right now.

"Hattie, please open the door. Please talk to me. Lucky misses you. I miss you." Then he said in a loud voice, "What's she doing, Jenny?"

Jenny reappeared. She'd just tossed back the rest of the M&Ms and chewed fast so she could talk without spewing chocolate bits. "Nothing. You should break down the door."

"Now that's a brilliant idea."

I glared. *So much for a good BFF.* With my forehead touching the door, I peered in the peephole and saw his forehead rested on the outside, both waiting for divine intervention.

He took a deep breath and said something I never-never, ever-ever thought I would hear, "Come on, sweetheart. Let's get lucky."

A word about the author...

Award-winning author Vicki Batman has sold many romantic comedy works to the True magazines, several publishers, and most recently, a romantic comedy mystery to The Wild Rose Press. She is a member of Romance Writers of America, Sisters in Crime, and several writing groups.

An avid Jazzerciser. Handbag lover. Mahjong player. Yoga practitioner. Movie fan. Book devourer. Cat fancier. Best Mom ever. And adores Handsome Hubby.

Most days begin with her at the computer, hands set to the keyboard, thinking "What if?"

http://www.vickibatman.blogspot.com

~

Also by this author
and available at The Wild Rose Press, Inc.
Temporarily Employed